I0655392

Alchemy's Angel

A Paul Marzeky Mystery

Stefan J. Malecek, Ph. D

DEDICATION

This book is dedicated with love and gratitude to all of the amazing and wonderful people I have known through the course of this long and often arduous lifetime, who have loved, encouraged, inspired, and supported, not only my continuing efforts to write, but also strengthened and uplifted my very will to live.

ACKNOWLEDGEMENTS

There are, as always, so many people who have directly or indirectly, contributed to the completion of this work. The following is a partial list at best.

For Topher Allan, and Harold Dick Jr., my two longest lasting and enduring friendships of this lifetime—for the countless stimulating conversations, loving support, and just the best of all that defines true friendship.

For Darel Grothaus, and Michael Hithe, more recent but nonetheless extremely deep, powerful, and enduring friendships that have encompassed so many experiences across a tremendous range of laughter, emotion, and transformation.

For Sharon Curtis and Tanya Stephenson, who had the strength, power, and courage to embrace me, hold me dearly, and love me through some extraordinary and amazing times. I will always love you.

For my friend and fellow writer, Jennifer Noel Taylor, for encouragement, deep conversation, and having such a good ear and compassionate heart. I love you.

For Andrea Scholz, my ever-faithful and brilliant friend and editorial assistant with so many job descriptions as to defy limits—great love and thanks.

CHAPTER ONE

A New Direction

San Francisco, January 1997

The fog horn whistle blew, deep and long and sonorous as whale song while the fog crept in on little cat feet, as Carl Sandburg had famously noted.

Paul loved San Francisco. He was proud to be an adopted son. There was just something about being a San Franciscan that totally turned him on, that carried him though countless trials and tragedies. He was more in love with her than he ever had been with a human woman. She was the Pearl of the Golden West. She was his constant, consistent best lover, always gave him what he needed—unlike any woman he had ever known. Her hills, her valleys, and vistas thrilled him, her architecture and ever-changing panoply of her population inspired him. He never tired of walking her fabled streets. Every day she supplied such an amazing spectrum of people and experiences, all the incredible variety of different languages, clothing, and lifestyles! On one particularly busy, vivid day, he had walked from North Beach to Chinatown, then down to Fisherman's Wharf (an increasingly rare visit, too many tourists) via The Embarcadero, over to Pacific heights and down Union Street, and then trailed Argüello to and into the aromatic eucalyptic enticements of Golden Gate Park. He had tallied twenty-five different languages spoken that day alone! (His academic mentor at New College, the revered Jekker DuBois, spoke thirteen languages, so he could have accounted for more than half of Paul's personal record day all by himself!)

There were always so many vibrant, intelligent, extraordinary, beautiful, amazing, articulate, educated, and artistic women around The City! Simply taking a walk to the grocery store he could end up meeting a trippy and intriguing woman. In the immortal words of Thomas Wright "Fats" Waller: "One never knows, do one?"

He had been well and genuinely loved by so many women, gorgeous generous creatures who had taught him the real meaning of love, and affection—though a full-hearted embrace at 0330 took an especially rare woman, unless, as during his glory days, it was accompanied by a big line of cocaine. Now he gave daily thanks for having been blessed with the grace of recovery, and leaving behind the pernicious addictions that had so plagued him for decades—and that had allowed him a window through which he had willingly jumped to freedom, and the beauty of enabling himself to finally translate his innate abilities into the "permission" (via educational credentials) to establish a private practice.

Paul loved setting his hours, keeping his own calendar, even choosing not to take on certain clients when he didn't resonate with someone—or, more rarely, just had a bad vibe. Once he had his Ph.D., it took him two months to get reoriented setting up his new practice; to not having class assignment deadlines, or being on-call for the local Community Mental Health Center. He also began assembling the next draft of a book he was writing about shame, addictions and "mental illness."

Even before he had his BA, he had written a first draft with the working title of "The Tyranny of Shame." The scope of it then was less broad and comprehensive than what he currently embraced. The years since had opened him to the possibility of shame being far more influential. In fact, he had come to believe that shame was the foundation of the most essential features of society—greed, addictions, trauma, permanent war, corporate exploitation. All were powered by, and defined, what were usually considered to be individual problems.

He longed to communicate the knowledge of his awakening without seeming like one of the many brain-damaged zealots who proclaimed their new "cures" and "breakthroughs" on late night television or the low, low price of just $29.99, plus shipping and handling. Being a practicing therapist gave him great joy, especially seeing many individuals actually change their lives, improved their relationships, and became better people. It was a wonderful way to spread joy, though somewhat slow and limited to just a relative few.

He would really prefer to present his findings—OK, OK, theories—in an academic setting, but he knew from his associations with the academic body politic as a student that he could never deal with the insane dogmatic machinations and the "publish or perish" ethos. As well, any new theory that was "paradigm busting" would require years of research and peer-reviewed writing of articles and books, and would essentially impede his personal spiritual progress. The possibility of being recognized and accepted by a major publisher, or recommended to one by a world class expert seemed far-fetched, even grandiose—leaving Paul on the horns of his personal dilemma while continuing to work on himself, and those who came his way wanting healing.

Many potential clients seemed to carry their mental and emotional programming, and all of the prejudices and unexamined resistance that surrounded core issues like badges of honor to be defended and even honored like sacred artifacts. It was as if dysfunctions were holy relics to be adored. Paul knew that his own shame had only slowly given way during his many years of therapy because of his willingness to surrender the well-guarded bastions of his fears, of having his tender places exposed, and potentially re-traumatized. He had been fortunate to have had such excellent and top-tier people with whom to work, and from whom he had developed his own style and pace of therapeutic pacing. He was giving back what he had incorporated through the many years of his apprenticeship.

He only booked two hour appointments. Usually it took a client an hour to get warmed up, ready to reveal the deeper hidden spaces of their hearts, to open up the contents of their souls for healing. The first hour generally consisted of hemming and hawing, resistance, half-truths, outright lies, diversions, and defenses of every sort. Paul had garnered a modicum of patience through the many years of both receiving and giving therapy. Though not generally known for patience, he had been educated by his clients' stories to listen to the space between words; to the silence between sentences, expositions, expletives, harangues, harassments, repetitions, retreats, and regressions. Such spontaneous silences often told more of a story than any words they might utter.

Paul had noticed that there were subtle signs that people showed when they started to open up, and were prepared to go deeper, to explore the chambers of themselves like a Nautilus shell, leading endlessly into the deeper and deeper territory that ordinarily remained hidden. It was one of the most important aspects of his continuing training as a therapist, that he accessed and utilized his inborn gifts, his empathy, to clear suppressed memories and lies, half-truths and screen memories that obscured the crystal clarity of that which was utterly, utterly real, honest, and true.

Previous experience in therapy provided a sort of "softening up" process that came into play, and facilitated deeper and more rapid penetration into the darker, and more obscure reaches of the human psyche, so Paul rarely took first-time-in-therapy clients. It was just too hard to crack the old armor and years of defending tender spots.

Opening oneself up to the deepest levels of shame required both trust and faith both in oneself and one's therapist. It was not necessarily a task that new clients took to readily. Unless one were stripped raw by a recent traumatic incident that had triggered old memories, such as the death of a loved one; or the ravages of drugs and alcohol had reduced one to "the bottom," and erased much of what might be considered to be "normal" resistance, it was extremely unusual for anyone to willing open up and disclose their shame without some measure of previous work.

Paul drifted off into a reverie, thinking about how status, money, and occupation lent an aura of power and authority; allowed people to avoid dealing with their deeper anguish about bills, mortgages, PTA meetings, tee times, promotions, sexual potency, new automobiles and houses—any and all manner of measures of 'success" brought about by "progress" in terms of contemporary society and its greed-orientated Social Darwinism, so often conflated with and mistaken for Darwin's original ideas about flora and fauna.

God it was amazing! Herbert Spencer and Darwin's cousin, Francis Galton, had misapplied his principles to the social world, contributing much to the philosophy that laid the foundation for the world as we know it today. (Ultimately such notions as "might makes right" and "white makes right" grew out of it). It perfectly suited modern Empire building, and legitimated it, concurrent with the development of the rise of technology that industrialized people, making wage slaves out of the populace in order to support the excesses of the few neo-aristocrats who controlled money and manufacturing, distribution, and transportation globally.

Some of Paul's academic research had focused around the topics of what Chomsky called "the manufacturing of consent" and the brainwashing of the populace that was deemed "necessary" in order for so-called modern civilization to arise—built on the deaths of millions of Native people by marauding Europeans and their superior weaponry. He remembered Charlie Tart once saying at a MENSA gathering that it is always in the best interests of the cultural elites that one's "normal" mind be not shadowed by too much introspection or insight, because it would dilute "the consensus trance" that incorporated control to be exerted over the population who were kept in thrall most of their lives in a quasi-hypnotic state.

Paul laughed to himself, then sighed deeply. All of the years of therapy he had had, and he still found himself profoundly pissed off at the way the world was run by lying, greedy, thieving politicians who used military might to further their own personal ends, and manipulate the global chess board. He especially hated the "super-patriots" who wrapped themselves in the flag under the guise of promoting a more comprehensive national agenda "for the good of all."

He had had the honor of working with the late great Jules Henry on a psychiatric unit in St. Louis, after the professor had lost his ability to lecture secondary to a stroke, and attempted suicide. Paul had had him as an assigned patient many times and they had "discussed" (Jules mostly scribbling on legal pads). Among the many wide-ranging topics they perused was advertising. The professor was of the opinion that advertising had been created to fan the flames of desire, especially in children, because it deliberately created the needs that permitted the culture to continue, because he famously believed that the young "must be trained to insatiable consumption of impulsive choice and infinite variety."

Paul sobbed briefly, then burst out crying as he reflected on the virulent, toxic long term effects of Columbus' invasion; most especially Spanish power abuse, and "authorizing" the Catholic Church to force Native people to convert ("The Book or the Sword"). They also inculcated slave mentality into Native people so they would accept the utterly failed strategy of "Christian" principles and its corrupted ethic of suffering in order to survive ("earning bread by the sweat of the brow"), like dysphoric music screeching and wailing through their very veins and arteries, internalizing seating abuse and addictions as if necessary to survive.

He himself had harbored rage in his heart for so very long—against Creator, his parents, the contemporary world systems—never releasing the screams and agony that lay buried in muscles, tendons, and joints, creating a lifetime of "accidents" and other injuries as his body attempted to manage the unmanageable; to accommodate the unquenchable desire created by the weight of foreign materials rampaging in his bloodstream, the quasi-machinery of a production line gone berserk; unable to stop it for the very longest time, driven, compelled to protect it from view, anyone's view, but most especially his own—so precious, so vital, so irreplaceable.

It had taken many decades of therapy and other personal work for him to even approach the golden shore he'd sought—even though it had entailed his becoming so emotionally constipated, and gaining so much weight as a result of not releasing the turgid contents of his heart—that he had gratefully stood before a group of men he trusted in a men's gathering, and confessed the depth of the effluvia of his heart.

He had cried for what seemed like hours, oceans of regret and deficiency flushing out of him until there seemed nothing could possibly be left. When he looked up, it was into the loving eyes of men who treasured him and his work as part of their own—and when he asked, they surrounded him, held him in their arms with simple human love, in recognition of his doing his own work in the midst of brothers who allowed themselves to feel with him, to go beyond the concrete strictures of the contemporary culture to see and be the love within themselves, without attachment to outcome, or expectation of return, seeing the loving light of the Creator of the Universe starting to shine, and to give it away to hungry souls everywhere he went.

CHAPTER TWO

Change is the Only Constant

San Francisco, April 1997

He introduced himself as "Willie Spieth." He was actually Wilhelm Augustus Dietrich von Spieth IV, the scion of a very old and revered Teutonic royal family. (There was probably a Count or Baron somewhere in there, but the client did not use it, and Paul didn't ask). He had only been clean for five months this time. He did not usually take anyone onto his caseload who was less than a year clean. He had been referred to Paul by a doctor who had helped Paul titrate other clients off psych meds, and Paul felt he owed her a favor. Besides "Willie" was willing to pay cash for each two-hour session. He was very motivated to stay clean, and make something more of his life than being the rich-kid Eurotrash trust fund baby he had been. He had a three day old stubble on his face and wore a black silk shirt open almost to his waist, blue jeans and enough gold chains to finance the takeover of a small bank.

"I left my Ferrari in the No Parking Zone! I couldn't find any other spot!"

"There's no guarantee you won't be towed!"

In and out of rehab from the age of fourteen, he'd lived lavishly off his family's money. When he was made aware that the provisions of his grandfather's will stipulated that, if he were not "productively involved" in some kind of meaningful activity (his lawyers were sorting this out), and managed to stay clean and sober for at least a year prior to the age of thirty, he would not gain access to the first half of his trust fund (a year and a month from now). It would then be held by the family trust until he was forty, and his life conditions reviewed again. This would happen every ten years until he was seventy, when in theory, he would have access to the multi-millions, no matter what reservations the estate's lawyers might have.

Paul was very skeptical when they met, but "Willie" convinced him of his serious intention to change his life, and "become productive" in some form or manner upon which he had not yet decided. He wanted it put into his treatment plan (and a copy sent forthwith to his attorneys). Paul did it, even though it felt a little like blatant manipulation. One possibility he mentioned was starting an elite drug-and-alcohol recovery facility similar to Eric Clapton's *Crossroads*, but, of course, it would require his grandfather's money to do so. Additionally, I told him that he had to focus on his own recovery first; that it was way too soon to think about such things.

Willie had initially requested an "hour's exploratory session," stating he would know "within fifteen minutes if we could work together." Paul insisted that he pay for the two full hours in cash up front. (Quite honestly the man was so arrogant that he almost doubled his usual rate!) As the end the first hour approached, he requested an immediate second hour. Paul resisted even though he had purposely kept his schedule clear. He did not want the young man to feel as if he could manipulate him because he had so much money. So Paul put him through the paces a little bit before the first hour was completed.

"All of a sudden you want more time, after wanting 'only fifteen minutes.' Care to tell me about that."

Willie squirmed in his leather chair—a tall, good looking young man, very stylishly dressed, his accumulated arrogance wearing away by the second as he began to seriously perspire. He sat upright, and gave Paul a half-smile, half-sneer.

"I figured you could use the money!"

"Nice try, but we both know better, don't we?"

"What do you mean?"

"There's a lot at stake for you. You're afraid because you've busted out of treatment so many times! And I may be your last

21

hope of staying clean, and hopefully making something out of your life."

"And?"

"I think you may be trying to use me like a line of cocaine!"

"What?" He was incredulous, though but he looked wounded around the edges.

"You wanted 'fifteen minutes,' and now, when the hour I insisted upon is coming to an end, you're in a panic—just like when the last line disappears from the bindle at three o'clock in the morning!"

"Damn! I guess I do feel a little…nervous…maybe even worried."

Paul just sat in essential silence.

"Fuck! I didn't want to like you!"

Paul remained impassive.

"But you're right! How long have you been clean?"

"Christmas Day will be fifteen years."

"Damn! How did you do it? Where did you rehab?"

"I didn't. I cut back initially to just using on weekends. Then one weekend a month. Finally, after three months clean, I took one line on Christmas Eve. It hurt my nose, even though it was Mother-of-Pearl. It pissed me off that I lost three months clean, and I vowed never to use again! And, I just haven't."

"Wow! That's trippy!"

"Thanks."

He glanced at the clock mounted on the wall equidistant between us on the wall.

"May I have another hour? Please?"

"That's fine. I just didn't want to feel like a drive-through window!"

CHAPTER THREE

The Beat Goes On

San Francisco, May 1997

$1000!

It was what Willie Spieth had insisted on paying him when he left his first appointment—ten crisp hundred dollar bills, or "Franklins" as he called them, peeling them off from a large roll in his pocket.

"You're worth it, man!"

When Paul received a check for the same amount from an insurance company, he reflected that he had worked five times harder for it than for the work he had done with Willie Spieth. He was finally making the kind of money he always felt he deserved. His regular hourly rate was within the community standard, but he felt it to be more a reward for the long and torturous road he'd tread during the many decades of learning, growth, training and credentials needed to validate his inborn empathy and healing abilities. In essence, he had always been right, and now he had the credentials to prove it. He believed in providing maximum value for his clients. It seemed miraculous. At $100 an hour, five client slots a week brought in $1000. Working so few hours would never make him rich, but it allowed him to keep his client load small and intimate. Even more importantly, it allowed him to really focus on doing his best work.

The completion of his doctorate was what he had always sought as the validation of his personal and professional skills. It had not turned out to be what he thought it would be—the pennant flying at the top of the Mount Everest of his mind. It was not a back-stage pass to hang out with the pantheon of gods and goddesses who lived in eternal Dionysian delight on Mount Olympus. His grandiose fantasies had been a diversion, an ego trip, to keep him from his real work—though he couldn't help but indulge in them. He reluctantly admitted to himself that he knew that their fulfillment would ultimately be empty and meaningless; would lead, inevitably and endlessly, to a cascade of yet more desires like the hungry ghosts of Buddhist literature.

The doorbell rang while he was still standing there, preoccupied with his own racing thoughts. Five shrieking, freaking times in a row. Paul cursed loudly through the front door at the intrusive noise-maker. Then the intrusive visitor started banging furiously on the door. Paul angrily pulled the door open, scowling.

"What?"

A scraggly man with several days' beard and stale alcohol on his breath was standing there. The reek of his stained, malodorous clothing assaulted Paul's nostrils.

"You have to help me," he whined as his fetid breath crawled over Paul.

"Who the fuck are you?"

"I'm a vet! They referred me to you!"

"Who in the fuck are you? And what the fuck are you doing here?"

"They gave me you phone number! Ya' gotta' help me!"

Paul took a deep breath into his belly, restraining his every impulse to punch the guy's eyeballs out. If they'd been in his office, he would have thrown him out of the window, and laughed as he recorded treatment as "defenestration."

"I do not 'have' to take you! Why didn't you call?"

The man just stood there, and looked at him blearily.

"When were you in the service?"

The question seemed to startle him. He stepped back two steps, looking confused.

"Well, when were you in?"

"Uh, 1965."

"OK. When did you get out?"

"Uhm, 1965."

"How long were you in?"

"Four months."

"Four months, huh?"

The man nodded.

"What kind of discharge did you get?"

"Medical."

"Because?"

"They said I was Manic-Depressive! But I'm not," he said agitatedly, flailing his arms.

"Leave NOW, or I will call the fucking police! MOVE!"

He could afford to turn them away. He no longer had a Clinical Supervisor who required him to take every client assigned to him—especially children, despite having repeatedly requested that he not be sent anyone under the age of thirteen. I mean, what was he supposed to do with a two-year old whose mom wanted him on meds; who'd only asked for therapy when she found out it was a requirement for AFDC (Aid for Dependent Children)?

Sometimes you just couldn't lead with compassion. He rarely had to get heavy and rude, but it was a part of his PRN repertoire. The more he mourned the many losses of his life, the stronger he became, the better he felt, the more correct he felt being exactly how he felt, in every moment. His oldest friends knew him to be honest and forthright, but his ability to be so with relative strangers had grown stronger recently. Someone had once said that he was known to "take off his clothes in public" because he had been known to be open in public, even having cried unabashedly in front of strangers.

He was reminded yet again of the curse of high intelligence, and the loneliness that often accompanied it. He considered going back to school again, to focus on "gifted youth" and their trials and foibles. These bright, often emotionally misunderstood and alienated young people tended to be the most difficult-to-reach, and to help navigate the world better. After all, he had experienced much of it himself.

From the time he was very young, he had always felt so estranged, so profoundly discontented, with common everyday life; and, as he grew older, with the way the planet had been run for thousands of years as a for-profit agency by the cultural elites. They never changed, just kept using everyone based on malicious mandates that had imposed deficiency, and induced craven hunger—and completely destroyed any lingering desire for autonomy. This created a "Flatland" orientation that completely denied the contours of the natural world. The net result was abandonment of any valuing for anything that could not be weighed, counted, or measured, including peoples' lives. This process became known scientifically as "reductionism."

It seemed that the resulting life of despair and uncare had been passed from generation-to-generation. The world seemed to be getting more and more insane, the more clear and sane he became. Yet he kept going, day-to-day-to-day, always striving, always seeking a greater light, a jolt of upliftment and awareness. It was this upward trajectory that kept the ever-recurrent waves of depression and despair from forever dragging him down, and ultimately disrupting the upward arc of his life.

CHAPTER FOUR
Diving Deeper

San Francisco, May 1997

Michelle de Vares ground her cigarette out just before entering Paul's office for the first time. She was a tall, thin, anxious-appearing woman of in her early forties. Her long, brunette hair had red-tinted tips. She was wearing blue jeans, an emerald green silk blouse, and high-heeled, lace-up black boots. She'd worked all the different psych units at St. Mary's for over eleven years, and had recently begun experiencing a severe depression she couldn't shake. She'd been prompted to take "medications" by the psychiatrist to whom her insurance plan had sent her, and had flat out refused. One of her co-workers had given her a referral to Paul.

She came into his therapy office, the third bedroom of the house he was renting on Twenty Third Street and Hoffman, up by Twin Peaks. It was a bit off the beaten path for a therapy office, but it was extremely comfortable, and that contributed to the quality of his work. He slept in the master bedroom, and used the second one as a writing office, where he kept case files, did the bulk of his composing of fiction and other writing, and editing. It kept all the confidential materials completely safe, and he never had to make adjustments to the many piles, stacks, books, or other assorted paperwork that were inevitably strewn about his writing desks.

Paul seated himself in one of the matched pair of leather-bound captain's chairs situated opposite the love seat where she sat.

"If you'll give me just a few minutes to review your paperwork."

He made notes as he read, observing his new client above the edge of the clipboard as he did, putting small stars next to information he considered relevant enough to ask about during the first session. This also added to the growing database of information that invariably created a pattern that indicated arenas to be uncovered, and indicated directions for treatment.

The first part of the intake went well, if a little desultorily. Filling out paperwork was always at least a little boring—personal information; insurance information; confidentiality agreement; agency agreement (as to hourly rate and payment); and assorted federal forms. Pretty routine, but it gave him an opportunity to begin interacting with a new client in a relatively safe mode. It also provided time for the client to relax, open up a little, and begin to melt into the therapeutic bond that allowed the transformative work to take place, the connection that eventually healed the broken trust precipitating all emotional disturbances. Transference in therapy was to be expected, with the therapist assuming the role of whomever the client might previously failed to connect in significant emotional ways through abandonment, abuse, addictions, or "mental illness" in the family.

Next, they worked on compiling and ordering the information required for the Psychological Evaluation (if requested, as for example, by court order); or, more often, the Comprehensive Mental Health and Substance Abuse Evaluation, including histories of various sorts: social, medical, psychiatric, occupational, legal, substance, as well as a complete mental status examination to code the diagnosis necessary for billing purposes. This would, in turn, become the foundation for the Treatment Plan that, developed with the client's input and assistance, would guide and shape the content and context of the sessions to follow; and, coupled with the case notes, would provide "evidence" of the work for a clinical review, or an audit. (You never could tell when the bean-counters would ask for some form of documentation to justify payment).

Michelle radiated a strong sexual energy that seemed quite natural. Paul was intensely aware of her radiance, though she did not vamp or flaunt herself in any superficial way—though her pants were tight and an extra button opened on her blouse allowed an occasional glimpse of the tops of her breasts. (Paul had to admit he enjoyed it. He was a guy after all!) She seemed unaware of how magnetic she was—what Jung called "shadow," wherein that which one hides, suppresses, or denies is held, and has an effect on, the individual's behavior in a way that Freud would have called "unconscious." Despite this titillation, she was, after all, a client, and hence verboten. Not only was it unethical, it was illegal. Besides, he had heard stories about how complicated therapists' (and clients') lives had become when these kinds of dual relationships were created—leading to endless complications as well as lies, shadows, and just plain bullshit!

There was often much to be gleaned from the observation of a client's repose (or lack thereof), people often doing things in relaxed postures that they did not (or would not) do when they knew they were being observed. Michelle chewed on her right index fingernail briefly, then pulled her hand away from her mouth as if fearful of being seen. Though she looked comfortable in silhouette, she was clearly anxious.

She settled herself on the small couch, holding a wooden clipboard on her lap that captured the required paperwork, noted down her information, and then signed the relevant sheets. Tears filled her voice as she briefly sketched her growing despair about the work she was doing, most especially forcing medications on involuntarily admitted patients who refused to take oral doses, and assisting in Electroshock Therapy (ECT). She also noted that she was experiencing "relationship problems" without explicating exactly what she meant.

"I know we talked about some of this when we first spoke, but just to be really clear, let's hit a few high points again. OK?"

Michelle nodded, and started to reach a thumb nail toward her mouth, and stopped when she noticed that he noticed.

"We have a confidentiality arrangement, unless, of course, you reveal to me that you are guilty of child or elder abuse; or if you are immanently homicidal or suicidal. And, as per the Tarasoff 'duty to protect' ruling, I am required to do what I am able to protect the potential target, if I sincerely believe you mean great harm or homicide."

In 1974 the California Supreme Court opined that therapists have a "duty to warn" prospective victims. In 1976, the ruling further determined that when a therapist assesses "… that [the] patient presents a serious danger of violence to another, [the therapist] incurs an obligation to use reasonable care to protect the intended victim." Further, that: "The discharge of this duty may require the therapist to … warn the intended victim, or others likely to apprise the victim of the danger, to notify the police, or to take whatever steps are reasonably necessary under the circumstances." Having such a patient hospitalized as a "danger to others" under the provisions of the Welfare and Institutions Code 5150 also qualified.

She nodded impatiently, then said "Yes, yes. I know. I've issued Tarasoff warnings before."

"I also want to mention that I really appreciate your stance on 'taking medications' (he said, making air quotes), and I will never recommend that you do. In fact, my practice is exclusively psychiatric medication free, although I do have an MD associate who has helped me detox clients off meds."

"Thanks. I appreciate that."

"If you ever have any questions about anything, please ask. I do not want, in any way, to add confusion or misinformation."

She nodded, and smiled faintly.

As he read, he'd checked several informational sections, and starred three others. She had been rather vague about her drug and alcohol history; and she had noted that she had very intermittent memory recall of her earliest childhood. This last was almost always an indicator of early childhood trauma, often sexual. Such folks often exhibited amplified sexual energy, created out of the deficit of abuse, and intensified because that had been the only way they got attention from their perpetrators. This was certainly not definitive—some people just had strong sexual energy. The other thing he noticed was a long list of allergies, both to medications and to foods. He often found this to be indicative of a delicate nervous system, conditioned by stress and reactive to triggering sources—though he sometimes joked with his clients that it showed they might be from another planet!

"I know you mentioned 'periods of depression,' and 'problems in your primary relationship.' Would you please tell me some more about either of those?"

She hesitated for just the slightest measure, then flicked her tongue to touch her bottom lip He had a moment of self-doubt (which in itself wasn't unusual), then reminded himself that he knew what he was doing, and he was damn good at it.

"Well, let's see. Martin and I have been together for eight years, since I was thirty three. He's older, forty seven. A doctor at UC.

Podiatrist. Makes great money, better than me, but we do really well together. We own a house in Ashbury Heights, on Belvedere, near Tivoli."

He just looked at her with a silent prompt in his eyes, then she continued.

"We…we've always had a great sex life. I mean I love sex, and he's always been very considerate, a really good lover. But the last six or eight months, I've just been feeling…off, distant even…when I want to make love."

"'Off?'"

"I mean I really love him, and I really love sex, but…I don't know. Sometimes lately when he touches me, I just feel cold…empty."

"And all this started six or eight months ago?"

"Yes."

"When did your depressive bouts start?"

"Around the same time, but I've always been intermittently depressed. I really don't think there's a correlation between the two, not per se. I've had periods of depression before, and didn't feel really desirable or turned on. But this feels different."

"'Different' how?"

"I'm sure the depression is causing me to lose the desire for sex, but I think the desire started failing first. It made me depressed."

"Tell me more about 'made me depressed.'"

"I started feeling less capable…less interesting as a person, less desirable. Then when I gained seven pounds, I got even more depressed."

"'Less capable.' You mean at work?"

"Well there too, but less interesting to Martin too."

"In what way?"

"Our conversations. It used to be that we could start a conversation that would last for days sometimes. He has an undergraduate degree in psychology, so there's always been plenty for us to talk about."

"And?"

"Our conversations were sometimes the best foreplay we ever had—we'd both just get so stimulated!"

"OK."

"Maybe we've just been together too long. Maybe we're getting stale."

"Ah!"

"What does that mean? 'Ah!'"

"I could tell you I've just had a deep and dramatic insight, but that wouldn't be true. I don't lie."

"Well thank you for that. But what about the 'Ah!?'"

"Good catch! You talked about your conversations, and how long you two have been together, but you didn't mention the possibility of something more basic being in play."

"I don't understand."

"You might have fallen into depression for any number of reasons, and your relationship might have suffered from lack of interest or enthusiasm—one of the main signs of depression."

"OK. But what might these other possibilities be?"

"You or he might have fallen out of love. Maybe one or both of you is working too hard. You might have started remembering some traumatic material. We'll explore these as we go along, but first I have to ask you a really basic question, one that I always ask of clients who are depressed."

"OK."

"Are you prepared to be angry?"

"About what?"

"Just generally. Are you prepared…willing, to be angry?"

"But I'm not an angry person!"

"I believe that depression is anger denied or suppressed, for whatever 'good' reasons. Therefore when someone begins to be less depressed, they almost necessarily become angry, at least transitorily."

"Oh," she said, as she mulled this. "That makes sense. I guess I do…shut myself down sometimes, not tell the truth as much as I might. But how does that add up to depression?"

He thought for a moment, then shared one of his favorite metaphors.

"Let's say that truth has weight. And every time you speak it, you either set it free, release its energy; or if you suppress it, and you have to carry that energy. You think, 'No big deal. Just a little weight.' Maybe it starts out with you attempting to spare someone else's feelings, or protecting an abusive parent. You develop a habit of not telling the truth, and voila! You find yourself carrying around an extra ten or twenty pounds, and seem to have no idea how it got there. But setting out to simply lose weight will not get you where you want to go, because, in this scenario, the weight is comprised of little untold truths."

"I can buy that. Now what?"

"Let's say you make a real commitment to always telling the truth. Sometimes it's easy, sometimes it's a lot harder. And all the people to whom you used to lie, they expect to get a pass. When you start nailing them for it, demanding the truth; some people won't like it. They want you to stay false. They get angry and upset with you."

"OK. Then?"

"Let's look at the other side of the equation. You find yourself getting angry when others expect you to lie by default. Eventually you get so strong in your truth that others expect it. Then you get into an encounter with one of your parents, for example, and all of your work comes up in your face. You want to lie! To avoid your truth! And you suddenly realize that you learned to lie to protect them! How would you feel?"

"Pissed! I'm pissed! I was OK just a minute ago, but suddenly, I realize I'm angry! How did you do that?"

"All I did was describe a couple of scenarios to illustrate a point. I touched something in you. But it shows you're ready to work!"

"Thanks. How did you know?"

"Just a feeling mostly, but the fact that you're looking for the source within yourself is a good sign."

"But what about the anger?"

"You may have been eating anger for a long time, maybe even in 'little ways,' and not expressing it, so you can get along better. If you start telling the truth, you might find that you're more aware of your anger with yourself or others—either for lying to yourself, or letting yourself down."

"OK. Let's say you're right. How do I deal with this lifetime of anger I may have stored up? That I don't even know I necessarily have!?"

"First we're going do is take a deeper social history, and then I'm going to ask you to apply your psych training to help me design your Treatment Plan the next time we meet. One of the things we're going to explore is your family history—how you learned to interact with others in dysfunctional ways. But before you go today, I'll show you a simple breathing exercise that we'll use at the start of every session. You can practice during this next week, and you can use it anytime you feel depressed or anxious. How does that sound?"

"'Breathing exercise?' How is that supposed to help anything?"

Paul stifled a small frisson of irritation, then smiled.

"What the main difference between life and death?"

"Do you always answer a question with a question?"

"There really is a point here."

"OK. There are so many differences between them, but…"she said, and then went silent for a moment, brow furrowing in concentration, brfore she snapped her fingers.

"Oh! I know! Breath!"

"Exactly! Very good!"

She laughed and blushed, a rosy glow spreading up from the neck of her blouse.

"Most people don't get it so quickly!"

"Thank you!"

"Some part of why anxiety develops is that when you breathe in a shallow manner, it prevents all of the carbon dioxide from leaving the lungs. CO_2 builds up, and replaces O_2. If you breathe CO_2, you will die from asphyxiation pretty quickly. So by breathing deeply, you will saturate your lungs and your whole body with incredible vitality, allowing yourself to relax more deeply."

"OK."

Paul sat up straight in his chair, and cupped his hands in a receptivity mudra, then closed his eyes.

He instructed her to follow his example, and said "Now breathe in deeply, pushing your belly out so that the bottom of your lungs fills completely. Release your breath as if out through the bottoms of your feet. Let's try one breath."

After they had both taken a breath, he noted that she looked quite a bit more relaxed—face softer, breathing more deeply.

"On this next breath, breathe deeply into the bottom of your lungs; and breathe as if you were breathing in through the top of your head. Breathe into your heart, and then out through the bottoms of your feet, releasing all of your tension into the molten core of Mother Earth."

Paul instantly settled more deeply into his body, entering a very expansive altered state, and went deeper into his center as boundaries faded. He kept his eyes closed, and spoke again.

"OK. Let's do seven breaths together. I will count so all you have to do is breathe. I'll make a small 'OM' when we've done seven breaths."

Part of him stepped aside from his core, as he managed to sink deeper and deeper into his entranced state, and in another separate compartment, keep count. He became aware of tensions in her body, and made mental notations of a couple of possible areas to investigate.

"OOOOOOMMMMMMM!!!!!!!!!!!"

He looked up as he opened his eyes, then said "Flutter your eyes softly before you open them, and come back completely into the room. Then just sit quietly."

She did so, and he noticed that she seemed much softer, more calm and composed.

She spoke quietly, and said, "That's amazing!"

"Isn't it wonderful? Now, I want you to practice this every day. It's best in the morning, even just the seven breaths, and then any other time you feel called to do so. Especially if you have trouble getting to sleep. It usually takes less than a minute. And you can do it anywhere, even when other people are around."

She stood and approached his chair as he stood. She reached out her hand, and they shook.

Paul asked, "Next week? Same time, same station?"

"Works for me. And again, thanks."

He walked her to the door, and immediately went to his writing studio to transcribe his case notes while they were fresh in his mind.

CHAPTER FIVE

Lost in Time

San Francisco, April 1997

Paul awoke at 0303 drenched with night sweats and trailing the remnants of a Technicolor dream. He could not remember any details, just that he awoke with dread, plagued by the immensity of the problems of the world, and a sincere desire to do something about them. Such dreams were not uncommon. Neither was his frequent contemplations about how to help— and the accompanying frustration that often left him tearful and with a profound sense of hopelessness. He sincerely wished he could give more, be more, do more. It was his therapist's albatross, always wanting to better alleviate the pain of a suffering humanity, do so more deeply, more efficiently with less intrusion and obstruction from insurance companies and the vested interests of the pharmaceutical industry. As hard as he might try, there was always a certain amount of bleed-through from the enormous amount of dysfunction he saw and with which he dealt every day, most especially in his private practice, but in the world-at-large.

Sometimes he felt as if he were on the verge of unravelling this mystery, what he believed lay at the very heart of not only his own dysfunction, but that of the entire planetary system. Other times the seawalls of his heart felt as if they might be crushed by the hundred foot tsunami swells of sorrow that overwhelmed his mighty craving to understand and attain true and lasting peace.

Sometimes he cried. Sometimes he screamed. Sometimes he prayed in supplication like a small and wounded child without resources, for release from the tendrils of haunted memory that bracketed his bizarre, Kafkaesque childhood.

So much of it circled around what he considered his constitutional inability to release his rage against his sadistic father, who had diverted his own severe depression into taunting and berating Paul for being too sensitive and "unmanly." What were to become Paul's great gifts of empathy and attentive listening were initially mocked and punished for many years because he was so sensitive on the one hand and actively suppressed by his father on the other. He had been deeply conditioned not to cry, look angry, or indeed, express himself in almost any manner. Being anything other than a bland, vacuous blob was likely to evince any manner of disapproval from taunting, vilifying and cursing to outright physical abuse to force submission and give temporary respite to the raging fires of his father's heart. His tremendously negative behaviors always seemed related to some kind of gender aberration as he was frequently equated with being a "pussy," and therefore infinitesimally "less than" the man he was expected to be by his father, the father whose love and support he deeply craved to help define his own boundaries.

Paul early learned to celebrate being more aware and intelligent than his progenitor, always celebrating his triumphs and insights secretly in order to avoid even more violence. It had taken many decades of therapy for him to release the depth of his rage— especially during a time he called the "Marianas Trench" of one of his depressive episodes, when he cried every day for a year, even twice memorably, for twelve hours in a single day. Such experiences had allowed rays of sunshine into his heart and kept the flow of his faith in his essential self, strong enough to endure repeated episodes he had experienced in almost Crusader-like fashion questing for his own wholeness and perhaps even to forgive his father.

His intuition had repeatedly prompted him that what he saw as the dysfunctions of the Universe were way beyond his pay grade; and to apply himself to allowing himself to even more deeply let go of his own grief and delusions, that had so often run aground on what was commonly called "reality."

He snorted derisively every time he thought of the term—so completely trite, so abusively used! Most people referred to their own "reality," as THE reality, the equivalent of the comprehensive whole, the far greater, far more vast "Reality." The former was simply "naïve reality," the projection of one's own experiences and judgments onto the whole of life—and most usually used to criticize or condemn the views or opinions of others when they differed. "Be realistic!" was a most despised dismissal he had heard many times.

Many people used the word in an attempt to make a final argument when they foundered in the depths of a deep, philosophical conversation, and wanted desperately to be proved "correct." It seemed a specious comfort using the word as a declaration of propriety, even a seemingly unbreakable bastion against their own fears and powerlessness. This happened even in San Francisco, the place he considered to be perhaps the most enlightened in the whole of the US of A. Even in the metropolitan area wherein many people had a history with LSD, he still encountered brainwashed individuals who used the term "reality" to castigate the views of others that were not in accord with their own.

He had always considered his high IQ to be a shield and a sword against the commonness of "normalcy," but it only exacerbated his loneliness and sense of separation. His topics of conversation, humor, philosophy, fears, shame, and, in truth, his entire array of his expression, often seemed foreign, even "mentally ill," to many. he had used to utilize this tendency to further reject himself and others—at least until he was several decades into therapy around his deep well of self-depreciation. It felt sometimes as if he had been instructed to not have lived his life as he had, though he would have missed so many incredible journeys and adventures otherwise.

He used this odd distinction to wedge his way into the crass, commercial world in order to survive, always believing in his uniqueness and ability to write. Perhaps it was initially agony that drove him to write, attempting to express the inexpressible, even as the words poured forth out of the deep vaults of his heart. When he wondered why he didn't just get the fuck out, out of this body, out of this world. In spite of that, he always strove to stay embodied, to stay on the planet, to keep struggling, to keep striving, to keep writing—even though there were days when the only thing he could think about was jumping in front of a fucking train!

San Francisco, April 1977

It was raining like a son of a bitch when he ducked into the New Montgomery Bay Area Rapid Transit (BART) station. He had prepared for the weather and was wearing his lined London Fog knee-length car coat with the attached hood, and his almost-knee-high Frye Americana boots. He was well protected from the unusually cold spring rains, but his internal weather was craggy and abysmally depressed.

He had recently been spiraling down dark, dank tunnels of hopeless melancholy. He had thought such awful declines of mood when he got clean five years ago on his birthday. Once he quit the mighty cocaine, he truly believed he might never again have to climb back out of such a deep emotional black hole.

He had wallowed in the hollow ecstasy of blaming his parents for their wretched ineptitude. He still struggled with the idea of personal responsibility, even if had made the choice before birth. And had, until very recently, coasted along in a kind of vanilla fog. Then suddenly the entire mélange of his life seemed to ensnare him, as if he had been in suspended animation; as if he had been awaiting the right concatenation of events, experiences, perceptions, and attitudes to explode into his waking life. It felt like the emotional equivalent of a meteor smashing into the Earth at 65,000 miles per hour.

He stood looking down the tunnel at the approaching train, as rain dripped off his coat. The compound wah-wah of the Doppler Effect struck him as he crept minusculely nearer to the concrete platform's edge. He pictured himself jumping, flying through the short space, consciousness disappearing forever, pain gone, blessed darkness, suffering alleviated—solidified more and more strongly with each nanosecond's passing. His chest, filled with intense sorrow, liquefied as a flood of dopamine, endorphins, and opioid peptides transported him into a supernally quiet altered state that released him from all joy and sorrow as liquid electricity gushed through his heart, his loneliness and cupidity disappearing into a blinding cloud of light.

For just the smallest possible fraction of a fraction of a second, the scintillating possibility of changing his mind flashed—just the slightest tang, a pang, of regret that he could not do so, would not do so enraged him, his inability to manage his own life, the powerlessness, the turbulent, tumultuous moods that had always drove him.

He shifted his stance slightly, bent his knees, calf muscles tightening, ready to spring, edging closer, ever closer. The nose of the train suddenly became visible. He inhaled deeply, stomach acids *congealing, tears falling freely, and a small shriek squeaked from the back of his throat, a prayer from the depths of his heart to gods known and unknown erupting, as he asked to be welcomed when he arrived disembodied in the invisible world—and breathed out as HER voice trumpeted through his every cell in the very next meaningfully measurable span of time, a Planck time (10^{-44} seconds).*

"STOP!!!"

It was HER, Divine Mother, Queen of the Universe. He didn't know how or why. He just knew. SHE had always came at critical moments.

"YOU ARE NOT ALLOWED TO LEAVE!"

HER voice froze him, infused him as with curare, a rippling contrecoup wave that smashed through his cranium, a super-megaton explosion of joy bursting in his heart of hearts as the putrid, constricted weight of his sadness and abandonment pouring out of his eyes in a gout of tears, and out through the bottoms of his feet in a mad torrent. Then, he started coughing and choking, and a huge deluge of body fluids poured out of his face. He felt as if his body was jerked, twisted and tossed by a pair of six hundred pound Sumo wrestlers, and he fell by the side of the platform sobbing uncontrollably as strangers made repulsed faces as they passed him by.

The most extraordinary healing balm started radiating through him, and a thousand thousand concentric waves of soothing balms telepathically salved him, unguent words and potion pictures filling his every available mind space as SHE spoke into the immense silence.

"THERE IS YET WORK FOR YOU HERE."

CHAPTER SIX

The Spirals Continue

San Francisco, June 1997

"…rumors…"

"Wait! Wait a minute! Go back! Please repeat what you were just saying! There was something in there I missed!"

Mandy Quentin turned and looked directly at him.

"Were you sleeping?"

Paul rapidly blinked his eyes, hoping to disguise the fact that he had been spaced out thinking about something else entirely when his subconscious brain signaled him that he was missing something potentially important.

"No, of course not" he answered honestly. "It's just that something in your voice, maybe, not necessarily the words, that struck me suddenly without my knowing exactly why. That's why I want you to repeat what you said because I remember the tone of your voice, but not the words."

She was a slightly corpulent thirty-something woman with poorly cut blonde hair. She was dressed in what he called "thrift shop chic," because she probably bought most of her clothing from high-end stores that featured the discretely recycled dresses, blouses, jackets, and frocks of society women—usually no more than one season old. She had told him about all of the bargains she had procured—Versace, Gucci, Chanel, Lagerfeld, Ann Klein—especially since she had had her stomach "stapled," allowing her to lose almost a hundred fifty pounds, though it hadn't truly healed her innate compulsivity. He had begun working with her initially as part of her pre-surgical requirement for therapy, and continued working with him afterward.

She looked at him askance for a moment, as if not sure whether she should believe him or not, then reiterated her previous two sentences.

"I was just saying that I had heard from a friend of mine Joanie who works at the nail parlor—she told me that she had heard a rumor from another of the women who works there, that one of her customers told her that she thought she had seen Bill, my Bill, walking on Mission Street with this really young woman holding hands..."

"Wait! Wait a minute! What does any of this have to do with what we have been discussing?"

She stopped mid-sentence, mouth agape, eyes wide and questioning.

"Well," she sputtered, "you know I've been...having some...difficulties with Bill lately."

"Yes. And how do your sexual problems relate to this, really, third-hand and unsubstantiated rumor?"

"Don't you see? If he has another girlfriend, it's no wonder he doesn't want to have sex with me!"

"Again, this is a totally unsubstantiated rumor! You have no proof!"

"But..."

"No, wait! Listen to yourself! 'She had heard from another of the women who works there that one of her customers told her that she thought she had seen Bill...' Come on! That is so superficial, and you're using it as an excuse to blame Bill."

"But he hasn't really wanted to touch me lately! We haven't had sex for weeks now!"

"Have you talked to him about it? Have you even talked to him about the two of you coming in some time together?"

She blushed, and lowered her head before mumbling "Well, no."

Paul took a deep breath, tamping down his anger, before continuing.

"Come on, Mandy. What's really going on?"

"I…just always thought that…if I lost weight, a lot of weight, like I have, that, you know, I would be…that men would find me really sexy. Not that I want to cheat on Bill or anything! Just…I want guys to look at me; to want me!"

"And?"

"I still don't feel sexy! Nothing has really changed!"

"So you look radically different, but you don't feel any different?"

"Yes! Exactly!"

"Why do you think that is?"

"I remember you telling me before I had my surgery that this might happen…that it might be more than just my weight!"

"And?"

"Goddamn it! You were right!"

"I don't care about being right! I only said it to point out to you that the weight might be a symbol of your unhappiness. Your depression is just a symptom too. You invested so much in losing weight as an answer to all of your problems. Now you've dropped the weight, and you've still got problems. We still have to deal with what's really eating you!"

Mandy teared up, then buried her face in her hands, and started sobbing.

Paul resisted his counter-therapeutic impulse to comfort her. He allowed her to continue releasing until she stopped naturally, and looked up at him expectantly with tears still streaking down her face.

"Now what?" she asked beseechingly.

"Now, Mandy, it's time we really get to work!"

CHAPTER SEVEN

Heart Triggers

San Francisco, July 1997

Why not me? What the fuck is wrong with me?

The old rancid mantra hammered at him, slashed at him—even though it had long lost its zest. Even though it had lost its power to move him, it refused to let him go—Paul still occasionally felt twinges of what he sarcastically called "negative incentive" that intensely spurred him on. He sometimes imagined Gautama Buddha sitting in meditation under the original Bodh tree in Bodh Gaya assaulted by all of the demons and desires of his entire timeline. He felt a total kinship with him, as he assessed his own intrusive pictures that pulsed, and reverberated around him like a dying star, tormenting him like the most hopeless junkie aching for a big whack of smack.

Why not me? What the fuck is wrong with me?

It seemed such an inane question, an eternal conundrum. What woman in her right mind would want to change the emotional diapers of a man who was constitutionally incapable of loving himself?

Why not me? What the fuck is wrong with me?

The disparity between where he was and where he felt he should be in his life lent a great deal of credence to his continuing self-torture and the sense of victimization—though in his heart of hearts he knew he was ultimately responsible in a functional manner for all of the phenomena that he experienced as his life—again, even though he ultimately "knew" that the Wholeness of the Whole was responsible for everything, and that he, as a reflective or mirroring agent, was responsible only for finding out that this was, in fact, the case—and to cease identifying with the brokenness in favor of the greatest possible wholeness. As reputedly attributed to Buddha, "Enlightenment is a series of disillusionments."

Why, oh why, did it seem so impossible? Who in the fuck had ever promised that he would get to be happy anyway?

Paul ruminated some more, then swore he was experiencing an impossible possibility—that he was actually feeling the hemispheres of his brain ache, shrieking with enervating pain that seemed to have achieved a separate consciousness that was delighting in unmercifully torturing him, vibrating with strains of ancient rhythms and rhymes; and tormenting him with the echoes of his loneliness.

———

San Francisco, September 1994

It was a warm September night in San Francisco, the cold summer months of June, July, and August having passed in a welter of gusty winds, fog, and chilly temperatures that always ambushed tourists wearing white patent leather shoes and short pants.

Paul and his inamorata, Rhea Carlton, had had an early dinner, and as the spark of passion grew from their conversation, as it often did, they made a post-haste pilgrimage to the bedroom. A stream of clothing started at the portal between the kitchen and dining room, and was strewn willy-nilly all the way to the bedroom in the back of the large apartment they'd rented together on Vallejo near Franklin.

Both were panting by the time they got to the bed. She reached down, grasped his penis around the base, and squeezed—then slipped the rest of her fingers around it as he moaned and reached for her. She laughed and pushed him away.

"Not yet, big boy!" She laughed again. She released his throbbing cock, and turned over, presenting her beautiful backside to him. She'd

been a dancer her whole life, and he was got aroused every single time he even glanced at her buttocks. She allowed him a brief squeeze, then pushed him away and turned, threw her arms around his neck, and kissed him deeply. She was the best kisser he had ever known, putting her whole self into osculating without restraint, transmitting her essence like a hungry flower to the light of day. He reached down and rubbed his fingers in the silkiness of her as she moaned and drew him to the bed.

They kissed again and he massaged her left breast. She slid under his fingers like silk, and the stiffened erectile tissue of her nipple grew even tauter. Small moans slipped from her throat that cut right through him and deepened his sexual arousal. His dick unbelievably hardened even further. Her kisses kept enflaming him, her mounting sexual aromas and excited vocalizations!

An absolute flame of desire flashed through him as he kissed his way down her belly, caressing both her breasts with his hands above his head. Her hips rolled from side-to-side as she hoarsely whispered to him. He continued to work his lips down her belly to the clean-shaven mound of her Venus.

He appreciated yet again how much they both treasured clean-shaven baby-soft genitals. They sometimes made a ceremony of removing their pubic hair together. She especially loved the feel of his silky smooth balls, and he had developed enough trust to allow her to shave them.

He licked her swollen clitoris, flicking his tongue, applying tiny bites and touches, then sucked gently, twirling his tongue, and pressed down slightly. His receptor cells reacted immediately and he recoiled when he buried his tongue in her, assailed by a vile scent and an acrid taste! He must be hallucinating!

Something…assaulted him, enveloped him, wrapped him in sticky tentacles!

IT COULDN'T BE! IT. COULD. NOT. BE!

He fell back onto his heels, a rictus of disgust twisting his face. Wave after wave of nausea rolled through him, a wild mélange of pictures hammering him like a wild ocean's rage.

HIS MOTHER!? HIS FUCKING MOTHER!?

He gagged, empty stomach cramping, seeking to expunge contents it did not have. Then gagged again.

Sharp knives twisted in his belly, his stomach lining penetrated by scalpel-like pains shooting through every neuron. Sheets of bright scarlet pain rolled through his head as yellow-orange flames sizzled down his brain pathways. A continuous reel of distorted images from his earliest years filled his aching cranium.

He saw himself as a dissociated boy-child kneeling between his mother's thighs. The smell!

THE SMELL!

IT WAS TOTALLY FUCKING REAL!

Rhea sat up abruptly, body having completely lost all of its glorious sensations, now and forever consigned to the depths of her hippocampus.

"What? What?" she said. Had Paul had a stroke?

"PLEASE! DON'T TOUCH ME!"

"What? What's wrong?"

"IT CAN'T BE TRUE!"

"What? What?" She asked, and attempted again to reach out to him.

"DON'T TOUCH ME! PLEASE!!"

He shrank further from this wonderful woman love of his life. He fought against his every instinct to be touched and comforted. His every cell cried out to be held—and was simultaneously repelled, filled with maximum, total fear. He felt ashamed to the very root of every single nerve, every hair follicle. He watched as wave after wave of shock poured through him, torn loose from even the most remote outposts of his sanity in opposite directions, unable to withstand even a yoctogram of additional weight upon his soul's fragile attachments.

He was so frozen by shock and shame creating an impasse as solid as a an massive iceberg of frozen rage and desire completely conflated, every vital energy dissipating, then reverberating through him into the present as if flashed through the decades as if they had never existed, his ability to communicate utterly contaminated.

It would yet be decades until he was able, through dint of massive effort and much personal work, to recover his memories, and restore some semblance of beauty and illumination to his soul. He was yet to spend decades avidly, even savagely, pursuing sex at every opportunity, always seeking that missing link of love, to fulfill the deep unfillable craving in his heart, fruitlessly searching for the love within himself.

CHAPTER EIGHT
Birth and Rebirth

San Francisco, September 1997

Paul was frequently struck by the enormous greed that infected the bulk of humanity. Though ostensibly working to "make a living," most people were enthralled by, and vaingloriously driven to emulate the "lifestyles of the rich and famous." The net result was eighty hour work weeks; massive expenditures for "defense contracts" to "preserve our way of life," continually invading Third World countries; a pornography industry that takes in $3075 a minute; and a massive spectrum of addictions from cocaine and heroin to gambling and shopping—all designed to keep the system going full speed, and with only very few who had the courage to examine the true basis of it, and even less to ask "Why?"

It boggled his mind to realize that there was more than enough food grown to feed every single person on Earth when instead 15,000 children starve every day because an allocation of resources favored a very small number of extremely rich people made a few pennies more per second around the clock—or, as Edmund Burke once said famously, "All it takes for evil to thrive is

73

for good men to do nothing." Distracting the population with televised events and the manufactured "spin" of governmental lackeys was what Walter Truett Anderson called "the politics of the spectacle." The Roman poet Juvenal referred to it as feeding people "bread" and keeping them distracted with "circuses."

Paul had carefully schooled himself to look beyond the traditionally sanctioned avenues of therapeutic approach, developing his own idiosyncratic methods, amalgamating his education and experience to create a therapeutic approach that blended technique with intuition and empathy. Building an empathic container with his clients permitted them to safely release old and hidden emotions relatively easily—especially during the second hour of the session when defenses were loosened and the sense of connection was enhanced.

Though Willie had had brief moments when he started to break down, even crying once, it had taken months of concerted effort for Paul to get through to him. The young man had so much money, and had been so insulated by his family's privilege, that Paul decided to treat him as if he were a true hysteric—telling him the same information repeatedly until he got it, and his words had eventually made an impression. He wasn't dense intellectually, but he'd been so effectively indoctrinated by his culture and upbringing that he'd almost developed "negative hallucinations"—a condition in which one does not see things that are actually there. In Willie's case, he genuinely did not see suffering, poverty, or corporate destruction wrought by worldwide globalization. To his entitled mind, it was all more-or-less "natural."

"Don't you see, Paul, there really are haves and have-nots!"

"Oh, here we are again—back to the same old Social Darwinist line!"

"You may have a point, but if those with money and status don't…guide the world, then we'll all be in a mess! Total anarchy!'

"And you sincerely believe that we're not 'in a mess' now?!"

"I would say that overall, my family has done far more good than harm!"

"Since when?"

"My family heritage dates to the Thirteenth Century."

"And?"

"We have always been good…patrons."

Paul laughed in spite of himself.

"'Patrons?'"

Willie turned red in the face, and then sputtered "You know what I mean!"

"Probably, but why don't you explain?"

"I meant…my family have always treated the peasants…the people who lived on our land…well."

"How do you know?"

"It's what I've always been told!"

"And you've bought into it?"

"I…I don't know. Yeah, I guess."

Paul simply sat in silence, waiting.

"Oh fuck you, man!"

"Fuck me? Why?"

"You look so fucking smug right now!"

"'Smug?' No, I look like I see you fooling yourself!"

"Fuck you! My parents are good people! You're just jealous because I'm rich!"

"And being rich has sure been a blessing, hasn't it?"

"Fuck you, man!" he said, rising from the couch.

"No, fuck you, man!" said Paul, and smiled.

"Why are you smiling at me, you fucker?" he said, as he sat back down.

"Because I think we just touched on a very tender spot! Want to work on it?"

"What do you mean?"

"There's at least two, maybe three, potential therapeutic issues here."

"Like what?"

"First your belief system. Another, your family's money. But I think that possibly, underlying them both, might be another shadowy, hurt place."

"Oh really? What's that?" he spoke very belligerently.

"Beyond the family's money, and what you believe they believe, we need to talk about how you honestly feel about yourself."

Paul was expecting another explosion, maybe even his client to walk out, slamming the door.

What he received instead was a thoughtful look, a false start attempt to speak, followed by a scowl, a head shake, and finally angry words that emerged in a tear-choked voice that was more a bleat.

"I still think you're a fucker! Goddamn it!"

Willie cleared his throat, blew his nose, and tried again.

"You've got the kind of recovery I want! If you have to ask the kinds of questions you've been asking for me to get that kind of recovery—then fine! Fuck it!"

Still Paul was silent.

"And…I don't like how you talked about my family! But you're fucking right!"

"About what?"

"About me!"

"What about you?"

"I…My parents never loved me! I just sort of…ignored it!"

"Why?"

"Because I always had plenty of money, drugs, and women!"

"And?"

He shrugged and smiled.

"Still do, except for the drugs!"

"And?"

"Goddamn it! Being stoned, fucking hard, and driving fast are only times I've ever been happy!"

"Good! Good! Excellent!"

"And what do you not like about yourself when you're not high?"

"Not high?"

"Precisely!"

"I...Oh fuck you! Do you always ask such hard fucking questions?"

"Willie, I'm only asking because I already know the answers!"

"What?"

"We been dancing with each other for months. Every time we start to get anywhere near one of your 'tender spots,' you withdraw or make jokes, or set up some other kind of diversion."

"Like what?"

"Sometimes you act like the old Willie Speith, man of the world, on top of the game. Now were going to have to peel your off your mask!"

Willie just stared at him.

"What no anger? No jokes? No stories about three day parties in Monte Carlo?"

Then just for a second it looked as if Willie's face would implode before he replied.

"No. Not this time. I don't want to hide anymore."

Then he started crying.

CHAPTER NINE
A Healing Life

San Francisco, November 1997

Paul believed that Otto Rank, Wilhelm Reich, and Stanislaus Grof were right in their belief that human birth was the most significant trauma of one's life. And perhaps he might not yet have sufficiently torn down the walls that protected his denial of the buried memories of his own birth. It was in the arena of interactions with women that what he called his "failure," his lack of integration, was most evident. Was he radiating so much shame? Maybe women sensed his un-resurrected codependence? Or was it his own shame about his shame that women felt and therefore rejected him?

Yet he felt he had always been as true and clear as he had been able to be at every stage of his life—and had always been frustrated by his relative inability to express himself more fully. He took great comfort in the sensitivity his father had maligned and the idea of being an artist. As John Lee had so beautifully written:

> For all writers, the proof of love of self as an artist shows in the way we arrange our lives: do we give ourselves the time to do what we love, do what we must? To achieve balance, to be able to enjoy (and write about) lovemaking in its highest form, you must fall in love with the Inner Artist.

Such words infused him with inspiration, and a sense of rightness in pursuing his path; imparted to him a key piece of the puzzle with which he had so long struggled: He had become the lover he had always sought, having projected his golden desire for wholeness and completion onto an idealized woman, seeking his own unity through another. He had seen the improbability, the impossibility, of this, the utter paradox it presented: looking for himself outside of himself because he had been shamed into believing that his inner self, his Artist, was unworthy and to be avoided—and needed buttressing in order to survive.

Of course, there was pushback and recoil from this deformed strategy, adopted so many decades ago, designed by all the machinations of the then-cultural ethos, to cripple him just enough so that he would, without too much struggle, take his place as just another cog in the great Newtonian machine, willing to accept whatever a insensate and dehumanizing machine-culture was willing to provide within the very limited intelligence and microscopic morality it offered, to anyone unwilling to assert himself and demand more. The most glaring aspect of this were the taunting and demeaning voices of his childhood that still tortured him in moments of greatest stress— echoing the vicious, slashing diatribes and harassment he had internalized during his youngest years, that had, at times, seemed salacious enough that he considered that they might be auditory hallucinations, and himself schizophrenic!

Of course, the greatest benefit that had accrued was that he had been given the opportunity to look at the ineluctable, even logical, progression of his life—all of the magnificent, munificent, and simultaneously disturbing and destructive, events that had flowed through him without any awareness of volition or choice. This created the totally unforeseen possibility of using these reflections in an entirely new way, he now being able to see that the poisoned flower of his early life had exuded toxic fumes and fragrances that had now produced the golden, succulent fruit of his later life for which he gave thanks many times every day.

The process had been a blessing well disguised. Paul was now able to look with some measure of gratitude at these archaic artifacts of his, these companions on his long journey through anguish and hunger, this apprenticeship of the soul; that had toughened his resolve to see beyond, to reach out to grasp the underlying cosmic meaning of such exposure; and perhaps see the golden land of emotional healing and release whose achievement would not have been achievable in any other way. It now all seemed to have been absolutely perfect and necessary, even though some of the reckoning and passages might appear twisted and bizarre to anyone who had not had the courage to stand in the fire of their own bellies and hearts, and survive—believing in something beyond, of which the exquisite horrors were but a flickering shadow.

He had used the heartache of his life to seek the fulfillment of this elusive phantom/fantasy. She was always cleverly disguised as a beautiful, intelligent, evanescent woman dancing in and out of view. It had taken many years of "falling in love" with totally unavailable women, and the consequent ridicule by self and others that always accompanied such losses that eventually led to his mourning, and learning to forgive himself for having fallen into this delusion over and over, despite his intellectual brilliance and his emotional fluency.

His obsession was always with his writing and courting his writing muse. He had shaped his entire life around creating time to write, always making whatever "work" he had to do to make money only a secondary consideration that provided for him to afford his writing habit. He had to admit that having an actual physical woman in his life might complicate his relationship with his Beloved who accompanied him everywhere, loved him, inspired him, catered to his needs literary and emotional; who had always been there for him, even (or especially) when he awoke at 0330, alone and lonely, though he could not reach out and touch her hip, or caress her in any of the many imaginably pleasurable ways he could with a live woman, but he could awaken the computer (it rarely complained), go to the keyboard, and start writing. The keyboard welcomed his intensity, his presence, his love flowing in whatever ways and whenever he expressed it; welcomed him and received him fully with more consistent relish than he had ever had with real live women.

The Muses Clio and Calliope came most frequently, goddesses of history and epic poetry, though sometimes Erato, the goddess of love poetry, came too, inspiring him to move emotionally into higher dimensional feelings and awareness. Nothing was more exciting than to feel the breath of the goddesses filling him with love and inspiration, ideas, pictures, thoughts, dreams, intuitions, to the cellular level of heightened awareness as his neurons and hormones unlocked and unblocked; as he was granted access to deeply hidden vaults of esoteric knowledge and information; as he drank deeply from the wellsprings of his native abilities as they awoke to the vast cosmic storehouse within him, to the entire spectral amalgamation of beauty and pain.

In these moments of touching Godhead, time flowed through him, fed him cosmic nutrients and disappeared back into the Void, offering him the opportunity to see and taste worlds beyond worlds, to bring back ethereal images of heightened interstices and intersections to write about, to paint bright, multi-hued, infinitely dynamic pictures of the greatest peace he had ever experienced, easing and integrating even the memories of pain and angst. He lived for such moments of such cosmic transport that were exponentially beyond even his greatest drug experiences in touching the Universal—so filled with joy and reverence that now all he wanted was to share this distilled essence of himself in some manner, to serve it as the most sumptuous banquet, to be savored and digested, bringing deep and fulfilling nutrients to each and every cell of every body of all who cared to partake of his gift.

Processing vast tracts of personal material had connected him to something far larger than himself in terms of addictions, and understanding the infrastructure that maintained an addictive society profiting from dissociation and deep anguish. He had paid enormous dues, and Paul would brook no "authority" naysaying him from sharing broadly all that he was, transformed and transmuted through the mysterious process of alchemy. He had submitted to the torturous process in order to be healed, to be freed of the tenacious pain, the reverberating sorrow that had allowed him to become a mature healer. There was no higher calling. He was finally able to fully acknowledge his lifelong distaste for the money and status requirements "the information business" demanded in contemporary society. An ancient Cree warrior had once asked what White people would do when all of the fish were gone, the rivers poisoned, and the trees cut—would we eat money?

The work had led him to deepen his love of doing therapy. He was grateful to, and always thanked, his clients. "I got as much out of the session as you did. I grow from doing this work."

It wasn't psychobabble. It was the truth. By reaching deeply within himself to give to others, he found a deep wellspring of hope, courage, and power—ever-renewing, and always effulgent—as if it were the Eternal Fountain of Youth. The more he gave away the better he felt. Not that he didn't charge for his services. Not a chance. No way. He had been known to jokingly tell a client: "When my landlord doesn't charge me rent, you'll get free therapy!" But this was soul work for him. He billed far less than creepy psychiatrists who were charging $150 (or more) an hour for dispensing brain-damaging "medications." He walked his clients through their psychic and emotional storms; helped them trace out and follow the pathways of their memories; to integrate their lost power; to recover the original magnificence buried in, and obscured, by addictions and phobias; and to resurrect the buried glory obscured by dissociation and regression.

It was the only job he'd ever loved! Funny that it had only taken him more than half a lifetime to find it!

CHAPTER TEN

Losing to Win, and Other Strategies

San Francisco, December 1997

Massimo Baldestari was a third generation San Franciscan EMT (Emergency Medical Technician) who had been referred to Paul through his informal network of contacts at San Francisco General Hospital. He was a smallish, swarthy, good-looking young man said he was having marital problems. He suspected that his wife, who was ten years younger, had been seeing a man even younger than she. He had difficulty making eye contact he shared that he had no real proof, just suspicions. Paul's first inclination was to take his client at face value.

The longer they talked, the more agitated Massimo became about her ostensible infidelity, and demanding without ever providing anything more substantial than his "sneaky feelings." At that point, fifteen minutes into the session, Paul started seriously doubting his veracity. He continued attentively listening, and Veronica seemed not to have exhibited any lessening of ardor or affection—but Massimo nonetheless had been feeling increasingly helpless and depressed. His biggest "proof" was that he had developed occasional impotence. A dozen possibilities came up in Paul's mind from his internal encyclopedia, and he pointed out to Massimo that his fear and anger might be affecting his performance.

"But I am telling you! I know! The bitch is cheating on me!"

"Do you realize, Massimo, how crazy that sounds?"

The young man sputtered and spit, then answered, "I don't care! I am *Italiano!* We just know things!"

"I have some understanding about intuition. And, I'm not saying that what you're feeling is wrong. I am simply stating that perhaps, just perhaps, your premise is incorrect, or skewed even, by the emotions that are feeding it."

"What? You think I am making this up?"

"What you're feeling is totally real for you. How you arrive at those feelings is something else altogether, something we will definitely be exploring. What I question is the possibility that the current situation is reflecting something, or reminding you of a past situation in which you felt helpless and out of control—even impotent, in the sense of not being able to do anything about it."

Massimo looked stricken, then suddenly thoughtful. The tirade stopped, perhaps reflecting even his runaway train of thoughts. The young man's eyes took on a distant gaze that was almost glazed, as if he had departed on a deep inner journey.

Paul sat silently, secure in his knowing that any spoken word, any *bon mots,* could easily disturb the inner process the young man was having—maybe even prevent him from producing whatever meaningful emotional flowers he was germinating. Paul closed his eyes, and went into his breath—in through the top of the head, down into the heart, and out through the soles of his feet into the molten core of Mother Earth. He had taken only four breaths when his client roused him from his reverie.

"Hey! Hey, Paul! I think... Maybe."

Paul sat and waited, watched semi-shock and incredulity melt from his client's face, and be replaced by shame and disbelief.

"I got this…I don't know if it's a memory or not. Maybe I made it up. But I just keep smelling cigars!"

"OK!"

"I can't stand the smell of cigars! Never could!"

"And?"

"I don't know! I don't! It's just what came!"

"OK."

"It reminded me…"

"Of?"

"Not totally sure. Something from childhood."

"Nothing more specific?"

"Reminds me…I don't know...of my Uncle Tomassino."

"Nothing more specific?"

Massimo snarled, and slapped the coffee table in front of him."

"No! Goddamn it! What does this have to do with Veronica?"

"I don't know. You brought it up. I'm just trying to follow you."

"Take a breath, Massimo. It's OK. I was just asking."

He ducked his head and mumbled.

"I'm sorry, man. I know you're just doing your job."

"And my job is to help you. Maybe we've gone far enough for today. Are you feeling complete for today?"

Yeah. Yeah, I guess so."

CHAPTER ELEVEN
Fruit of the Harvest

San Francisco, January 1998

While many clinicians claimed that much of the import of suppressed memory (what Freudians would call "repressed") might remain hidden behind the veils of the distant past, Paul did not believe that such materials would ever yield to even the most concerted efforts of hammering with cognitive therapy. He was of the opinion that the childhood hunger for love and recognition got projected onto adults to seek "success" in contemporary culture with the expectation that they would achieve through intellectual and cognitive approaches what had been missed as an infant or child. Paul believed that such rich and primal materials were far more deeply hidden, and only rarely recognized as underlying the very real issues affecting society. They were almost never taken into consideration by the tenets of cognitive therapies in attempting to heal what such approaches were only considered to be "personal issues" that were to be taken separately and out of context of the larger impingements of societal mandates and proscriptions.

Paul's own history of addictions and recovery, as well as those of hundreds of clients he'd treated, had led him to believe that the very nature of contemporary Western society was predatory, creating trauma by its very nature (traumatogenic), as well as addictions (addictiogenic), by denying the primacy of emotions, and attempting to quash, deny, or manipulate them in children for the preservation of the existing order and the accumulation of profits—much in the same manner as Freud had done in denying child sexual abuse as being the key to his original "hysterical" clients that led to his creation of the Oedipal and Electra complexes. And buttressed the malicious underpinnings of a society based on sociopathic organizations that dated to the birth of the East India Company (EIC), the original corporate raiders, granted royal charter in the year 1600.

Paul's early experience with traumatically-induced internal oppression had led to understanding and integrating it when he first had therapy in the Army. His scholarship had continued to grow through graduate school when he was able to take up a more formal approach. He had become convinced of the power of cathartic work in releasing individuals from their internal chains and shackles.

He had long ago become aware of the presence of analog "people," though he preferred to think of them as subpersonalities (within the main personality), versus alternate personalities (alongside the main personality) as in Dissociative Identity Disorder, (what had previously been called Multiple Personality Disorder). He saw what were generally called "personality tendencies" toward self-depreciation/self-aggrandizement might actually be analog children, who might be addressed as emissaries from the Spirit World—as real, even perhaps more so, than the commonly accepted world of illusion and appearances, each of them carrying important pieces of the larger puzzle of the individual, and all of them playing a part in what was perceived as "survival" through exaltation or suppression of various moods and emotional states.

Paul first experienced the necessary inducting light-trance states during sessions with his own therapists. It had helped him to retrieve various aspects of the love, comfort, recognition, and connection of which he had always felt deprived. He had uncovered the truth of many of his variously-aged inner analogs (what Stone and Stone called "sub-personalities"). He had trusted enough to allow them to speak the truth of their own idiosyncratic experience; to speak in an accurate and genuine voice—not how he thought they should speak, but to have a precise and unpretentious voice, as if he were, in fact, they.

This had led him to new levels of awareness and maturity—and to become the champion of all of his child states, assuring each of them in turn of his love and protection. They learned to love him back. He had adopted the technique, and adapted it to his own personality and style as a new empathic tool to use to help his clients free themselves. After marinating for most of a lifetime in a caustic shame had led to him to create an alchemical sphere from which to emerge, as if a phoenix birthing itself from its own ashes.

He feared investing too deeply in this most recent awakening, but he was inspired by Wilber's stance that everything was "already always perfect;" and that, therefore, everything that had ever transpired in his (and every other life) was always perfect and necessary; was completely and intimately crafted in its most exquisite details that unfolded to provide the exact specifications for the life experiences required for the every individual, every everything, to evolve and become more relatively whole, to become more of that for which he or she or it had had initially coming into this life—no matter the artificial sense of separateness, of isolation, of closed off inviolability imposed by aberrant contemporary cultural or temporal mandates.

All of which implied that the wholeness of the Whole was always present, always all-embracing, ALL, actually, if one were to consider it in great enough depth. Everything is alive. It is/was/will always be all that is. There is no true separation, no true apartness or distance. The ALL is always perfectly what it is, the essence of all there is, whole and complete from the most massive planet to the most submicroscopic particle, even to dark matter. To anthropomorphize it a bit, the ALL was/is, always will be there patiently waiting to be greeted; waiting, as it were, to welcome each and every seeming individual with open arms and the fierceness of the love for which one has always waited, longed-for, yearned-for as if time really existed. It was, as Mick Jagger had once sung, under completely different conditions, "It's just a breath away, a breath away, yeaaaaah."

This conclusion left him feeling that the whole idea of "free will" was ludicrous, just such a cruel joke, even a delusion. If there were truly "free will," it would be manifest throughout the Universe. One's kidney, for example, could decide to go on a trip to Florida. He knew it sounded absurd, and that most people only applied the concept to human beings, (though this called into question exactly how much sentience and intelligence the average human had). It was related to the extremely common belief that everyone had a mysterious sense of control over their own life events; that anyone could alter events at will—whereas Paul believed that, being part of the Oneness, we were moved by cosmic events and forces far beyond our pay grade, to do incomprehensible deeds and embrace completely transcendental states (at the furthest infinite "end" of the spectrum).

We are all, always, connected to the whole of the Universal will. The notion that we are all completely separate autonomous individuals running around doing our own will seemed the utter peak of absurdity. That it was frequently used to cajole and manipulate individuals for often abusive (governmental) reasons was beyond doubt. And it encouraged individuals to believe that they could somehow escape the heavy burdens of responsibility for their actions! Jesus! Talk about delusion!

He found it impossible to believe that any government, religion, or corporation existed that did not demand a renunciation of personal power, and the embracing of some level of what was so often called "order" that was essentially abusive to the human spirit; that did not create a dysphoria that affected and infected everyone, germinating a low-grade depression that weakened the immune system and eroded the human will—though, as Tart had observed, such a maneuver was very useful to keep citizens manipulated and coerced into to obeying whatever the mandate *du jour* happened to be, out of the fear of being reduced, in any given arbitrary moment, to a pile of groveling ordure by a nameless, faceless bureaucracy; to seeking a specious mercy, and being willing to do penance of any sort to be allowed back into the fold, just to have a taste of the illusion of being approved of, and belonging to, Big Mom and Dad. The best possibility was actually having autonomy and belonging (to a different, higher order) simultaneously. He did not believe that The Universe demanded that one give up one's sense of wholeness (autonomy = "having one's own law" = true self-possession) in order to approximate the feeling of wholeness and love. There could be no actual conditions on love.

As a child he had developed a default strategy that he later came to call "losing to win." Attempting to deflect his father's violent tirades, he learned to shut down his emotional expression. The danger was real and actual—and the very people who should have been providing him safety and protection were the ones from whom he was at the most risk. He had had to learn to placate an angry parent when he himself was filled with despair and rage (therefore to "lose"), in order to keep from being hurt or abused more, even killed (therefore to "win"). Or conversely, to ameliorate a parent whose emotional needs were so overwhelming that he had twisted the events of his internal landscape to accommodate their aberrant views. It had seemed like a sound and logical strategy at the time, though he became so inured of it that he became like a strung out junkie searching for an early morning score, dancing like an insensate marionette to the distorted tunes of others. He had to admit that, at least retrospectively, these lessons in early aberrance had inevitably brought him many life lessons. (It was only decades later that he finally realized that this was his first lesson in "inverse parenting," or the kind of role-reversal in which the child becomes the adult to his or her parents).

As a result of doing his own work to unravel such gnarly notions that he had internalized to survive, he had developed one of his primary therapeutic approaches, deepened using his natural empathic ability to assist his clients in unfolding their own therapeutic evolution (even revolution). By having lived and digested it, he could draw from his life experiences to share the empathic nutrients and emotional minerals these initially damaging experiences contained—akin to the scarring that many tribal initiations inflict to signal one's maturing to adult status.

He always felt he got vastly more than he gave; blessed that his clients' desire to heal allowed him the opportunity to bolster his own continuing recovery; deepen his own personal magic, and utilize the balm of the words and feelings he shared—distilled and refined, run through flasks, retorts and alembics, evaporated and distilled to the purest essence he could muster—and offered as a gift from the Creator, Source of All. It was the highest high he ever experienced.

CHAPTER TWELVE

To and Fro Goes the Way

San Francisco, February 1998

"Cigar smoke. I had a flash about why I can't stand the smell of cigars. They remind me of this friend of my Uncle Tomassino's. Haven't seen this guy in twenty years. My uncle's dead now, but I ran into this old friend of his at Gino and Carlo's. I just immediately wanted to kick his ass!"

Paul waited a beat, then gestured with his hand.

"Go on," he said.

"It gets hazy after that. Just the smell of his cigar made me sick to my stomach. Then suddenly I got really, really angry. I just wanted to kill him!"

Paul waited, already aware of what was coming—more a feeling than a thought.

"I…I think he might have…touched me… when I was a kid."

"What's your belly telling you?"

"My belly hurts…like cramps. It aches…I feel sick, like my belly is all black and sticky." H estopped for a moment, then looked up, and said "But I am fucking pissed off too."

Paul himself had benefitted many times from deep emotional release that did not allow for anyone else's fears or concerns. The truth was primary, and knew no boundaries. The essential purpose of therapy was to get free of old emotions and the dysfunctional patters they generated. So he was completely comfortable leading this young man into a cathartic release; and his therapy office was lined with six inches of soundproofing insulation, enclosed by a false wall. He had no fear about his neighbors complaining, or the cops getting called. His office was good for up to 10,000 decibels (the equivalent of a massive heavy-metal rock concert, or being up close and personal with a Rolls Royce jet engine).

He encouraged Massimo to just let go with whatever he was holding. He instructed him to allow his body to have its own way, to simply open his mouth and let his belly speak.

"UUUnnnnggh!"

"Louder, man! Let it go!"

"UUUUNNNNNGGGHHH!"

The client was gripping his belly, clearly in great discomfort, but he was still far too restrained, at least as far as Paul was concerned. He could feel the depth of what lay there.

"Let your belly speak! Open it up!"

"AAAAAAAHHHHHHH!!! FUCK! GODDAMN! MOTHERFUCKER!"

"That's it! More!"

"YEAAAAAAAAAAH! FUCK! MOTHERFUCKER! FUCK YOU! FUCK YOU! FUCK YOU!"

"Fuck who? Fuck who, Massimo?"

"MY UNCLE'S FRIEND! FUCK HIM!! HE HELD ME DOWN AND MASTURBATED ME!!"

"Go on! Tell him what you think!"

"FUCK YOU MOTHERFUCKER!! LEAVE ME ALONE!! LEAVE ME ALONE! FUCK YOU! FUCK YOU! FUCK YOU!"

"More!"

"I WILL FUCKING KILL YOU!! DON'T FUCKING TOUCH ME!!"

"Now you got it! Give it to him!"

FUCK YOUUUUUUUUUUUUUUUU! FUCK YOU!"

With this last outburst, Massimo collapsed onto the floor, sobbing his heart out, drool leaking like a hydrophobic baby.

Paul put a box of tissues and a glass of water near the man's right hand, and resumed his seat, allowing as much time as he might need.

A few minutes, maybe as many as ten, went by. Massimo got up from the floor, and took a seat in the leather chair next to Paul's.

"I told my mother about what happened, and she didn't believe me." His voice was filled with both sadness and anger.

Paul nodded his head, and gestured for the young man to continue. Massimo took a deep drink of water, and blew his nose several times, and then wiped his face.

"She told me to not 'to make waves.' Then she slapped me when I cried!"

Paul allowed the silence to speak for itself, then asked what had happened next.

"I decided 'Fuck her!' And stopped trusting her!"

"And?"

"I never really trusted again…until I met Veronica."

Paul just looked at him quietly, and asked him what his body was telling him.

"My belly is tender, but not cramping anymore. I…I've been so afraid she doesn't love me anymore!"

"Why?'

The younger man started sobbing again, then reached for another tissue, wiped his eyes, and looked imploringly at Paul.

"I don't know."

"Massimo, I think you do. Come on. Tell me. I see it in your eyes."

"Veronica…reminds me of my mother!

"Ah!"

"I've been freaking out ever since I ran into that asshole! I wanted to kill him!"

"And?"

"I wanted to kill her too!"

"OK."

"I'm just so goddamn ashamed!"

"Of what happened?"

"No! I let the fucker get away with it!"

Paul could see that there was more, and decided to wait patiently for it to tumble out.

"But when I saw him, he was just this bent-over old man with a three-toed walker!"

Paul thought he could see the process, and asked a critical question to clarify.

"So what did you do with your shame and rage?"

"What do you mean?"

"It doesn't just go away. What happened to how you were feeling?"

"I'm not sure what you mean."

"OK. Did you go out and scream? Beat up a tree? Drive a hundred miles an hour?"

"No. I just…sort of kept it to myself."

"Did you share it with Veronica?"

"No. I was too ashamed!"

"And now?"

Massimo looked perplexed, the fine features of his face drawn as he looked distractedly up at the corner of the office ceiling.

"I wanted to tell her, but I'm afraid she won't believe me!"

"Like your Mom?"

"That sounds crazy!"

"I'm not saying you're crazy. Aren't you angry with her because she reminds you of your mother?"

"What'd you mean?"

"You had a sudden confrontation with someone from your past who harmed you. It brought up all of these feelings, and you couldn't follow through—you couldn't kill him, right?"

"Yeah."

"And your Mom shamed you further, right, when you told her?"

"I think you may be remembering the past and projecting it onto the present."

"OK! OK! And what? You think I'm turning Veronica into my mother?"

"You said you were too embarrassed to tell Veronica. Just like with your mother!"

"I don't know. Maybe."

"When did things start going sour with the two of you?"

"Shit! Right about the same time!"

"It might help if you tell her, clearly and honestly."

"I want to go home and tell her everything!"

"What do you think? How does your belly feel?"

He rubbed his stomach tenderly, and then said, "It's sore but it wants my sweetie to know all about me! I'm not afraid now! Not ashamed!"

"Then that's exactly what you should do, if you feel complete for today."

"Thanks, Doc."

"No, congratulations! You had the courage to go into that deep, dark place, and recover yourself. Good job! And leave me a message tomorrow, tell me how you're feeling. OK?"

CHAPTER THIRTEEN
Food—for the Soul?

San Francisco, March 1998

Paul was reverent about his alone time. Conversely he felt genuine heartache about not having a deeper human connection with a loving woman—though like many long-time bachelors, he believed he would have to sacrifice his solace in order to have her. He needed to be able to stay fluid emotionally, to keep his life flowing like water across a shark's gills. He dreamed of the day when he could write without having to work, though that might yet be decades in accomplishment.

He missed his real friends, the people who had proven their love and loyalty by being willing to be "there" for him through the many difficult years. And his dear sisters, who he loved dearly, but seeing them entailed visiting the dreaded Midwest. He had fled St. Louis, the city of his birth in 1966, thanks to a draft notice—and never looked back. He had lived on the West Coast almost thirty years and they had never visited, while he could barely be in the heartland three days before getting withdrawal symptoms for the ocean.

Maybe he was just deeply confused, or perhaps it had been his terrible role models, but it seemed that appearance versus essence, versus soul, had such a huge effect on relationships. Paul had spent countless hours in therapy dealing with his shame around body weight and body-image. He had even considered that he might have Body Dysmorphic Disorder because he viewed his body in such distorted ways. (Or perhaps his not feeling valued was reflected in the body weight as a way of having something to blame—a further obfuscation). He had always seemed to require mass quantities of food to fill the gaping black hole that lived in his belly consuming any and all magnetism that came within his gravitational pull—as if anything could ever hope to sate that aching, dyscrasic hunger that could potentially consume the Universe. It was a reckless, heedless ingestion disorder. Long before coffee, alcohol, tobacco or marijuana, opium or cocaine; before he had ever consumed speed or LSD—he had been a junkie! Even though underneath this ravaging, raging desire lived the desire to be whole and connected within himself—to be seen, to be heard, to be known—not even as an artist, but simply as a viable, lovable, worthy human being.

Much of his recovery had been Inner Child-related, or by other forms of regressive work aimed at allowing catharsis and abreaction. Now after all the years of detox and recovery from so many addictions; after all the healing work on himself; he had been brought to his knees, metaphorically and actually, by this original addiction—the overwhelming indisputable craving for carbohydrates from which he could not escape, no matter how much he deprived himself of cakes, pies, and pastries; no matter what eating strategies he adopted, or how much pleading he did with gods and goddesses known or unknown; no matter what austerities he practiced—fasting, vegetarian, vegan, raw foods; no matter his pleas to the One Who Is Always Listening—nothing seemed to prevail in the chiaroscuro battle that raged inside of him, the most insidious, vicious, demanding, and visible of all addictions.

He always fantasized that if, having ascertained the why of the emotional carbo-craving, he could graduate to ways to avoid using them and lose the weight! And thereafter integrate the energy into more healthful processes? Would he never again have to deal with all the shame and misuse of his vital energy? It was his most cherished fantasy. This possibility did seem to be the ultimate and profound reversal of process—wanting the outcome before having experienced the excruciating practice of having healed the shame that fueled it, layer after layer, to be integrated, and forgiven forever.

Like many topics he had tackled, he wanted so, so much to be able to just think his way through his disfigured emotions. As he often taught his clients, emotions were far more compelling, more primal, more driving. He had worked thousands of cases, and come to the somewhat excruciating conclusion that the cognitive work had to come after the emotional. It would then provide a structure for re-ordering the vaulted emotional spaces that had been emptied of all of the toxic elements previously so successfully suppressed, and hiding genuine self-love.

He was convinced—again perhaps delusionally—that his salvation lay in getting thin and staying that way—to eschew forever all of the sugars and other carbohydrates that he blamed for his horrible loneliness, for the belief that his size and weight kept him from developing a loving relationship with another—though it was, in fact, probably only his hatred of himself and his unwillingness to forgive both himself and others that led to the piling on of the pounds. He had to admit he craved that dopamine rush, that fleeting comfort that, like cocaine (in a different way), filled him with a sense of wholeness, wellness, and invincibility in the face of the toxic vulnerability that he had learned as a child. He "knew" he had adopted this stance at the time when good self-care would have threatened the loss of the extremely narcissistic relationship with his mother; when any such effort would have been seen as a withdrawal of his dependence on her—something she required at all cost, her needing him, feeding her, emotionally, intimately. She would not, could not, have borne him taking care of himself. He would have become stable, and expand a healthy desire to relationships with others instead of his waistline, and being stickily bound to her. She had needed him tied to her forever, endlessly providing her with everything she craved emotionally, as if he were a missing vitamin or hormone. It allowed her to temporarily keep at bay her awareness of deprivation and deficiency, her own addictions, losses, and hungers. He had been her toy from the very beginning, conceived as her personal emotional savior, reared to be an emotional slave to do her bidding because she could not get them met by her husband, the emotionally vacant and violent man she had married. What did a little kid know? Giving her oral sex had become his salvation. She was his altar, his refuge from the insanity of his world outside of their precious moments together, cementing his sycophantic, obsequious vulnerability toward all women left him fully at the mercy of his fluctuating moods—unable to either retrieve or therapeutically release his dissociated knowledge and information of her perfidy, doomed to spend many decades in search of an elusive woman who would unlock him, liberate him from the chains his mother had twined around his heart with barbed wire knots; that consigned him to immersion in eternal emotional turmoil, self-degradation, and self-repudiation to manage and carry the weight of his emotional burdens denied—in order protect his mother, the perpetrator; in order that she never be revealed for her crimes against him for which he had paid the eternal cost.

It was so fucking sick, all his many years in denial, and all shattered in that one night—the most powerful, earth-shaking flashback he had ever experienced! She had awakened his nascent preternatural sexual abilities, and fused them with his naturally developing desire for nurturing and attachment—and sent him down the path to healing his own soul and becoming the savior and champion of his own self! Indeed, a blessing and a curse simultaneously—the most insidious and beauteous conundrum to be unwound simultaneously in his heart.

CHAPTER FOURTEEN

The Haunted, Vaunted Streets of her Heart

San Francisco, September 1997

"It's all this skin," said Mandy, and for the second time during her appointment, started to pull out the edge of her blouse in an attempt to show Paul the excessive skin that had been vacated post-surgery. For the second time, Paul had demurred.

"Mandy, please! I do not need to see your extra flesh. I know it really bothers you, but I cannot help but feel it has become your new obsession. And I know it's probably an extra twenty pounds that you would like to have removed."

"Absolutely! The sooner the better, damn it!"

"The fact remains that you're still finding physical reasons for you to feel bad."

"If the goddamn insurance company would just approve the surgery…"

"Mandy! Please listen!"

She looked at him incredulously.

"What?"

"You haven't heard a word I've said!'

"What? No! Yes! Yes I have!"

"OK. What?"

"Uhh, you think that I'm blaming my extra skin since I lost all that weight."

"'Blaming yourself' for what?"

"Uhh, I…don't know…exactly."

"Precisely. That is exactly the issue I want to talk with you about. The whole point, really, of all of our work since you were pre-surgical."

"OK. What's that?"

"The same thing I keep broaching with you. There's something deeper than how you look that gives rise to you not feeling good about yourself—first the weight, and now the skin."

"But it's true!" she said in a pleading voice, pinching a relatively substantial mound of flesh between her fingers.

Paul sighed.

"I am not denying the extra flesh! But why do you think you look so disfigured?"

"But I am," she whined.

"I'm not going to argue with you about it. I know Doctor Fernandez has spoken to you about this already."

Paul had spoken at length with the surgeon after Mandy had signed a Release of Information (ROI).

"OK. OK. Let's try another tack. Settle yourself. Sit up straight. Uncross your finger and legs."

"OK."

"Now just breathe in as if through the top of your head into your heart, deeply into the bottom of your belly before you breathe out through the bottoms of your feet. Don't think about it. Just do it!"

"This isn't going to help!"

"Please, Mandy! Just try it! OK?"

"OK."

Paul settled himself as well, and started doing the exact same breath. Since he used it with regularity, he found a rhythm almost immediately. He almost immediately slipped into an expanded aura of peace and relaxation. He reached out energetically, felt the golden lines of connection with her, and synched his breath with hers, allowing the connection to flow out to her.

"Now I want you to keep breathing deeply and regularly. And I want you to feel deeply into the center of your belly when you answer me. Do not think about what you are going to say. Just listen, and see if there's somebody who lives there that wants to talk. OK?"

"OK." Very softly.

"I…I'm a little confused. I want to be an adult, but I'm not."

"Just keep breathing."

"I'm…just a little girl."

"How old?"

"Four."

"What's your name?"

"Man-dee." Child's voice.

"Just keep breathing, Mandy."

"This is weird!" Adult voice.

"Just trust the process. Take another deep breath into your belly."

"Now Mandy, I want you to tell me about yourself."

"Like what?"

"Are you happy?"

Long pause.

"Sometimes."

"Just sometimes?"

"Yeah." Soft and slow, stretched out.

"Are you sometimes unhappy?"

"Yeah." Again.

"Why's that?"

"I 'on't know."

"Is it your Mommy?"

"Maybe."

"Do you love Mommy?"

"Oh yes!"

"Does mommy love you?"

Long pause.

"I guess so."

"You aren't sure?"

"Mommy's always busy."

"What's she doing?"

"She's carrying a dolly."

"A dolly?"

"Yeah and she cries all the time."

"She does?"

"Yeah."

"Is it maybe your little sister?"

"Maybe."

"Do you like her?"

Long, long pause.

"No!" Very abgrily.

"Why not?"

Another long pause.

"Mommy likes her better than me!"

Angry. Defiant. Tears at the edges of her eyes. A huge angry squawk that sounds a little like a wounded tropical bird. Then a bark of a sob escapes, followed by huge cascade of tears flowing unimpeded down her cheeks.

"I tried to be a big girl!" Distraught adult voice tainted with strained child.

"I know you did."

"I did! She told me to be a big girl!"

"Who?'

"Mommy!"

"Where was your Dad?"

"I 'on't know." Little girl again.

"She told me I had to be a big girl!"

More tears and the beginnings of anger in her voice.

"Goddamn her! I was only four!" Full adult voice now.

"Fucking bitch! I was a child too!" Adult tailing off to sad child voice.

And now a massive burst of sobbing as Mandy repeatedly strikes herself on the thighs.

"I tried! I fucking tried so hard!"

As Mandy reaches for the tissue box, she opens her eyes.

"Jesus! Where the fuck did that come from?" Adult in the present.

"Welcome back, Mindy! Your little girl just got released—maybe for the first times since you were a child."

"Jesus! You know I remember it now! Why couldn't I remember it before?"

"I would venture to say that you didn't feel safe. You weren't ready."

"Jesus!"

"Welcome back," said Paul and handed her a glass of water.

CHAPTER FIFTEEN

Perchance to Dream

San Francisco, October 1997

He fell into a deep sleep, deep sleep during which he had a dream that cautioned him that his excess weight was part of what he had to endure on his "punishment tour" on Planet Earth. Sometimes he believed he was expected to withstand a great deal before he could be released from his commitment to being here in this body; that he would at some point at which he would have expiated enough of his "sins" to be released to go "home," which for him was always Alcyone, the brightest star in the Pleiades. He had dreamed about it so many times, visited by the ethereal beings who lived there; and having a life amongst people of similar high intelligence and spiritual consciousness, where he could genuinely feel and be himself amongst equals; where he could be seen and loved, cherished and appreciated by true peers, rather than having to endure the daily agony of living amongst those he genuinely considered to be savages. It was difficult for him to have compassion for them, especially as a world mass—though he did have a soft spot for vets and survivors child abuse.

Since most people found drugs to be a "problem" (most usually related to property crimes), he was seen as oppositional, even heretical, because he saw them as just another artifact of the fascist nature of the society in which they lived. He certainly sided with luminaries such as Thomas Szasz, R.D. Laing, Peter Breggin, and Loren Moser—all treatment professionals who upheld the belief in healing without the intervention of the deadly brain-damaging chemicals proposed (actually now mandated) by "mainstream" psychiatry's strictly biological approach—so hungry were they still to be an accepted by the medical hierarchy. (More than a hundred years after Freud, and still yammering to be let in the house!)

Most people assumed Paul would be full of derision and negativity toward drugs, being clean as long as he had been, but he was not. In fact, sometimes he said that "Drugs saved my life!" because in many ways they had, especially stimulants and LSD. They had helped him pull himself out of the giant hole of despair and depression in which he had from early on lived. Paul was especially offended by Nancy's Reagan's inane "Just say 'NO!" campaign. And he always had to correct people who said he was "clean and sober." Though he had quit drinking alcohol for eleven years, he was now able to have a glass of wine or a snifter of Drambuie every two or three months—a single drink with nary a desire for another, or to binge.

Most people, even vets, seemed completely brainwashed about the intentions, and disinformation, of the government—our ostensibly benevolent intent toward other countries and our own citizens; about "spreading democracy" globally; about fighting constant wars in the name of "freedom" (93 wars in Third World countries since WWII); about domestic and foreign surveillance; about the CIA's true purpose and its involvement in some of the most heinous crimes ever committed in the name of "life, liberty, and the pursuit of happiness"—all of the assassinations, genocide, destabilization of governments, murders, and false imprisonments—all of the vast network of fascist interconnections; and the corrupt venal network of government, and former governmental members working together to subvert the rule of law for their own enrichment, often using the International Monetary Fund and the World Bank to bankrupt the economies of other countries so they could be stripped of their rich natural resources "legally."

Even after all these years, Paul still felt split as a veteran about Vietnam, and about war in general. He felt split about a lot of things, especially because he was far more spiritually advanced than most of the people on Earth—mentally, spiritually, and emotionally—and was therefore superior.

One of his more difficult tasks was having to find a way to say "You're welcome!" when people thanked him for serving, when what he felt was a deep churning in his guts that threatened to erupt like a massive diarrhea, related to the lies and bullshit the fucking "G" (as he called it) represented, and the purposeful lies, that were served up to maintain the shiny image that politicians wanted maintained at any cost in order to cover up all of the blood spilled and the lives disrupted to honor that tarnished image.

He was proud of having served with his brothers, but ashamed of the larger venue in which it had taken place; that linked him to the slaughter of the Native peoples of this continent to steal the land we call "America," and all of the crimes committed since in order to hold it and its citizens hostage to this pseudo-benevolent, paternal image. It was goddamn disgusting! It was fucking insulting! It made him want to puke long, green streams of bile. Sometimes he felt completely ashamed of being a human being!

Even joining MENSA hadn't really helped, though he had met many interesting, exciting, even beautiful and brilliant people, with diverse and incredible backgrounds and histories. He felt a certain kinship being amongst a group of people whose IQs were guaranteed by psychological testing to be in the genius range—theoretically the upper one percent of intelligence on the planet. That did not, however, exempt them from all of the human quirks and foibles—in fact, it almost guaranteed that these human artifacts would be amplified, and they were. One of the reasons that he had not become too deeply immersed in this small, alternate culture was that the aforementioned quirks and foibles. They tended to trigger Paul into both exhibiting his own more freely, and contributed to his turning more deeply inward in self-examination, (even self-repudiation) at what he considered his failings. It seemed that whatever symptoms of loneliness and isolation he had hoped to avoid, were, in fact, compounded by meeting with these brilliant, beautiful people.

The problem was that he kept "falling in love" with extraordinary and unavailable women. It seemed an inescapable pattern: he'd meet someone interesting and attractive, have a conversation, or do some kind of processing together at a workshop; and experience exhilaration, joy, and a truly altered state in which he felt whole and fulfilled, as if he had never been damaged; as if he had never suffered through all of his years with desires and expectations unfulfilled and unfulfillable; as if he had not writhed and twisted in the throes of utter agony beyond bearing, the screams echoing though his soul; as if he had not spent tortured hours immersed in a rich and malicious stew of toxic memories and insults—and yet he believed himself to be well and truly "in love!"

He had had to repeatedly come to the not-so-amazing conclusion that he himself must be unavailable emotionally. The equation was inexact, though he firmly believed that there was a mirroring effect at work, in that he believed that everything anyone generated managed to find a correspondence in the Living Universe that manifested it in form. It related to what Michael Talbot had called *The Holographic Universe* in which every object or person was a reflection of every other within the Greater Whole.

David Bohm had said in a now defunct magazine called *Clarion Call,* that there is an "Implicate Order that exists as an ultimate physical substrate that underlies our present perception of reality. Although the parts appear to be distinct from the whole, in fact, because they 'enfold' or include the whole, they are identical with the whole. If we could invoke the precedent of quantum mechanical indefinability, we could leap to the idea of a united entity encompassing all space and time in which each part contains the whole, and is identical to it."

This was absolutely mind-blowing in its implications! And it led directly to the understanding that he could heal himself, not by having to eliminate all those "parts" of himself he didn't like, or would wish to get rid of, but by integrating all of these aspects of himself, which were, in turn, developed early to defend him against physical and emotional assaults perpetrated upon him. As such, it implied that there was no need of any kind of surgical removal of the artifacts, but simply allowing himself to feel the loss and grieve what had developed as a result of the most egregious boundary violations he had ever experienced. This would, in turn, lead to the connectedness, blessing and grace he well and truly craved, but also to love itself, fully and complete, needing nothing, being at ALL, complete unto itself, timeless and eternal, forever.

Paul awoke exhausted, lying on the couch in his therapy office. He felt as if his very bones had turned to dust. Deep waves of exhaustion chased each other through his decimated nervous system as if each of them were gasping for revenge upon the very body that had birthed them in flame and fury. He felt as if he were still floating in the dreams, as they were real and true, and he was not. He shook his head once, twice, and then heaved himself up off the couch. He pushed the button on the two cup coffee maker pre-loaded with his favorite blend of 2/3 French Roast and 1/3 Mocha Java, and headed for the shower. He had a two hour session scheduled with one of his regular clients in less than an hour.

CHAPTER FIFTEEN

Progress, not Perfection

San Francisco, September 1997

One of the miracles that had transpired during the course of our work together had been Willie's desire to reach out to his father. At first the elder Spieth had been very reluctant to have anything to do with his wayward son and heir, but after several attempts, Willie had gotten one of his attorneys to intervene with one of his father's attorneys—and they had arranged a conference call.

Willie had been brutally honest with his father—about his early life; the drugs; being bounced out of any number of top-flight schools; payments made to various and sundry individuals to keep him out of jail; the vandalism he had visited on the *Schloss von Spieth* once in the throes of teenaged angst and rebellion, not to mention various outlays of cash to the families of young women with whom he had dallied sexually.

And he apologized, an act that at first his father thought might be another of Willie's cruel jokes—and refused to believe.

"No, Papa, I really mean it! I…have been an arschloch! *I have hurt you, Mama, just about everyone!'*

"You're lying! It's just your grandfather's money you're interested in!"

"No, Papa! No!"

"I do not believe you!"

"I'm telling the truth!"

At which point, his father had hung up on him.

Twenty minutes later he was in my office, vacillating between being livid with anger, and sobbing out his frustration and shame.

"Fuck! I don't know how to get through to him!"

"He's hardened his heart against you, maybe for what seem like really good reasons."

"Thank God he doesn't have anything to do directly with the Trustee's Board!"

"But he has influence, no?"

"Oh hell yes! Some of the voting members have known my father all of his life!"

"OK. Let's look at this from another angle."

"What?"

"You want what you want…"

He started to object and Paul intervened, both hands open and palms out and up directed at him.

"I'm not saying that you haven't truly changed, and don't deserve your trust fund."

"OK. What?"

"Let me finish my thoughts, OK?"

"As I was saying, you want what you want and you're frustrated. You cannot change your father directly. Shit, he won't even talk to you. And you cannot yet directly sway the Board."

"OK. Right."

"So what can you do so you use your energy…in ways that will benefit you, versus getting further frustrated and angry?"

"OK."

"So how are we going to do that?"

"'We?'"

"Well, of course. You think I'm going to abandon you now, after all of the shit we been through together?"

"Thanks, man."

"So the next level of our work together will focus on you forgiving yourself for all of your own faults and foibles, so you don't make the situation worse."

"How's that going to change anything?"

"First it won't make things worse. It will stop you working against yourself."

"What?"

"When you're as angry as you can get, it doesn't help you. It makes you more determined to get you own way. You work harder to prove yourself right."

"Oh."

"So, if you can forgive yourself, then maybe you can forgive your father."

"But…"

"I'm not saying he's right, or that you are. I'm just saying that forgiveness can be miraculous. If you can stop being so (here

Paul made air quotes) "right" all the time, you might have a little more room in your heart to listen to other people, even your father."

Willie just sat there, head down, contemplating. Then he looked up, cheeks tear-stained, and broke into an uncertain smile.

"You think I can?"

"Absolutely!"

Then a glimmer of the old Willie reappeared, like a flashback out nightmare shadows.

"Goddamn you! I've changed so much I don't even recognize myself anymore!"

"And the way you used to be was working real well for you, was it?"

"Fuck you! I don't even know who I am anymore!"

"I would say that you don't yet know who you are going to become. Or even who you always were underneath the overlay of arrogance and rage you've always carried."

"And who is that?"

"Who you really are is emerging from the mists, now that the cultural overlay is disappearing."

"But who's that? Who will I be?"

"Are you willing to explore and find out?"

CHAPTER SIXTEEN

Tilting at the Proverbial

San Francisco, October 1997

He was such a good, even brilliant therapist—but he seemed constitutionally incapable of applying to himself all of the good and beautiful approaches he used with his clients. Physician heal thyself indeed!

Every time he convinced himself that he might actually be free of his rage, it popped up like an NVA out of a spider hole. He decided he probably could not live without it. He was so terrified of living without a sword and shield to protect his adult self from his remaining traumatic memories, his areas of seeming weakness and what he called "toxic vulnerability;" afraid that he might lose what small measure of self-possession and strength that he had gained. If he were not able to pull up a roar from deep in his gut and put the "laser beam look" in his eyes to push people away when he felt threatened, he might conceivably feel completely naked and regressed. This was totally at odds with his lived experience of letting go of anger and rage—he had actually always felt more emotionally flexible and "bigger," more available and able to function.

Paul was very frustrated sometimes wanting to make more of a contribution to the upliftment of humanity, which of course, would require his letting go of some of his more crippling personal restraints. He could sometimes feel his connection with a great change that was coming. He wanted to pass on lessons he had learned to younger men—even if that seemed more to be warnings about how not to live, what to avoid, and perhaps only a few shortcuts to a better way to live.

He had begun to forgive the deep sense of loss, remorse really, about things both done and undone—opportunities missed, failures to connect, or even times he had! So he decided he had to seek out a competent therapist with whom to process his emotions. He had friends, real friends, with whom he could talk about all of this, and he did; but it was almost always more like shared experience and some commiseration than the electric jolt he often wanted, and occasionally got, out of therapy.

He feared becoming dissociative again. He had been having difficulty remembering his dreams lately. It was a serious symptom for him. He was so often guided by them. Sometimes his dreams even provided narrative flow, dialogue, even characters and plot lines. Sometimes when he had creative constipation, he would go to bed and ask for a dream—and the Universe almost always answered. And then, there were the healing dreams that seemed to have been sent both for himself and others.

It was the ultimate male heresy, but Paul sometimes felt acutely ashamed of being a man, especially the image of the contemporary, old-style, knuckle-dragging male that had come to dominate planetary attention for the last eight or ten thousand years with the might makes right imperative. There was, of course, the deeper level. He was actually ashamed of being a human being on Planet Earth during these barbaric times. It smacked strongly of R.D. Laing's "ontological insecurity," that he interpreted as being ashamed of ever having been born. Even his brilliant intellect could not refute the power of the emotions he felt around this topic. He really considered most people to be backward, even primitive, and he was unable to dismiss it with even at the widest possible aperture of his emotional camera lenses. He felt so dislocated from life on Earth, feeling, that he did not belong here. Not just in the sense of not fitting in with the bulk of humanity because of his intellect or his refined sensibilities, but more the dreams and visions he had had most of his life of being from the far future, and having come here from the Pleiades, having come back ten thousand years to these times in order to be a part of a large committed group of individuals who came to support a humanity emerging from millennia of being spiritually suppressed and emotionally manipulated. He so strongly identified with Dane Rudyhar's New Group of World Servers promoted by the Theosophists, so felt himself to be an intrinsic part of them.

He wavered back and forth between feeling unloved and unwanted, and truly not belonging, because he was an inter-dimensional alien. He thought he might never escape it, to walk and talk free in the world as a fully-fledged man who truly loved himself, and the world into which he had been born, to which he had come with a mission from beyond. He had been experiencing some twinges of angst and uncertainty lately about exactly where he wanted to go with his life, and had hence decided to find a new therapist.

He sorted through all kinds of possibilities he had experienced—Holotropic Breathwork, Primal Therapy, bodywork-related therapies, hypnotherapies, and regressive work, parts work and Shadow Work, Jungian and Freudian psychoanalysis, psychodynamic and abreaction work; art therapy or biofeedback; co-counseling or cognitive; Gestalt or drama therapy; desensitization eye-movement; family constellation, Hakomi; humanistic, Logotherapy; milieu therapy, music therapy; Motivational Interviewing, ontological hermeneutics; psychodrama, rational emotive therapy; Rogerian, schema therapy; Transactional Analysis, Twelve Steps; Vegotherapy, Wilderness therapy. He decided he perhaps wanted a hypnotherapist, to help him get better access to his earliest thoughts, dreams, and perceptions; to answer questions about when he had first arrived on planet; about what Redfield had called "birth vision."

He had read the works of Stone and Winkleman (later Stone and Stone) describing "subpersonalities" in Voice Dialogue, pointing to the distinct possibility of there being an entire plethora of inner children and other personalities (such as an Inner Critic) that are rarely contacted or consulted, not even ever known and acknowledged by the individuals involved—and they therefore remained unintegrated and unavailable to be used by individuals; and held vital energy and information that could and would enrich the individual's life if released. He wanted to be a fully human male, even with his memories of another radically different life; to love his life and act as a warrior and protector for women, children, and the planet itself. It was a seemingly endless quest paralleling his journey toward being illuminated by the Great Light.

He trolled through his rolodex, put in calls to a dozen therapist colleagues he trusted, and checked through the Yellow Pages (with a semi-smirk about the advisability of finding a decent therapist there!). He had both a list of qualities he was seeking, and of potential outcomes. They were relatively flexible, except in one respect: he was going to get to the root of his crippling anger/rage issues, and he was going to heal his lifelong aching hunger for the "perfect woman." He knew he had to act rather quickly because he had started having seriously broken sleep (both waking up in the middle of the night and being unable to return, even difficulty getting down to sleep at all). As well, there were times when he felt his vital energy so dissipated that he just plain did not want to get out of bed; to just lay there and read all day, arising only for the bathroom and occasional food and drink. He laughed as he added both hyposomnia and hypersomnia to his evaluation of himself. But it was not an entirely bad thing, especially since he took advantage of the extra waking hours to either read one of the many mystery novels he enjoyed, or to get up and add more pages to growing his latest manuscript.

Rita Tallmage was a psychologist. She looked a lot younger than her years—tall, even statuesque, raven hair, with green eyes. He had met her at a party through her partner, Janine Gleason, a lawyer, at a party thrown to celebrate the publication of Janine's first novel, a courtroom drama, featuring, naturally, a lesbian Prosecuting Attorney who fights discrimination and sexual harassment while ferrying a case through court that should have been a slam-dunk, except that all of the witnesses start disappearing. Even the prosecutor (Carole Jenkins, although her friends called her "Butch") is frequently threatened and then abducted before justice prevails.

At any rate, they'd had an interesting conversation, and exchanged cards. When he called her, he mentioned that he wanted a consult, and they agreed to set aside an hour.

When he arrived the following Tuesday, she was taken aback when he mentioned that he was seeking therapy for himself.

"You've caught me totally by surprise. I thought you wanted to consult with me about a client of yours. That's why I quoted you my consultation rate."

"That's OK. I'm perfectly willing to pay. I'm wanting to do some more deep personal work, and I've set up appointments with several potential therapists. But we hit it off so well at the party that I thought I'd have a session with you, to see if we could work together."

Rita looked at him for a long moment, and then laughed.

"I don't know quite how to put this. My private practice is limited to women only."

Now it was Paul's turn to be embarrassed.

"Oh shit! I guess I really stepped into it! I should have been more revealing up front!"

"And I was trying to act more broadminded than I usually am, being that you're a psychologist too."

With this they looked at each other with guilty eyes, and small smiles. He started to chortle, as she giggled. Then they both broke out in a small wave of laughter.

"I guess that'll teach me," they both said simultaneously, and then laughed harder.

"Under the circumstances, I think this is a 'No Bill!' she said.

"Are you sure? It's partly my fault too."

"We both learned a lesson here today. I'm glad it happened."

"Me too."

Paul left her office, and decided he should be much more up front with the next therapists on his list. He really wanted a female therapist. Pamela Fernandez was a therapist with whom he had shared a married couple who had been referred for therapy by the court. She had taken the wife, and he had worked with the husband.

After several months of individual sessions, and numerous consultations together, they decided to work the pair together, with both of them facilitating. Another six sessions, and they were complete, marriage repaired, and he and Pamela on their way to being friends. All of which was wonderful, and precluded there ever being anything more because Pamela was married to a hulking body builder who owned a custom-design auto shop—and she was happy. So when he set up an appointment with her for two days later, she was happy to do so. He told her to determine if they could work together with him as a client.

After a spate of small talk, she asked, "So you're wanting to do some personal work?"

"Yeah, like I told you, I keep having these periodic depressions, but I know they're related to my old issues with my father. I believe I've introjected his rage, and I've always believed it was mine."

"Do you have a preferred approach?"

"Some kind of expressive work, something cathartic. I just don't want to carry this any longer."

"I don't really do Primal Therapy or anything like that."

"I understand."

"My best approach would be psychodynamic psychotherapy, with the intention that you will travel to those deep old spots and uncover the anomalies and inconsistencies."

"I'm really serious here. I need the emotional release!"

"I understand. I understand!"

"So how deep can we go, together? How willing are you told space for me if I plunge deeply into Inner Child work? Do you use it?"

"I know that Carl Jung originated the concept with the Divine Child archetype. Later Emmet Fox called it the 'Wonder Child,' and Charles Whitfield later dubbed it the 'Child Within.' It was in 1963 that Hugh Missildine wrote 'Your Inner Child of the Past' and made the idea popular. And then Roberto Assagioli brought it into context as a subpersonality within the framework of psychosynthesis."

"Wow! You know more about this than I do!

"Thanks!"

"Except I'm actually more interested in subpersonalities, like in Voice Dialogue."

"Is that going to get you where you want to go?"

"I don't know. I don't know!"

"How…I know you're not big on medications, but…"

"Fuck that! I'm really disappointed that you would even mention it!"

"Might help!"

"No! Never! Not in a million years!"

He left her office severely depressed, and pissed off that he had felt so close to his goal. But that she would even mention meds…Fuck!

That night he slept poorly again, woke up at 0300, reached out his hand as if to touch the hip of the loving woman he wished were there, cursed, turned on the bedside light, and read for almost two hours before falling to sleep. He awoke at 0700, groggy, grumpy, and with no memory of his dreams.

CHAPTER SEVENTEEN
A Surprise in North Beach

San Francisco, November 1997

Frustrated by his inability to find a competent therapist, Paul had been doing his own stress relief work—screaming at the top of his lungs while driving down the Peninsula, or while driving to the top of Mount Tamalpais; screaming into a pillow; beating the shit out of a stack of pillows with a plastic bat (something he had learned in Primal Therapy); even bashing a tree with a large stick on one occasion—all of which generally left him sobbing, sometimes for long periods, even hours; and hoarse, with a sore throat and aching belly muscles, and a blessed feeling of relief that sometimes lasted for days.

All of his strategies had helped reduce his angst, and actually seemed to improve his effectiveness in interacting with clients. He was acutely aware that his rapport with his clients had increased because he was more emotionally available.

He had been dealing more confidently with other men too—instead of ignoring them, or brushing aside any routine contact, except with other vets. In Vietnam he had experienced the most intense brotherhood possible; lived it, breathed it, every single moment of every single day; bathed in it, drank it, ate it, cried and screamed and exulted in it, every single deep rich, never-to-be-forgotten moment. He had been reticent, even reluctant to let anyone get too close ever since he had come home.

One day recently he had been walking around North Beach, and stopped in at Specs, the venerable institution at 12 Adler Place, just off Columbus. It was actually almost more of a museum, featuring a walrus penis hanging above the bar, (actually it looks kind of like a child's femur), next to the sign that says "All dogs found on the premises will be turned over to Chef Matsumoto for the Sunday luau," and an Alaskan king crab mounted on the wall just beyond the end of the bar. The walls are drunk with pictures, posters, notices ("How to Get a Drink" to the immediate left upon entering), shipping company pennants and drawings (pencil sketches of neighborhood notables done on cocktail napkins and framed, are especially prominent). Way in the back, near the piano, is a full-sized mummy case, whose face, on closer inspection, is a pretty good likeness of Specs himself, a gift from Dancer, a former Specs bartender who had serious artistic talent. Of course, there was a coin slot in the mummy's head, encouraging the long established tradition to contribute.

Glass display cases containing scrimshaw, American Indian artifacts, lapel pins, political pamphlets, a stuffed armadillo, even a stuffed mongoose locked in mortal combat with a stuffed cobra. Paul always seemed to find something new, even though he had been going there for years.

It was late on a chilly, windy afternoon, and he decided to have a double espresso and a snifter of Drambuie. He was sitting quietly (he may have been the only one) at a table scribbling in his journal, when this very energetic fellow—maybe a little bit younger than he—stopped by the table holding an espresso and a snifter half-filled with amber liquid. At first Paul thought he was being gifted a free refill, but he was quickly disabused of that notion.

"Mind if I sit at your table? Place is pretty crowded."

"Always is," said Paul, moving his hat and gloves from the other side of the table to an extra chair.

The man settled, and Paul automatically made a note of his features and dress in his journal. He sometimes created characters from such random encounters, even snippets of dialogue—most especially in San Francisco, where quirky people, artists, and just plain characters were the norm.

The man looked well-to-do, neatly dressed in a pair of pressed jeans, a blue Oxford cotton Brooks Brothers' shirt, and a decent pair of tasseled loafers. His hair was short, but well-cut, and he had an air of jollity about him. Paul felt inclined to talk to him for no reason at all.

"For a moment there, I thought you were bringing me a free refill!"

The other man looked up, smiled, and sipped from his snifter.

"Double espresso and Irish Mist."

"Double espresso and a Drambuie here!"

They both laughed, and then shook hands.

"Paul Marzeky."

"Darryl, Darryl Croesius." He said his first name like "drill," and Paul immediately started a mental file with that name for a character, and slotting in the details he had observed so far.

"Any relation to King Croseus of Lydia?" asked Paul off-handedly.

"Only the very astute ever ask me a question like that! Most people have never heard of him. Besides, there is an 'i' instead of an 'e' in my name, so the spelling is different."

"But still, it's pretty damn close."

"Surely is. And, I must admit, sometimes I wish I had his money!"

"Of course, but you might have suffered the same tragic ending if you did!"

Croesus was renowned for his wealth. According to Herodotus, Croesus encountered the Greek sage Solon, and showed him his enormous wealth. Croesus, secure with his wealth and happiness, asked Solon who was the happiest man in the world. Solon responded that Croesus could not be the happiest man because the fickleness of fortune meant that the happiness of a man's life could not be judged until after his death. Surely enough, Croesus' hubristic happiness was soon reversed by the tragic deaths of his son who was accidentally killed, followed, according to Critias, by his wife's suicide after the fall of Sardis; and then, of course, his own defeat and overthrow by the Persian king Cyrus the Great in 546 BCE.

"You seem to be quite the historian."

"When I got back from Vietnam, I started researching the history of Southeast Asia for my first novel."

"'Southeast Asia', huh?"

"Yeah. I travelled there pretty extensively."

"Where?"

"Taiwan. India. Vietnam."

"'Vietnam?' During the war?"

"Yeah. 1968-69."

"Were you on the front lines?"

Paul hesitated as he did when civilians asked questions like this, people who had no real idea what it had been like; and contemplated how much he could, or should, share with him. He followed his intuition in believing that this was not just a one-time meeting; that this was someone who could become a friend; and decided to sketch it out a bit.

"There really weren't 'front lines. We occupied strategic areas and worked to hold them, whereas the Viet Cong and the NVA fought a very unconventional guerilla war. In 1966, the First Cav got beat up really badly in the Ia Drang Valley. After that, the military decided to make it a war of attrition, using 'body count' as a measure of whether we were winning or not. (The guesstimate was that we had killed twelve of them for every of our own). The problem was that we had a limited number of men we were willing to commit, and they had millions to expend to get control of their native lands again. They were at war for a thousand years—the Chinese, the Japanese, the French, and then, after Dien Bien Phu in 1954, us. So body count meant absolutely nothing to them, and they knew they could not defeat us using conventional tactics."

"Jesus! I've never heard any of this. How old are you?"

"I'm forty one. You?"

"Thirty one."

"Ah!"

"'Ah?'"

"It makes more sense now. You were still in grade school when I was in the 'Nam."

"So, how do I ask about…?"

"Action is what you mean. So. I was not a grunt, in the infantry, not in a line company—in the sense of being on patrol and such, no. But I flew around on choppers a lot where I occasionally got shot at. I was in a lot of rocket and mortar attacks on fire bases and fire support bases—so in that sense, absolutely."

"Got it!"

"And I was a Social Work/Clinical Psychology Specialist, so I met with lots of guys comin' in out of the bush, dumping all of their emotional stuff on me."

"Jesus! That must have been heavy!"

"It was, but I've never been able to accept the label of 'combat vet'—even though a lot of the heavy duty combat vets have told me I'm one too!"

"Why not?"

Fuck! Paul thought, now I'm getting in deeper than I really intended. But, as he thought further, he decided to jump in.

"I've never believed I'd lived hard enough; never felt I deserved the title 'combat vet'! I was never a grunt. I never lived on the streets, shooting heroin."

"Wow! That's almost too much information."

"Yeah, you're right. I'm sorry."

"No. I'm…just…Most guys…except 'initiated men,' aren't willing to…be as open as that…Go so deep with a stranger."

"I've done a lot of work on myself."

"Yeah, it shows."

"But there always seems to be so much more to do!"

Darryl took another sip of his Irish Mist, and then looked at Paul above the lip of his snifter.

"I'm involved in men's work."

"What's that?"

"Drill" took a deep breath, set his snifter down, and took in the last dregs of his espresso, then smiled before looking directly into Paul's eyes.

"All men are taught to be savage warriors—staunch, eat our own pain, not cry, fight wars, and make money. We're nourished on conflict and violence. Nobody ever teaches us about cooperation, about helping each other."

"Yeah, I get fucking sick of it! I just wish there were another way!"

"That's what men's work is all about. I hang out with men who work at making the world better. We say 'I change the Universe by changing myself.'"

"Wow! That's fucking powerful shit!"

"Yeah, I think so."

"So how did you get into it?"

"A good friend of mine told me about what we call the Wild Men in the Woods Training (WMWT), a weekend training—forty-eight hours actually, Friday night through Sunday afternoon. We hang out with other men, learn new approaches to living."

Paul made a face, immediately skeptical.

"Is this some kind of cult?"

"No, not at all. There's no single leader, no ideology, or giving up your income. These guys are some of the finest men I've ever known—writers, artists, and business men too."

"Rich and poor?"

"All levels of economics, occupations, and temperaments too."

"I bet it's expensive as hell, huh?"

"Not at all, when it may change your life."

"Right! Five grand?"

"Nowhere near! $500!"

"I could manage that, especially if I could make it in two payments!"

"Easy, peasy!"

"Wait, wait, wait! We just met half an hour ago, and all of a sudden I'm signing up for a $500 training!"

"I'm sorry! You're right! You don't really know me, but you seem so ready for a change—I just thought that…maybe you might want to go!"

"No! You're right! I…I like the idea. I want another round! How about you?"

————

Then they'd each had another round, decided to stay in touch, and traded phone numbers. Darryl mentioned a men's group he attended regularly, and offered to bring Paul, if he wanted to think about it—which he did, almost obsessively, from the time they left the bar and went separate directions. Paul felt as if he had been offered a doorway into another, better world—or at least, to become a part of an effort to make the world better, not necessarily by him, but by those who would follow him, far, far into the future of the Great Unknown, a future not yet unfolded, waiting to unfold, far, far into the future where he could not, would not, be able to go.

He felt so connected with the vastness of living for the seventh generation from now of which his Native American friends spoke. That he could somehow be linked to such a tremendous possibility, such a far-reaching vision, simply reduced him to tears, tears that fell freely down his cheeks, and enriched the Earth with his expurgated sorrow, and his soul with its release—freeing him just a little bit more to walk taller, and more clearly, the path that stretched out in front of him. He felt so grateful, so filled with gratitude, so very, very glad to be being allowed to see, to touch this beautiful, as-yet-unfolded vision. It uplifted him, lent him the sense of being valuable, worthy, and loved—more so than he had ever felt at any other time since the moment he had taken human form.

He thought several times every day of signing up for the training. He felt drawn magnetically drawn, that there was something essential waiting for him out there, that would take him far better prepared into the future if he missed this golden opportunity, a prospect missed he would always regret.

He and Darryl had had several phone calls punctuated with a lot of laughter and witty repartee. Approximately a week after they'd met, Darryl invited him to the men's meeting he regularly attended that would include some other men who had attended his initiatory WMWT weekend with him.

They met at a large Queen Anne Victorian house on 26th and Diamond. There were eleven men ranging in age from twenty three to sixty one. There were three Latinos, two African-Americans, a Native American, and a bunch of White guys. They were construction workers, psychotherapists, artists, truck drivers, computer programmers, yoga teachers, and the unemployed. Five of the men had been through the initiatory weekend and some of the rest had signed up, though they all seemed to be aware of the processes, and utilized various aspects of the work in the meetings. They all had agreed to be as open as possible with each other, and to keep the confidentiality of all. All of this was elucidated after they had walked through a wall of sage smoke, and checked in with how they were feeling. At some point, one man started giving a long-winded explanation about why he was angry, and one of the more experienced men shouted, "Story, brother! Mercy, please!" which quickly put an end to the monologue.

Next, one by one, they went around the circle, and were prompted to look around and pick a man they knew least, and tell him something about themselves that they had never revealed to anyone before. By the time they had gone around the circle, there had been several bland, superficial replies, three angry outbursts, and one man who tearfully admitted that he had been abused as a child.

They took a short "bio-break" to drink water, and use the bathroom. When they re-gathered, the leader (called "The King") asked the men to take a deep breath into their bellies, and simply to feel into whatever they were holding there; and when it came their turn, to speak what that feeling was—only to do so as a sound, not words. Paul thought it a little odd, but recognized it as something that Fritz Perls might have used in a Gestalt session.

Paul was sitting on the furthest side of the room from "The King," who said he would model the work he had requested. He designated the man on his right hand side as the backup leader while he did his own work. He took a deep, deep breath—they could all see his belly expanding—and then he started what was at first a low hum, much like an "OM." He took another breath, and suddenly the room exploded with sound as the low murmur burst out of his chest, and then a growl like a wild animal angrily snarling erupted, as if his chest would rip open if he continued, but he did. The third breath erupted as if Hell's gates had shattered—and a weird mixture of half-slurred words, and even more animal sounds filled the room. Some of the other men looked a bit shocked; others opened their hands, palms out, toward the man, while a few, Paul included, seemed to swallow their initial fear, and allowed the desire to resist wash through them, and leaned forward expectantly instead. Paul heard another man's breath catch in his throat, and start to moan sympathetically, then noticed the tears flowing down another man's grizzly-bearded face—and felt himself responding to the primal output in the same way. Soon almost the entire circle was emotionally reacting as "The King" released a fourth and fifth time, eventually ending up quietly weeping in a fetal position in the center of the circle. His back-up spoke quietly to the group. He told everyone not to touch the man "who had just done his work," to "just keep breathing," and not to speak. Paul found himself sinking deeper and deeper into his personal store of memories and recollections, seeing streaming recurrent images of his father emotionally torturing him.

Fuck! I thought I was done with all of that shit!

Paul's thoughts echoed through him as he sat in the uneasy silence of his inner world. After the initial waves had driven through him like a raging hurricane, he found himself inexplicably quiet. He became increasingly sad as the trickling tears turned into a Biblical deluge. Soon his entire shirt front was drenched, and he went in search of a box of tissues.

As much as he hated to admit it, he still had deep canyons and crevasses within himself wherein were hidden unexpurgated rage and sadness that had failed, in spite of all his efforts, to be healed and integrated.

By this time, the designated "King" had made it to his chair again. The man sat quietly, still flushed, and then emitted a silent sob as he wiped his face and brow. Someone brought him a large glass of water, which seemed to restore some of his former *robusto*. Paul, amongst several others, sat in a kind of muted silence bordering on shock. John, "The King," had really exposed himself in front of a group of men in a way that most men would not have done, especially in front of strangers. So, it was with a certain amount of relief that they received the announcement from the backup man that the next portion of the meeting would be devoted to going around the circle—any man could pass—giving feedback to the man who had "worked," not advice or criticism, rather what each of them had felt, insights, greater awareness about personal issues, and such; and that "any man may start."

Paul found himself strangely moved, and raised his hand to speak first, not something he would ordinarily do. He took a deep breath before his emotions crept into his voice, wanting to speak as honestly and clearly as he could.

"I...don't...know exactly what to say, but," Paul said, looking at John, "I want to say how much I admire your bravery and honesty. I've never seen anything like it, except in therapy." He took a deep breath then, and suppressed a tear. Though his voice filled with emotion, he continued.

"I've done a lot of work on myself, but what I saw you do today, and all this incredible support…It's beyond anything I have ever experienced. I see a whole new level of faith…and hope, now. Because of you," looking at John, "all of you. I want to just say thanks, especially to Darryl, for bringing me here."

The backup man, Bobby, held up his hand, and said, "Giving thanks is something we reserve for the next round."

"OK," said Paul, "I just want to say that I have been deeply, deeply inspired today. Thanks."

Paul sat down, and started crying, feeling a vast relief wash through him; feeling that he had been gifted with a totally new direction for his life, gifted by the Creator—and feeling that he had done absolutely nothing to deserve it. It was true grace, pure grace, perhaps the most uncontaminated he had ever experienced.

CHAPTER EIGHTEEN
The Next Step Forward

San Francisco, November 1997

The day after the men's meeting, Darryl called him to ask about his continuing reactions. When Paul enthused excitedly about feeling new possibilities related to being more authentic, to be more able to honestly connect with other men. "Drill" asked about his finances, and Paul wondered why.

"There's an initiation training next weekend up in southern Washington, about an hour north of Portland. If you want to go, you need to let me know in the next couple days so I can help you make arrangements to get there. In fact, if you sign up, I'll get a chance to be on staff!"

"Far out! We could fly up together!"

"Aah, that probably won't work. I have to be there twenty-four hours before you. But I can help make arrangements for you to get picked up at the airport, and we can fly back together!"

"That'd be cool! Sign me up!"

"Just like that? We haven't really talked very much about the weekend!"

"Look! You did the training. A bunch of the men at the meeting did the training. I got so fucking high hanging out with you guys! I want to do the weekend!"

"Wow! OK! I'll get you the paperwork later today. Can you afford to pay the whole thing up front?"

"Five hundred? Right?"

"Right?"

"Yeah, I can handle it. I'm going to make a reservation. Are you flying back Sunday night? Will we get out in time?"

"I know some people in Portland. If you stay over and fly back Monday, we can. I guarantee you'll want to take the day off anyway."

"Just not too early! How about like 1 PM or so?"

"Works for me!"

_____

Washougal, Washington – November 1997

Compared to the glitz and glitter of Baghdad-by-the-Bay (as famed columnist Herb Caen used to call it, invoking exotic sights and sounds, not the panorama of war), the trip up the tree-lined, river-gurgling Washougal River Road (only an hour north of Portland) was truly rustic. It was also damn cold, with already freezing rain falling in a steady sheet, and snow, at least flurries, predicted for the entire weekend. Camp Melacoma seemed a bit foreboding as Paul approached, in the back seat passenger in a van-load of men who had gathered from all over Oregon, and scooped him up at the Portland airport on Friday afternoon.

There was a definite air of anxiety that pervaded the vehicle, as one or another of the men speculated about various aspects of the initiation weekend they had heard about (not that likely) mixed with gossip and rumors (far more likely). There was also some small talk amongst several of the men, a pair of whom were brothers from a small town near Eugene, but mostly there was a mood of expectant excitement mixed with a mild-to-moderate fear, though they were all trying to put a brave face on it.

They had stopped at a place called Fred Meyer, a gigantic grocery/department store that seemed to have just about any kind of consumer item imaginable. They spread out through the store and raided it extensively, buying bottled water, snacks, prepared foods from the delicatessen, pens and paper, gloves, scarves, long-johns, and other items—despite having been explicitly instructed that their needs (food and other) would be taken care of, and not to pack excess "stuff."

As they turned up the muddy road to the camp, the buildings appeared out of the mist like ancient animals coming to a pre-historic watering hole. Even in the wind and the rain, they appeared slightly shabby and under-maintained. There was a barrier across the road to the entrance to the camp, and they were greeted by a grizzled, fierce-looking man in a long green poncho holding a plastic covered clipboard with a long list of names.

As he approached the van, his face, impossible as it might have seemed, actually tightened, and he scowled at Dave, the driver.

"What do you want?"

"We're…we're here for the training."

"What training?"

"Wildman in the Woods."

"And what do you want?"

"I don't know what you mean."

"What did you come here to get? What do you want?"

"Oh! Uh, well, you see, I've been in therapy for a long time…"

"I asked you what you want."

Dave was clearly nervous, and started to stammer. One of the brothers, James spoke from the back seat.

"We're here because we want to live in a better world!"

"I didn't ask you!" said the Road Warrior (as I later found out he was called). I want this guy," he roared, gesturing with a thumb toward Dave, "to tell me why he came here today!"

Dave shook his head, and replied, "I want to be a better man!"

"OK. We'll see if you got it in you. Who else is in this vehicle?"

Dave stated our names, and the man checked us off on his list.

"Drive into the parking lot. See the man there."

This inauspicious beginning elicited much speculation—some angry, some fearful, some querulous—on the way to our designated parking area, where we were greeted by another grim-visaged man, this one clean shaven and wearing a blue poncho.

"Park your vehicle over there. Take all of your belongings with you, and lock your vehicle. You will not be returning to it until Sunday."

"What about the food we were supposed to bring?"

"'Take all of your belongings with you, and lock your vehicle. You will not be returning to it until Sunday.'"

We gathered our belongings, food, jackets, sleeping bags, extra shoes and boots, and a dozen Fred Meyer bags.

He pointed and said, "See that man!"

We trudged up the path, looking like a disjointed millipede with Tourette's syndrome. There was yet another grizzled-looking man standing in the rain who told us to "Wait" until we were called individually, and then to knock, and wait until we were told to enter through a shabby wooden door.

When one of the men standing in the queue started to talk, he was told to shut up.

"Maintain essential silence, unless you are asked to speak!"

As soon as he entered one of the tattered barracks, he became acutely aware of the "small mouse problem" they were having there at the camp. The smell of mouse urine was pervasive, overwhelming even, and jokes about "roasted mouse feces" on the menu stopped being funny after the first two hours.

One by one by one, we were funneled through the door; had our names checked yet again, signed paperwork, had photos taken, were issued a number sticker to be kept "visible at all times," as well as a colored bandana, handed food off; and told to gather our belongings, and "see that man," yet another grim looking fellow in corduroys and a flannel shirt, who asked us to contemplate, not answer the question he put to us one-by-one.

"Who do you serve?" after which we were ushered into a huge, flood-lit, chaotic room, with man men issuing orders in loud voices, and the echoing refrain, "Men are waiting," surrendering most of their personal possessions, and being questioned repeatedly why they had brought so much extra stuff—had they not read the instructions?," and were then summarily searched, before being shuttled into a room lit by only a candle, and reminded again to "keep essential silence." They sat there—some quietly, some anxiously, some angrily—for the very longest time.

At length, they were told to use their bandanas as a blindfold, stand, and, forming a single file line, to allow themselves to be led into the next room, where they were seated on pillows on the floor. When instructed, they removed their blindfolds, and saw they were sitting in the center of a huge room, with klieg lights shining on them, and surrounded by a circle of men dressed all in black, with ash on their faces.

After being allowed in, they had been divided into color-coded teams, and operated mostly out of them for the weekend—to the last lingering bittersweet moment when they all said a silent good-bye to each other and the staff as brothers. Every single moment had been filled with adrenaline-surging, dopamine-whirling, non-stop, balls-to-the-wall, power-pulsing, cell-amplified, blasted wide-open emotions, gut-wrenching tears, insights, screaming, shouting, epiphanies, the cries and grief of ancient hungers and needs finally fulfilled, deep heart-felt connections—and love.

He'd never forget the crazy staff man who had covered himself in phosphorescent "glow sticks" and appeared out of the midnight blackness like an illuminated ghost, as they wandered through the scrub and brush, through the hills and over little bridges. At one point on Saturday afternoon, somebody had failed to post a gate guard. This couple drove up, parked, and got out of their car just as he and the thirty other of his new brothers walked by naked (all in a collective altered state). None of them paid any especial attention. By that point, they all thought it was just part of the process.

The thread that connected all of the activities was a massive, amazing sense of connection, of brotherhood. It was completely unique in his experience—one of the most liberating, most exhilarating, powerful and abreactive experiences of his life. He had never in his life attended a gathering with a bunch of total strangers, and come away in love with a hundred men!

———

Paul's experience in the aftermath of the weekend proved to be as devastating as the weekend had been uplifting. It started simply enough. At first Paul thought he might be catching a "cold." He was having some trouble breathing out of his right nostril. It was the one he suspected had been partially remodeled during his cocaine days—so he didn't think too much of it for the first couple of days. He had had frequent sinus infections through the years, and other breathing difficulties. But as the days went by, he started feeling increasingly worse—drained of vitality, muscle aches, fever. He suspected he might be developing one of his tremendous, often horrendous, physical collapses after making a huge emotional breakthrough. It was a lifelong pattern.

He loved altered states, and thought he was ready to endure a certain amount of distress in order to accommodate his newly awakened brain states. He was not yet fully cognizant of the fact that he had experienced a vision of an entirely new lifeway, and that much of what he had previously believed just had to go. (He found out later that the word was peripeteia, a sudden turn of events where everything one has previously believed to be true turns out to be false). Paul loved (though also feared) believing too strongly in his visions. He had been misled by his visions generated by too much LSD (most of it while tripping alone), and other psychedelics, the first 150 times during his first year home from Vietnam. It had allowed him to ride the biggest, highest, most powerful and mind-blowing wave of consciousness he had ever experienced, releasing him utterly from all of the boundaries and barriers of the prison walls within which he had lived previously—and then dropped him from the peak of the crest directly into the frothing trough of the wave; left him delirious and delusional, filled with the visions without having done the underlying emotional and psychological work necessary to ground them sufficiently. He had worked extremely hard on that, and now he sought to avoid making that mistake again—though the alteration from the weekend had been cleansing and healing of the past, and had opened a doorway to an enhanced present and a potentially more glorious future without the intervention of substances of any type. but still he knew he was susceptible.

When he woke up on Monday morning a week later, he felt lethargic and considerably worse than he had a week previously. He had purposely kept his client load light that week, seeing only long-term clients with whom he had a well-established rapport that provided him a much easier ingress and egress from sessions. It was not that he put out less effort and attention, just that it took a less deeply empathic focus because these clients were already in the groove of diving deeply. New clients in the initial meetings always required him to be much more broadly empathic in order to capture clues that might better delineate their backstories; and occasionally he had to be confrontational when the client was clearly not telling the truth, or trying to present a false picture of him or herself. And he also had to pay far more attention when formulating the Treatment Plan to better facilitate their work together.

But that day, he struggled up out of bed, had two cups of coffee and a protein shake, then took a shower, and dressed in a clean pair of jeans and a Polo shirt, his favorite emerald green one, to see his twelve o'clock client, a very astute and intelligent woman in her mid-thirties by the name of Shannon, who worked as a programmer in the Transamerica Pyramid. She had been referred by a colleague when he felt the woman might need deep trauma work. He had wanted to refer her for medications, and she refused, choosing to see Paul instead, having heard of his reputation regarding psych drugs.

They first did some deep belly-breathing—usually just a count of ten, but with more experienced clients like Shannon, he allowed the client's needs to guide the initial part of the session, and listen for any subtle change in breathing rhythm that signaled a readiness to begin the shared work. He had found that this technique calmed and centered both him and the client, and put them on the same page emotionally.

This woman was someone who tasked him most deeply to fight to keep from showing the depth of his emotions. He felt a strong connection with her empathically (and, he had to admit, a certain sexual attraction, despite the fact that she was essentially very straight, and he preferred hip women).

Today, with his less-than-robust immune system, he was having a really hard time staying focused.

His thoughts kept straying to his WMIW weekend, and the opportunity to open himself up to long-suppressed emotions and terrors—territory he had previously explored in therapy and psychedelic excursions, but had magically gone deeper on the weekend. The images that kept appearing in his memory field today were quite intrusive, and kept bringing him to the verge of inappropriate tears in the middle of the session. He felt especially sensitive to the waves of dysphoria and sadness that were wafting off of his client.

Although he had run the scenario so many times that it was almost boring, it still contained a lot of juice for him. His less than robust state of health amplified the vividness of the images tremendously.

It was late fall. He was four.

Daddy loved brains. In his innocent child-mind he believed he could convince his father to love him, change all the sour faces and harsh words, never a smile...if only he could figure out a way to win him over!

He knew he was really smart! There had to be a way!

And suddenly, he had it! A question so big, so…powerful! He would show Daddy he <u>was</u> worth it!

He wanted to be wide-awake when Daddy got home (very late as always), so he took his afternoon nap instead of running away and fighting with Mommy.

He was too excited to sleep, so he just lay there rehearsing his big question—see the big smile on Daddy's face; feel his cheek when he picked him up, hug him, really love him!

At dinner, he even ate his vegetables. Ugh! Frozen broccoli again! Watched I've Got a Secret *and Perry Como. God! What was with Mom and "Oh Perry!" all the time? He hoped Daddy would be home early. Then he had to go to bed, to pretend to sleep, head flooded with happy pictures!*

And he heard the back screen door slam. Daddy! Daddy always came in the back way, down Grand Avenue, half a block over on Alaska, and then down the alley.

He threw back the covers, and dashed out. Daddy kissed Mommy, and went to his closet. Standing in the closet door, he took his hat off, and unwound his scarf as Paul came flying out.

"Daddy! Daddy!"

He threw himself onto his father's left leg, and Daddy reached down and pushed him gruffly away.

Paul tried again, tugging excitedly on his father's pants leg.

"Daddy! Daddy! I have to ask you something!"

His father pushed him away again, even more roughly.

"It's really important, Daddy!"

Using both hands, he pushed Paul away yet again. Paul smelled the rotting odor of Daddy's bad moods, but it wouldn't stop him! Couldn't stop him!

"It's really important, Daddy!"

Snarling, his father turned toward him.

"What the fuck is it?"

Paul stood tall and beamed.

"Where was God before He created the Universe?"

The last syllable left his mouth as an eight foot tall, nine hundred pound Monster roared and stepped out of his father. Eyes black and filled with hate, he bared his razor-sharp teeth, then exploded like a nuclear device erupting.

"WHAT? WHAT DID YOU SAY?"

Paul asked again, determined to win his love.

"Where was God before He created the Universe?"

The berserking monster roared like a hydrophobic bull.

"WHO TOLD YOU TO ASK ME THAT?"

Paul started freaking, backing away, sweat suddenly pouring from every pore and orifice.

"Nobody, Daddy! Nobody!"

"LITTLE FUCKING LIAR!"

He wanted to turn to his mother, to her sheltering arms, but he was frozen to the spot.

"YOU'VE BEEN TALKING TO YOUR UNCLE FRANCIS!"

"No, Daddy! No! I thought it up on my own!"

Daddy made a brief appearance in the mist, then the Monster backhanded him, smashing him in the face. Paul sailed through the air, and his head smashed into the wall opposite.

"LITTLE FUCKING LIAR!!"

Suns and stars whirled, ringed planets living their multi-millennial lives twirled as his eyes strobed stereoscopically. He moaned, shocked and paralyzed with fear and disbelief as his mother flew into the room, nightgown billowing behind her as Paul dazedly recorded the unfolding events of his life as if on a television screen.

Mommy savagely pushed Daddy away, as a short, swarthy Japanese man with a topknot, wearing an emerald green kimono embroidered with red-and-gold dragons, stepped out of the top of Paul's head, went into a crouch with his katana sword drawn, approached Paul's father—and in one clean swipe, he removed Daddy's head, which rolled to a stop, eyes wide and staring at Paul.

"Hey! Hey! Are you there?"

Shannon was looking with alarm at Paul, and snapped her fingers in front of his face. "I thought for a moment" she only semi-joked, "that maybe you were dead!"

"No. I just had a bad night's sleep. Please, let's continue. Where were we?"

CHAPTER NINETEEN
Spiral Journey

San Francisco, December 1998 - January 1999

After Shannon left, Paul called his service and instructed them to cancel all of his appointments for the following week, and to reschedule them for the week after. Surely he would be well by then, even though he felt a creeping indolence seeping through his nervous system like a multi-legged parasite.

He took a giant dose of Chinese herbs, and heated some chicken broth. It was all he could handle, yet it was terribly soothing—so much so that he had a second large mug full. He went to his favorite love seat, and put his feet up on an ottoman, intending to muse for a few minutes on the nature of life and psychotherapy. Instead, he fell almost immediately into a tortured sleep, punctuated by scaly, serpentine creatures that seemed to have no eyes, but instead sought Paul out by sense of smell—and seemed to know exactly where he was no matter where he hid in the gigantic cuboid city made entirely of white rock. He awoke with a start, and ran to the bathroom and experienced the first of many episodes of diarrhea he would have over the ensuing weeks. He was immediately soaked in a clammy sweat, though he cooled rapidly. After washing his hands twice, he felt his forehead and neck, and noticed that his body temperature had to be high. He usually ran about a degree below "normal;" his hands and feet were almost always very warm, even hot sometimes, to the touch.

He lurched down the hall to his bedroom, tearing off his sweaty clothes as he went, and dived into bed. He glanced at the bedside clock and saw that it was only 2010, insanely early for him. He lay for a minute with the covers off, exulting in the chilliness of the air temperature as his perspiration evaporated. Then, as if struck by a cosmic bolt, his entire body chemistry shifted, and he started shivering uncontrollably, teeth chattering, and perspiration pouring out of him. He swiftly slid under the cool sheet and pulled it and his wonderful wool Pendleton blanket up over him. He was almost immediately aware that it would be insufficient to warm him, but he was too cold and chilled to do anything about it. He fell again into a torpid, restless sleep, pursued by nameless, faceless demons of severe ill-intent, who nonetheless, were repelled any time he stopped and turned the full glare of his eyes on them. When he next awoke, it was with a completely closed right sinus, and a dry and aching throat. He was also still chilled, though he forced himself up and out of bed to drink two glasses of water with ten grains of aspirin through chattering teeth, and then retrieved two additional blankets from the hall closet.

He tumbled into bed again, and fell into a sodden, dreamless sleep during which he felt as if he were wide awake and experiencing exactly what he believed otherwise he was dreaming—and awoke at 0332. He threw off the covers and lay in the king-sized bed, shivering and soaked in sweat. As the moisture cooled, he felt an immense surge of well-being, and had a fleeting thought that the cleansing had passed through him remarkably fast. He jumped up and went into his writing studio, brought the screen to life, and re-read the last paragraph. He immediately picked up the thread of the narrative he'd been creating. He wrote for a long timeless time and, when he looked up, he realized that he had created three and a half new pages, including dialogue, and completed a chapter. He leaned back in his leather executive chair, and closed his eyes for just a moment at 0610, intending to contemplate what he had just written, especially a really brilliant spate of dialogue.

And awoke with a start, shaking and shivering, cursing the ague that gripped him—and made his way back to bed as swiftly as possible, having first stopped in the bathroom again. He crawled under the blankets, and groaned in deep pleasure as his lower back relaxed. He closed his eyes, fearing the very worst—that he might be down for two or three weeks, as he had been in the past with "flu-like symptoms." As he slipped into the edges of somnolence, as vivid, Technicolor dreams immediately swallowed him—and took him on an exotic journey to Hong Kong, Bucharest, and Papeete, but they were oddly colored, and shaped by distorted, wavering boundary lines. The dream seemed to last for decades, but when he awoke, summoned by the telephone he had forgotten to unplug, it was only 0922, and he spoke briefly, and incoherently, to someone seeking a new referral. He asked the man to call back the following week.

As he lay there, soaking wet, and wanting so much to change the sheets, he realized he did not have a scintilla of energy to devote to the task. He decided he had to endure his extreme discomfort, closed his eyes, and decided to breathe into it. As his breathing deepened, he felt his consciousness shifting into something resembling a half-awake sleep, something he remembered was called hypnagogic, and exulted in the floating, soft, altered state that preceded him falling deeply into a profound slumber from which he awoke in a panic, and ran to the bathroom again. It was 1247.

He returned to lay in bed for the longest time, minutes merging with hours seamlessly, and he battered and berated himself almost ceaselessly for the negative invectives of not being strong enough, for self-repudiation, and the assault of old shame-based flashes of garbage memories he had long hoped dissolved. And sincerely wished, not for the first time, that the mystery samurai who had taken his father's head had been real in actuality, and had really done the deed he had hallucinated in his concussed state all those years ago. A crimson/turquoise flash shot through him as he had a blinding realization that all of his old torments were being flushed from his body, though he could not hold onto the acuity of this awareness—though he tried mightily, wanting so much to believe, and was reminded of a famous line from Demosthenes: "Nothing is easier than self-deceit. For what a man wishes, that he also believes to be true."

It was then that he remembered the last time he had seen his father alive. Paul had gone to take care of him so that both of his sisters could get away together for a once yearly fishing trip. There had been a small portion of his mind in which he still harbored resentment and a desire to kill him, but when he saw the wizened up old man hobbling across the floor toward him, he burst out crying. His father was completely uncomprehending, standing in front of him, as Paul thought to himself, "Oh my God, this is not the raging monster who once tortured and tormented me! This crippled up little old man with the greasy hair is not the gigantic asshole who once abused me! I just can't kill him!"

He remembered Nin's line about writers living life twice (she might have been citing Proust). In his reverie, Paul saw all of this as clearly as if it were taking place right in front of him, and he felt his rage wilt and shrivel like a time-lapse orchid in an acetylene flame. And he sobbed deeply into the day or night, he knew not which. He sobbed and sobbed, acutely feeling the import of all of the years he'd lost pursuing the love of another, and learning how to love his own nascent self, having not had it granted naturally to him. It was the kind of crime against him, the likes of which so many, many children had suffered through many the millennia of pain and torture, shaping the quality and nature of society through mean and vicious techniques of suppression and violence, teaching crimes against the self to be repeated endlessly and unabated, through uncountable ages and eons. Then Paul cried again, sobbing for what seemed like weeks, in mourning for the tremendous loss of all of those innocents who had ever taken birth, who had come into human form with high and great expectations only to find the snarled tangle of delusion and disinformation awaiting them, a sticky net that was the contemporary ruling power's template on Planet Earth. It seemed sometimes that God Him/Her/It had totally abandoned the track of evolution for the delightful spirits coming in, deserted them totally to the specious intentions of the oligarchic plutocrats and their dark agendas.

––––––––––

Time folded in on itself during the ensuing days and nights, weeks even, as he vacillated between a certain bright clarity that always seemed to accompany his altered states, and being plunged into the deepest, most dank pools of murk and despair that he had ever known. He awoke several times to change the sheets, innumerable times to drink water and visit the bathroom, the latter of which visits had shifted from dreaded diarrheal expurgation to feeling as if his abdomen were filled with a ten pound block of cement he had swallowed whole, and was unable to release—the net result being his sitting on the toilet, sometimes reading his current choice in mystery novels, or a *Sun Magazine*; sometimes just sitting there in agony waiting for the simple ciliated columnar epithelia of his intestinal tract to develop enough strength and power to eliminate the accrued toxins.

Then one night in the midst of this almost surreal melee of inter- and intra-connected events, connected by an avalanche of psychedelic and phantasmagorical ideation and images, he had the best night's sleep he had ever had, or so it seemed. He awakened to go to the bathroom (yet again!), and when he fell back asleep, almost gloating because he felt that he had reached the bottom of whatever cycle he was in; feeling that he was going to start coming out of this huge twisted journey on which he had been traveling, and from which he seemed to finally be graduating.

He fell back asleep, and was plunged into the thickest, soggiest, humid jungle he had ever seen. Which was, in and of itself, not that big of a deal.

The problem was that he was sitting in a gigantic iron pot filled with water, his hands and feet tied behind his back, while the area under it had been cleared down to the soil for approximately twenty feet all around. Unimpeded by his inability to move, bird and insect songs filled the air, chirping, clicking, and tweeting their clamorous joy.

Then their voices disappeared, and a vacuous stillness replaced them, a silence so complete that it seemed as if all of the oxygen had been sucked out of the air. Into that clarion quiet brusquely spoke a deep, reverberant voice, crackling with resonance and clarity.

"WE'RE GONNA BOIL YOUR BONES, BROTHER!"

Paul smiled in his delirium-induced reverie. He knew instantly that he was about to experience a classic "Shaman's Death." It was a process in which one was metaphorically reduced to bones, either by boiling or burning, signaling the death of the ego of a spiritually aspiring person, and the subsequent rebirth into a higher level of spiritual and psychological awareness from which one could, would, even should, be enabled to go forward in a new and heightened manner. Paul knew it signaled the end of the ordeal through which he had been travelling, an ordeal that was so much more important, so much more fraught with depth and meaning than he had even considered possible—the end of the ancient processes by which he had forever disempowered himself, kept himself down, unchanging, not evolving, unwilling and unable to recognize the Great Light that lay within him. Now he cried with joy and gratitude mingling as the vestigial elements of grief and mourning flushed from his every cell, and a clarified tone-note sounded resoundingly, clearly signaling a new vision, a new beginning, a newer, better way to be and live in the world-at-large, and embrace that ineffable eternal Light that is a million, billion, trillion times more beautiful and brighter than any other.

CHAPTER TWENTY

Slowly Rocking On

San Francisco, March 1999

It was actually another week and a half after that extraordinary dream that Paul felt as if he were human again, and even more days after that before he reinstated his client schedule. He felt as if he'd been put through the Heavy Duty cycle of the Universe's commercial washing machine several times—light and airy, almost floating yet also very firmly grounded and powerful. All of his clients had had to be rescheduled, and most were glad to see him.

Of necessity, his first week back was far busier than usual, but that was really good by him. He felt renewed and uplifted after recovering from his ordeal, the power of the Shaman's Rebirth surging through him as he re-established his working routine. Usually he never saw more than two clients in a day, but this first day back, he gave himself only thirty minutes between visits so he could squeeze in five and still start at ten o'clock, but that meant he was not done until ten o'clock that night. This was totally fine with his last client who liked the latest appointment possible, and delighted to have his at eight o'clock. Paul was exhausted by the time he was complete, and he finally had time for a quick dinner and a final coffee before putting his feet up, to listen to some music. He decided on some Van Morrison because he was good for the nerves.

His thoughts turned to his father yet again, though this time the rage did not. He felt as if it had been washed away in reverie of the ceremony. Another aspect of the healing process began to take place, as he was reminded of the last time he saw him alive.

Paul had spent two weeks with him—fixing meals, running errands, doing laundry, but mostly hanging out watching TV, which provided the backdrop for some of the real conversation for which he had longed and questions he had always wanted to ask. He even got his father telling reminiscent tales about his childhood, which had, after all, been almost a century ago. Several times they had even talked about their interactions when he was a child, precipitating in some of the most the most poignant exchanges they had ever had. Paul ranked them with the time he and his father had stood in front of his mother's casket, holding each other and cried without shame.

By the time his sisters had returned from a much-needed vacation, he and his father had fallen into a very comfortable routine, sleeping late, eating casual meals whenever they felt hungry, watching a regular retinue of television programs, and sharing—more attitudes and opinions than actual facts and memories; long conversations about ideas philosophical and contemporary, such as their shared hatred of Ronald Reagan, who was, for the both of them, nothing more than a "B-Grade actor."

When it came time for him to leave, they were both feeling quite attached; feeling, actually, that they both wished they could spend even longer together. But Paul had put off his "real" life long enough, and his sisters were back and ready to re-establish their program with their father. On the day Pe was to leave, they shared an experience Paul would forever after relive in his thoughts and reveries.

Paul had gotten up early, even though he did not have to leave for the airport until one in the afternoon, ran a final load of laundry, prepared his father's breakfast, and then set out his morning medications next to his coffee. Paul showered and dressed, then packed. He still had two hours, but he felt the anxiety growing as both he and his father acutely felt the immanence of his leaving—though neither of them knew at the time that it would be their very last face-to-face meeting.

They both tried to maintain some semblance of normality, but the anxiety kept intensifying. Paul was feeling it even more powerfully than his father, so he dressed, and set his bag on the front porch, having already called his cab, and been told it would be there in half an hour. His father stood in the doorway while Paul stood one step down, facing him, smoking yet another cigarette.

"Well, Pop…"

"It's been good to have you here, son. I'm glad you came."

"Yeah, I wish I could stay longer, but I gotta get back."

"No! No! That's OK! Your sisters are back."

"I know. I'm really grateful for them."

"Me too."

"I…I've always wished we could have gotten along better when I was young."

"I know. Me too."

"We've sure been through a lot of shit together," said Paul, tearing up.

His father looked directly into his eyes, tearing up too.

"But the important thing is that we still love each other."

At this Paul burst out crying, burying his face in the sleeve of his shirt, then looked up, and they hugged.

They both looked up as the cab turned at the head of the block. His father straightened up, and raised his hand to his right eyebrow to salute.

"Good job, sergeant!"

He saluted him back, one of our longstanding rituals.

"Thank you, lieutenant!"

Then he gave him a great gift, one for which he had waited my entire life, one that he had never heard before and for which he had longed like the arid earth for life-giving moisture. He looked him in the eyes, and spoke.

"I'm proud of you, son!"

Though part of his mind was adrift on undulating waves of the past, Paul's eyes snapped to with an almost audible click, as his attention rapidly returned to the present. He sighed deeply, loosened his neck, and sat up, intending to get some sleep. He had reached a good place to stop, and wanted to be totally clear in the morning, to hit the keyboard fresh and full of energy. The book kept calling to him. Indeed, he had even dreamed parts of it—enriching the continuing narrative, characters, even an exchange of dialogue. He sometimes thought of his dreams as the sleeping version of his intuition.

He felt himself growing stronger every day, more open, more aware, and more ready to once again tackle the often taxing problems of his clients. He genuinely got both a great deal of satisfaction from, and grew personally through, each one of them.

Since he'd established his practice, he had bucked the trend of what he called the "shrinking hour" in psychotherapy, one that was rarely an hour's clock time. It had been a "fifty minute hour" for years, allowing the clinician ten minutes to write up case notes, get a drink of water or a cup of coffee, and go to the bathroom, if needed. Then it became the "forty-five minute hour," in part to align with HMOs and insurance companies required "suggestion" that clinicians bill in fifteen-minute increments, with any seven-minute segment being billable as a quarter hour. Paul had heard that many clinicians had taken advantage of this new "requirement" (far more convenient for the "bean counters," certainly not for the client who was ultimately considered, and even now called a "consumer"). To him it was the extension of corporate greed into his sacred healing art.

Prisoners were now being called "consumers of penal services," as the trend toward greater and greater privatization of prisons spread, making it the fastest growing industry in the world. Corporate dollars being invested in owning prisons seemed to be considered by the venal power structure to represent a legitimate and viable way to make yet more profit.

Paul always gave his clients a full two-hour session, and always gave himself at least a half an hour, usually an hour, between clients. He rarely saw anyone before noon, often working until nine or ten o'clock at night. (He actually preferred working through the afternoon and early evening). That left him free to write, read, and pay bills, et cetera prior to shifting his mindset to the healing of others.

After all, true healing (a trademark he had thought to own at one point) required that he be able to give freely of his own resources. In order to hold space for others; and to offer his very best, he had to be at his very best. This required, in turn, almost continuous maintenance of his own well-being. So he was learning to be generous with his own beloved and most precious self—in marked contradistinction to the many years when he had been his own worst critic and judge. Part of this had come about as a direct result of doing extensive Voice Dialogue work, in which he got not only to acknowledge his inner children, but to dialogue with them. He had come to love and appreciate the energy that they (albeit in analog form) held for him.

Acknowledging their presence in his psyche had freed him of having to create ways of either avoiding or obfuscating the energies they represented in order to have a life that he wished for himself, without the repeated intrusions of analog, disparaged, and unintegrated children who often, very inappropriately, took over the active portion of his life when he least expected it. He had found that unintegrated subpersonalities seemed to have a life of their own—carrying all that was hidden or suppressed, including what Freud had called the "masochistic superego." He had once lost a perfect opportunity to have sex with a beautiful nurse he had courted for weeks when he found himself completely unable to perform, even after she had taken off her blouse and bra—and he too had been unable to stimulate his manhood, despite the best efforts of both of them.

CHAPTER TWENTY ONE

Considerations

San Francisco, April 1999

Paul had initially marked him as a bullshitter and a narcissist. They had met casually at a watering hole he very occasionally visited on Union Street called Tarr and Feathers. It could be a pretty rowdy place at times, but had toned down considerably from when he had used to meet coke customers there twenty years previously.

Johnathan Rothstein owned a bookstore just off Union where Paul had sometimes found obscure psychology volumes as well as hardbound art books (a special favorite). Johnathan claimed some not-too-distant relationship with the famous gambler and financier Arnold "The Brain" Rothstein who had corporatized organized crime. He did have a "New York accent" (Paul wasn't really as good at distinguishing the different ones as he was able those in San Francisco, easily picking out a variety of Asian accents and able to distinguish Cantonese from Shanghainese for example). So Paul was initially drawn to believe that he might be genuine.

They talked sports (John was a Raiders fan, Paul 49ers); books (John did seem to know quite a lot about his chosen trade); wines (John's ex-wife was a professional purveyor of high end reds); and, in the end, they traded business cards.

"I might call you one of these days. Everybody I know tells me I'm crazy!"

"Crazy can mean a lot of different things, especially for non-professionals. My very brief assessment tells me you're not, at least clinically!"

So it was with some surprise when Paul got a call from his service one Saturday afternoon, stating that Johnathan was on the line and wanting to speak with me.

"Just take a message. I will call him back."

"I already told him that. He insists he needs to talk to you right away."

After connecting the call, Paul inquired what the urgency might be.

"Paul! Thank God! I really need to talk to you. Professionally, I mean. I have no idea what your rates are, but I don't care!" He seemed in some form of manic flight.

"Wait a minute! Wait a minute! Answer my question first and then I will assess whether to take you as a client."

"Oh!" said Johnathan, voice suddenly defeated and deflated.

Paul waited for the man to resume.

"I...I know I must seem really crazy now...to you. I've been thinking of calling you for a week or so, just kept putting it off. Now I'm kind of having a crisis and so I called."

"That's not really how I operate. I'm in private practice. I have a regular schedule and office hours. So why don't you tell me briefly what's going on and let's see what the next step might be."

Johnathan launched into a rambling monologue, with lots of self-referencing and tangential sidebars, about how, despite his money and social connections, he felt lonely and devalued. After listening for a few minutes, Paul interrupted him.

"Johnathan, I know you're upset. But you still haven't told me what this 'crisis' is!"

"Oh! I forgot. I was just trying to give you the backstory!"

"Don't need it! Don't want it! What is going on right now?"

"I met this woman, Camille. Gorgeous. Dancer. Former model. We been dating for a couple of weeks. I been taking her all the great spots. Fairmount roof for drinks. Ballet. Le Trianon. You know what I'm saying?"

"I get the drift."

"And she's been nice. Friendly. Not what I would call receptive though."

"Yes. And?"

"We haven't had sex!"

"And?"

"Well, I feel…diminished!"

"Why?"

"I've been spending all this money on her, and we haven't had sex!"

"So?"

"So I feel devalued. Worthless!"

"Because you haven't had sex with her?"

"Yes! Of course! Wouldn't you?"

"That's neither here nor there. So this is your crisis?"

"Yeah! I've had a few drinks, and got to thinking about this. And, you know, I feel really depressed. Worthless."

"I would suggest, Johnathan, that we make a regular appointment—sometime early next week—and talk about this at greater length. I think your feelings of worthlessness existed long before this. You could really benefit from some work. Let me flash the service back and they'll fix you up with the earliest appointment I have available. Remember to set aside two hours."

Stefan J. Malecek, Ph. D.

208

CHAPTER TWENTY TWO

Paying Dues

San Francisco, May 1999

Since his initiation weekend, Paul had been feeling much lighter and more self-expressed, though he was still haunted by some of the psychic weight from the past—and wanted desperately to find a way to release more of it.

He made a checklist of behaviors that triggered him, and thence, began to track down the essence of them in order to heal them. He knew he was still carrying grief unmourned. He knew he had to design how he wanted to live in order to more fully express himself spiritually and artistically, be the man he had always wanted to be.

One really vexing question for him was: how much responsibility did he personally bear for the actions of others, especially how they affected or triggered him? He frequently asked this of himself, of the Universe (which still hadn't replied!). How much of his father's rage had he introjected, and re-enacted, as if it were his own? How much responsibility did he bear for the actions of others who had triggered him? He was especially pissed off that sometimes people implied that it was all his responsibility! And he adamantly refused to be responsible for his childhood! Disavowed it completely! Such a line of reasoning implied that he was responsible for his pre-birth circumstances! (In odd moments of reflection, he believed he might have been, but was totally puzzled about the mechanism).

He'd be goddamned if he would take responsibility for how he had been treated! He could own that his reactions to the primally fucked up behavior of his father were his bailiwick, but not the original violence and denigration. That was clearly his father's projections, the disbursement of his own shame onto the small and relatively defenseless Paul, who, with his not-yet-developed nervous system, was at his mercy. Otherwise he would most assuredly have killed his father long before; would, in fact, have killed him the first time his father hit him, maybe as soon as he was born!

Sometimes he saw it as such petty bullshit, yet the potential of carrying around the toxic materials to interfere even further in his life than it had was just too great, too onerous, to manage any longer. He hungered mightily to live more in tune with his own principles, needs, and aspirations. How could he be so smart, a certified fucking genius, and have such seemingly small, niggling pains and obstructions interfere so massively in his life? It was enough to piss off the Pope!

He always got especially upset when his rage rose in seemingly "inappropriate circumstances" (even though it was triggered by those people or circumstances, it interfered with the clarity or purity of his vision of himself). It always generated a titanic inner struggle—he was torn between expressing his emotions as he was really feeling them (his God given right!), or squelching the desire for a more appropriate time (or in a more appropriate manner, such as his therapist's office). There were various stages and phases in between these two on the spectrum of human emotion that sometimes left him simply speechless and gasping like a large fish trying to breathe out of water.

He did feel a certain taint of victimhood from his childhood that was just extremely bothersome. He often vacillated amongst the options, though generally managed to keep his contexts straight. He had very rarely ever allowed a client to see the depth of his distress. Parties or large group gatherings made him uncomfortable. His desire to be open and vulnerable was very often overridden by his desire for quiet and privacy. He was also acutely aware of the potential shaming about being too open, especially in uncontrolled groups of individuals. He only really felt safe when he was in a circle of trust—or, far better, by himself or with one individual.

His opinion of women had been severely warped by his mother's illicit attentions and attitudes toward him, and he had worked mightily through the years to combat and ally, integrate actually, his earliest fears and suspicions of women as manipulative, cunning, and predatory. He had been blamed by women at different times for all of the ills of <u>man</u>kind. Until his initiatory weekend, he had thought that most of his interpersonal problems were with women—and then he discovered the depths of his issues with men! He had been so triggered many times during that weekend; and, thankfully, had the good fortune of making the acquaintance of Alan Hightower, the Ritual Elder, who was also a psychologist. He had paid especial attention to Paul, and always had some process or other that provided a balm for his aching mind—and allowed him to swiftly get to the root issues that were only proximally related to other men, and were, in fact, all related to his father, from whom he had extended his distrust and hostility to all men.

Unfortunately, this man whom he had come to trust, lived on the far north coast of Oregon, in a town called Manzanita. Paul would have loved to continue working with him, but it was not really possible, since he didn't do telephone work, and Paul was not able to travel frequently enough. Perhaps if it had been

Portland he could have managed it, but the four hour round trip to Manzanita from the airport would have been prohibitive.

With Paul's permission (signed and faxed), Alan forwarded brief case notes related to Paul's work on the weekend to a Mankind brother who had a private practice in The City. Ted Riser was a tall man with thick white haired worn shoulder-length, in his sixties who had done his Mankind weekend just three years earlier, and contributed to the Mental Health Resource Team. These men were mental health professionals who reviewed the medical questionnaires of all potential candidates, and participated on the weekends as a silent-until-needed resource, in case of a mental health emergency (though they usually only advised the leaders and other staff, not the initiates themselves). It was to this man that Paul went, seeking some kind of father-substitute perhaps, or at least someone to hold space for him in a therapeutic manner such that he could continue releasing his old, moldy disaffection with his father.

Ted had a sunny second floor office on Sacramento Street near Presidio Heights. It was filled with a variety of indigenous artifacts—an exquisite Navajo rug that had been beautifully and meticulously woven and framed took up the center of one entire wall; Mimbre pots and other collectible jugs and vessels stood illuminated on a glass table in a small alcove; a peyote priest's water drum sat next to what looked like a hand carved Native flute on yet another glass table. There were two bunches of fresh flowers in vases—one on his desk, and another on a small, slender, dark wood (he thought it might have been mahogany) pedestal near the entrance to the room. Three of the walls of room itself, and the twelve foot ceiling vault, were painted an off-white that had a slight iridescence to it. Sunshine poured in through a series of small, rectangular windows that flowed across the one wall that was painted sea-foam green.

Their first appointment had been limited to filling out paperwork, brief discussions about the symptoms he wanted to address, some shared experiences in WMIW, colleagues they knew in common, and setting an agenda for treatment. This latter seemed simple for Paul: He had requested two hour sessions, once a week initially, and wanted to not spend a lot of time going over old ground, but intended to write a brief bio and treatment summary that would enhance the voluminous case notes and evaluations that either had been, or were being, sent from various past providers. Ted at first balked around the idea of two hour sessions, and seemed to want to spend what Paul considered to be an inordinate amount of time on "old ground."

"I know from long experience in my practice that it takes most people an hour just to warm up, and get to the really juicy stuff. I seem to do my best work during the second hour too."

"I'm just not used to that format. One hour sessions seem to work really well for me and my clients."

"But not for me! I really must insist. Otherwise I will pay you for the first session filling out paperwork, and we can immediately terminate. I am very staunch on this point."

"I will consider it if you will consider spending a little more time than you would like on your personal history. It gives me the opportunity to get to know you better, admittedly more slowly than you might like."

"It sounds like we have a deal in the making here!" Paul laughed, leaned forward, and they shook hands.

They spent the remainder of the session discussing some of the comments that had been made on previous Psychological and Psychiatric Evaluations. Both essentially purport to make a definitive diagnosis of an individual's behavioral template and features. These were measured in what were called "the five axes": Axis I: Primary diagnosis of mental illness, such as Schizophrenia, Major Depression, et cetera; Axis II: Any personality tendencies or disorders: Narcissistic, Borderline, et cetera; Axis III: Any medical issues that may be significant and/or contributory, such as diabetes, history of brain injury, et cetera; Axis IV: Psychosocial Factors that may be exacerbating the primary presentation, such as lack of employment, mentally ill sibling, et cetera: Axis V: Global Assessment Scale (GAS): A number between one and a hundred, chosen to indicate the individual's level of impairment, generally between 30 and 60, with the lower numbers reflecting serious impairment of dysfunction.

The primary difference was that the Psychiatric Evaluation was performed by a psychiatrist (who was a medical doctor), often with the intent of providing a basis for prescribing psychiatric medications. Paul had had both at different times, and had assessed himself frequently as well. He placed his GAS somewhere around 50-55 generally, but when he had been severely depressed, he had put it more around 40-45. (With a score somewhere in the 30's, one was usually a candidate for psychiatric hospitalization as one was too severely impaired to function equably in one's daily life).

The highlights of Paul's evaluations were generally: Axis I: Major Depression; Posttraumatic Stress Disorder; Cocaine Dependence by history (in long term remission); Marijuana Dependence by history (in long term remission); and Alcohol Dependence by history (in long term remission), even though this latter was not quite accurate in that he had stopped drinking for eleven years, and was now able to enjoy an occasional glass of wine or snifter of Drambuie without it causing any deleterious desire to become addicted again. He questioned whether he had ever actually been an alcoholic (since being able to drink at all should have categorized him as an non-alcoholic, at least by Twelve Step standards that said one could never drink again once having recovered; but that was highly debatable in his opinion); Axis II had variously read through the years as: Borderline Personality Disorder (or tendencies); Narcissistic Personality Disorder (or tendencies); and/or Histrionic Personality tendencies; Axis III listed his history of multiple fractured bones; a head injury when he was thirteen in an automobile accident, and such; Axis IV generally included living by himself, social isolation, a tendency to reclusiveness, and some reference to his early childhood chaos.

Although he had been in therapy on and off for many years; and although he was himself quite a skilled practitioner, Paul always approached therapy as a client as if he were not too highly prejudiced in certain directions, and to certain conclusions. For example, he sometimes clashed with other clinicians around the idea of "re-stimulation" versus "catharsis" in terms of expressing and expurgating traumatic material in therapeutic approaches. Paul had always been a big fan of more Dionysian methods (versus Apollonian) in which he sought support for, and granted himself permission to have, crying, screaming, shouting, growling, moaning, groaning, screeching, shouting, sobbing, throbbing emotional releases.

In like manner, he felt that it was totally justified (indeed necessary) for him to express his anger and rage. (He had loved Primal Therapy!), totally believing that he should not have to carry all of the old pain and shame and fear, but rather, should freely self-express himself in whatever ways he felt he needed to relieve his heart and soul. Conversely, there were those who argued that such behaviors simply cut new grooves, as it were, in the mind and psyche; and created deeper, perhaps more serious, issues that became stored in the tissues—actually making things worse rather than better.

Of course, Paul vehemently disagreed with this latter approach, as he did with any kind of behavioral modification or any essentially cognitive approaches. These he deemed bland, boring, and superficial. He wanted the depth. He wanted the meat! He loved the intensity, lived for it, always had, though some had said that this was more symptomatic or indicative of his primary diagnosis than an actual life choice. Most people, including many clinicians, supposed that he was driven to excess and intensity as a matter of traumatic adaptation rather than a healthful and healthy lifestyle choice.

Of course, Paul always argued that there really was no such thing as societal health, or healthy people; and that the social network of the entire planet was damaged and traumatized—and it had been set up that way, was owned and managed that way purposely, because the plutocratic oligarchs were happily benefitting from the pain and shame of others—an obvious case of *schadenfreude*. Paul found it to be intolerable and unchangeable, hopeless, and completely fucked up. It was both a symptom of his depression, and the actuality of the world in which he lived—both a precursor and a result thereof simultaneously

Paul trudged through a long conversation about his past symptomatology, treatment implications and approaches, historical precedents, and then traded a few small insider jokes about therapy and therapists before they started discussing, in broad, general terms, a treatment plan. This last was generally necessary to structure the flow of treatment such that it, at least ostensibly, met the stated needs of the problems for which the individual was in treatment. It was also a document deemed absolutely necessary by insurance companies for recompense. It was supposed to guarantee a formalized framework in which the work was being done, and at least, a minimum of incompetence and a container within which to function.

They finished at ten minutes past the allotted two hours, and Ted looked at amazement at his watch when he saw how absorbed he had been in their work. He then expressed how thoroughly satisfied he felt with what they had accomplished—and then, a little more sheepishly, conceded that Paul had been correct, in this instance, for insisting on the two hour format.

Paul felt so refreshed that he decided to go for a walk. He walked up Sacramento, turned left on Argüello, and into Golden Gate Park.

CHAPTER TWENTY THREE
Further on Down the Road

San Francisco, June 1999

Michelle arrived early. She was dressed casually and comfortably, and looked as if she were actually rested for a change. They had spent many sessions working on her sleeping patterns, various breathing techniques, and relaxation exercises. Michelle had declared that it was more important for her to sleep well than to delve into her periodic depressions and the growing emotional gap between herself and Martin, her partner of almost nine years. Of course there was no way to separate the various strands of braided wire without touching upon all of the others, but, as far as he was able, he kept the boundaries tight and correct, focused on her expressed needs and desires.

"You look well today!"

"Today? As opposed to lately? Or since I began seeing you?"

"Wow! You tongue is certainly sharp!"

"Isn't that part of some kind of sexist reference?"

"Wow! I was just making an observation!"

Michelle's laughter trilled.

"Sorry. I didn't mean it to sound so sharp!"

Paul gestured to the door to his office.

"Shall we?"

She took the leather captain's chair to his left (as opposed to the quite-comfortable love seat that occupied the space across from them). When they had settled themselves respectively into their chairs, Paul casually asked "Is there something on your mind?"

"No," she answered automatically. Then cast a thoughtful look at him.

"Actually there is."

"OK."

"I know I asked to not talk about Martin. And I appreciate you've been respecting my choice."

"I always try to keep my word."

"I've been having weird dreams lately. Not all of them about Martin, but some are."

"OK."

"We used to have a pretty good sex life."

"I remember you told me."

"It's…gotten worse. I mean we're really good friends, but I just don't feel sexual toward him anymore."

"Has this been gradual, or…?"

"I has been. It's not like there was a single event."

"Is it just him? Do you still feel sexual? Sexy?"

"I do get twinges, but I haven't met anybody. I'm just kind of blah about sex right now."

"OK."

"But…oh this is so weird!"

Paul sat quietly and waited.

"It's…these dreams."

"Tell me about one."

"I've been blaming myself; that I'm not sexy enough; or working too much!"

"And?"

Michelle scrunched up her face, the suddenly jumped out of her chair.

"I think Martin's turning gay!

"What?!"

"He seems to have developed a new friendship with one of the tennis instructors at the health club. And the guy is a flamer!"

"That's no proof!"

"I know! I know!"

"What else? Feels like there's more."

"I…oh shit!"

What? Come on. I'm sure I've heard worse!"

"It's…Oh goddamn it!"

"What?"

"I followed him to the health club!"

"You stalked him?"

"I guess."

"Wow! You are a trip! And?"

"They played tennis for an hour or so."

"And this is proof he's gay?"

"Well, no. They kissed each other—and then went into the shower room with their arms around each other!

CHAPTER TWENTY FOUR

A Kindergarten of the Mind

San Francisco, September 1999

The months had been speeding by in a blur. His own therapy sessions, a private practice that was thriving, long walks all over The City, especially his beloved North Beach, lower Clement Street, parts of the Upper Castro, and on Twin Peaks, and in Golden Gate Park. He had also been making journeys to Muir Woods, Mount Tam, Stinson Beach, and Bolinas in Marin too.

The net result of all of these various forms of therapizing left him moderately-to-severely exhausted. While this came about as a result of the healing process he was experiencing, releasing what seemed like eons of traumatic grunge—and this, in turn, facilitated him taking a nap three to four times a week, usually in the afternoon, which had the added benefit of granting him a second writing period most days. He was moving forward swiftly with the book (still called *Brotherhood* at this point). He had developed the fever of competition, feeling the proximity of wholeness he knew, just knew, would be his personal prize for completing this latest and greatest version, one in which he believed he had finally found his true voice, his literary voice, thirty years after he'd come home, twenty years after the very first draft. He felt it deep in the marrow of his bones, that this latest version would be extremely powerful, and might actually give him entrée into the world of publication.

Though it still beggared the question: Perhaps sheltering vivid recall of injuries was really all that kept him from more optimum health? Or did he maybe need even greater recall to finally heal his analog children, and his precious self.

If he was the only one keeping himself from being the man he always wanted to be, from having the life that he wanted, the he was the prime perpetrator of all of the crimes against himself, though he had learned at the hands of the ultimate masters of deceit and manipulation, shaming and the maceration of the soul—his parents.

This led directly him to pre-life choices, when the "he" that was him did not yet seemingly exist, and had chosen the life that "he" had subsequently lived; chosen to experience all of the weird and wacked-out things he, as Paul, had, some of which he now regretted, even lamented or wished he could re-live in a different manner, if he had had the prescience to have avoided the reefs and shoals that had beset his ship of state; that had reshaped his path to illumination, instead blaming all of those who had filled crucial roles in his unfolding drama. But the nothing would have been the same. He would not be, could not be, the man he was had he not been the man he was.

Paul had early learned to conflate blame and responsibility. They were entirely different concepts, yet his father had always used the former while meaning the latter, so Paul had always felt blamed and resented—and resisted responsibility because blame always felt so shitty.

He was himself the only one he ever had to forgive for all of the years of torture it seemed impossible to release; a violent, vicious, parasitic demon that self-replicated despite his every effort; that ate at him, tore at him like myelin-destroying Parkinson's, eroding the very fundaments of his soul—and nowhere to hide; no escape, no salvation, no cure—and none of his self-abnegation could ever satisfy that deep craving, no matter how Herculean his efforts; only the massive efflux of tears and toxins from his body gave him the strength to go on, to keep on living, to keep on giving, to keep on writing, this sacred work alone the only holy mandate of his life, the very raison d'être for and of his life.

It was his wilderness outpost, his bulwark against the raging elements, his sanctuary in a ravaged world gone mad, the one and only place where he felt he could abandon all pretense, all obfuscation, all distraction, all lies and untruths; where he could be truly, and really, really real, sit naked before the keyboard and pour out his heart's discontents and his soul's most twisted fears and desires without thought or care of judgment or repudiation, self or other. It was the only respite he, those passing moments of ecstasy, so alike yet so completely different than the throes of orgasm, or being immersed in a spectacular dream—especially so the "novel dreams" that came every six weeks or so, bringing plot lines, sub-plots, narrative, characters, and dialogue; even occasionally a complete manuscript, once an entire organized crime novel had stretched out seamlessly across three nights dreamscape!

Any number of his therapists had commented on his behavioral patterns as being components of Posttraumatic Stress Disorder (PTSD), that originated in the dark, dank crevices of his childhood—and had been severely exacerbated by his experiences in combat psychiatry—the aftereffects of which he still suffered; would likely always experience, and re-experience for the rest of his life, though hopefully and theoretically, with lessening debilitating effects and reactions. As he had frequently said, "I will always have the memories, but I don't have to carry the emotional weight of them."

He had finally come to the conclusion that he should, in fact, give thanks for ALL of his experiences as the torturous path of his life had led him to the here and now, to being a man he truly loved and admired.

CHAPTER TWENTY FIVE

Progress, Not Perfection

San Francisco, October 1999

Mandy had pestered her Primary Care Provider for almost a year before he decided that perhaps her repeated bouts of rumination about suicide, and increasingly intrusive thoughts about her worthlessness (based on her body size and weight), might qualify as medical necessity in her case. Bariatric surgery was not usually considered to be so, often dismissed as "cosmetic." It was only when the insurance company's Board of Review representative agreed with Paul's diagnoses of Bipolar Disorder Mixed, Obsessive-Compulsive Disorder (moderate to severe), and Body Dysmorphic Disorder (severe), all of which seriously contributed to the variety of delusions that grew in her mental garden—that the bean-counters granted her permission to proceed.

The net result of all of this dialogue was a serious constriction on her medical spending plan (unless of course she wanted to pay almost double her current rate, out of her own pocket because her employer was unwilling). Thus her desire to have the approximately 25 pounds of excess skin removed was quashed immediately, followed in short order by a reduction in the number of visits to Paul she would be allowed per month (down from twice to once).

"I'm still so pissed about only being able to come once a month!"

"What is it you're actually pissed about? Go deeper!"

"Oh shit! You always say that!"

"It's true! There's always a deeper level!"

She whined, a momentary intrusion from her 4-yearold—a not uncommon behavior.

"I on't know!"

"Come on, Mandy! I know you're scared!"

"Little Mandy is!" A dissociated, regressive way of phrasing it.

Paul walked her through a progressively deepening series of breaths, listening and synching himself with her.

After a few minutes of this, Paul spoke softly but firmly, asking her to flutter her eyelashes before opening her eyes, and coming back to the new present. Her eyes had a smoky quality that had been appeared recently, that gave her a sense of depth and quality he had never seen with her before. He poured her a glass of water from the sapphire-colored crystal flagon on the side table.

She drank deeply, then Paul refilled her glass before she cleared her throat.

"Wow, Paul! That was awesome! I just wish I could remember better when I start to drift away (the term she used for dissociate).

"But you picked up the cue right away! That's so much faster than when we first started working together!"

"I know! I've been doing my homework!"

Especially with her only attending once a month, it had been imperative that she practice new techniques and develop new habits on her own time. They had worked on breathing exercises of various sorts as well as surveys, questionnaires, and various personal histories (the latter to help her remember the biographical facts of her life, rather than the confabulation to fill in gaps in her memory, what she called "making stuff up").

"So, what triggered you today?"

"I guess I'm still pissed off because they won't let me get the other surgery," she said, and grabbed a thick fold of skin. "I guess it triggered my…self-loathing, all my not-good-enough stuff."

"I tend to agree with you. But it seemed like you might have been triggered before you got here. Did you have a bad day?"

They had had lengthy conversations about mirroring, and attracting what one feels rather than what one thinks. Paul considered this to be an extension of his dismissal of so called "cognitive therapies."

"Yeah, nothing special, just stuff. I'm getting better at managing."

"Your mother?"

"A little, but that's always there. I don't give her power anymore…not like I used to!"

"What's working best for you?'

"Mostly I've healed enough of my old memories that she can't get in there and fuck with me like she used to!"

"And you said you were still pissed at the insurance company."

"Yeah. They're just corporate assholes. They have no idea how therapeutic it would be for me to have the follow-up surgery. I'm…still pretty intimidated by my size."

"And what's your latest revelation around that?"

"It's just another way that I internalized the abuse. It's really old, and I have to 'unlearn' the old behaviors. I look forward to really not being bothered by her, especially since she keeps it up in the face of all of the amazing work I've done."

"That's right! Not to repeat old behaviors, but to do it with awareness of not doing it. It will become truly natural."

"Because I am really working at completely embracing…everything. I know it sounds kind of "woo-woo," but that's what I want."

"So you really believe you can create this out of whole cloth."

"Yeah. I really do, as long as I keep working on my whole agenda as much as I can!"

Paul sat quietly, chin in his upturned palms, eyes a thousand miles away.

After a long timeless time, Paul sat up.

He looked at Mandy, jumped up, and extended his hand.

"Thanks. Really! Thanks! I appreciate it. I have to give it some more thought, but I think you might be onto something!"

CHAPTER TWENTY SIX

The Return of the Voodoo Child (Thanks, Jimi!)

San Francisco, January 2000

Paul was very grateful for the end of all of the "Y2K" bullshit, the numeronym for the year 2000 software problem. There had been so much nutty, media-generated hysteria, including police throughout the world securing emergency bunkers for themselves; a marked increase in the popularity of wilderness-survival boot camps; and even an NBC made-for-TV movie about the coming "disaster." All of the hullabaloo, all of the "computer fixes" and other proposed technologically-oriented nonsense did nothing but promote far more fear and anxiety (off of which many industries prospered).

One thing Paul found especially irritating was having to write "19" before the year of his birth, as if just using the "47" would lead anyone with half a brain into the error of believing him to have been born in 2047 instead. It was a minor issue, but still a pain in the ass. Of course, government intrusion almost always was, especially since he believed that there was way, way too much of it already, interfering in the intricate details of citizens' lives. Paul was still a believer in the old-school idea that a government's first duty is to protect and enrich the lives of the populace. Conversely, government had many agendas, the least of which was its stated purpose—especially since bureaucracy-on-steroids had lent itself to help create many billionaires.

He had done extensive research into the media-hyped hysteria used as a method to induce and exponentialize fear in the populace—most especially with the intention of manipulating what Herman and Chomsky had called "the manufacture of consent," an insidious process through which lies, obfuscations, disinformation, media-generated hysteria, and fear for personal safety, were used to twist public opinion into appearing to be in agreement with the hidden agendas of Big Government and Big Business (which owned which these days was a good question, since they were both primarily interested in power and control, and making exorbitant profits at any cost).

He had always been a big fan of George Bernard Shaw's take on such issues that he had never been shy about stating publically:

> I am, and always have been, a revolutionary writer, because our laws make law impossible; our liberties destroy all freedom; our property is organized robbery;

our morality is an impudent hypocrisy; our wisdom is administered by inexperienced or mal-experienced dupes, our power wielded by cowards and weaklings, and our honor false in all its points. I am an enemy of the existing order for good reasons.

For Paul, the biggest aspect of the "non-problem of Y2K" was related to the fact that it had any existence at all. Before the advent of more modern computing, data processing for business was done using unit record equipment and punched cards, most commonly the 80-column variety employed by IBM. These had dominated the industry for decades. One of their significant space-saving tricks was to leave off the first two digits of the century. As early as 1958, there were those who, as a result of work on genealogical software, foresaw the problem portending. Bob Bemer spent the next twenty years trying to make programmers, IBM, the government of the United States, and the ISO (International Standardization Organization) aware of the problem, with little or no response.

Starting in 1998, the phrase "Y2K" first appeared in TIME in a story that explained the problem. Though most prognosticators cautioned that the necessary programs would get fixed in time, the fear of a fallout was still scary enough for TIME put the hysteria on its cover in January of 1999 under the headline *The*

End of the World!?! (In this same issue ran a full-page ad for Buspar, proclaimed to significantly reduce anxiety!)

It fucking figured! Big Pharma and all the other plutocrats would use absolutely anything to make more profits! Creating fear and hysteria was a flagrant attempt to magnify and exploit people's most ancient dread. Another aspect of the "new reality" that Paul especially resented was something called "unbundling," the extraction of a previously free service from a package of services included with the original price (such as airlines now charging for baggage), re-packaging it as a paid service, and selling it to the consumer. The same was about to happen with airline meals, he had been told.

It was all related to ideological hegemony, to which he had been introduced at New College by his favorite Professor of all time, Jekker DuBois—one of the most brilliant people he had ever known. He had learned the concept, and come to understand it in one of his earliest weekend seminars involving cultural change and the crisis in belief systems. The insidious tentacles of ideological control and manipulation had spread throughout the world as the working philosophy of power.

Althussur had called ideology "Ideas imposed by society and embraced by individuals which determine our lived relation to the real, in order to maintain the status quo." This was done to assure the maintenance and reproduction of wealth, and allow for a dominant class that would control society through owning the means of production and distribution. Kavanagh had noted that the existence of any society is only possible because its citizens hold a mental image of it, and carry that around within themselves.

This whole line of thought had set his mind on fire. He had used the knowledge starting with his first paper at New College; and it further influenced both his Master's Thesis and his Doctoral Dissertation; even ended up as a key plank in his book on shame, in which he had explicated it as the underlying foundation of all societal phenomena—his version of Freud's *Civilization and its Discontents.*

He reflected on something Walter Truett Anderson wrote in a book called *Reality Isn't What It Used To Be.* "The great games of modern politics, the by-products of democracy that often threaten everything democracy was meant to be, are the games of opinion molding: propaganda, brainwashing, programming and deprogramming, advertising and public relations." One of his cohort-mates at New College, a truly bright mind named Jocelyn Kopes once said, in an unpublished paper, "Propaganda is to democracy what violence is to totalitarianism."

Paul shivered thinking of how broad-spread and insidious the system actually was. It was one of the factors that occasionally led him to the edge of his sanity, as he look down into the never-ending cascade of shadows at the very edge of the abyss, the infinite hall of horrible mirrors that inevitably thrust him into dark thoughts of suicide and non-existence.

Paul always thought about "having to make a living," wage slavery, as a perfect example. Such ideas get reinforced through laws, advertising, and the media, needing no further need of reinforcement for an undiscriminating and obedient populace, as the cultural elites make disembodied corporate decisions not based on morals, ethics, or environmental concerns. Ideological hegemony's development had been so incorporated the cultural biases that they had become integrated into the psyche of the society as "acceptable," and were acted out in daily life as if they were "correct" and "proper"—and very rarely questioned!

As if it had been designed to interrupt his reverie, his business line rang. It had a markedly different tone than his personal line. He felt inclined to let it ring through to his service, and allow his lethargy to take him back. If it were important, the service would call him on his private line, which they did within moments.

"Dr. Marzeky here."

"Doctor, this is Helene, at the service. I have a Mr. Baldestari on the other line. He seems pretty upset. He's crying and wants to talk to you right away!"

"Thanks, Helene. Please connect us."

Massimo had terminated therapy four months earlier, after working on his memories of childhood sexual abuse had reached a kind of impasse, a ring-pass-not beyond which he was unwilling (or unable) to go. Both he and Massimo felt he needed a little break before continuing. He just simply refused to discuss any other relevant issues about Veronica. Paul had told both Massimo and Veronica to call at any time, should either of them feel the need for more work, individually or together.

"Massimo? It's Paul. Dr. Marzeky."

A huge sob burst through the telephone receiver, followed by a strangled cry of desolation.

"Paul. Doctor. You gotta help me!"

"Just take a deep breath, and tell me what's going on."

"She's dead! Veronica's dead!" He started sobbing again, a wail of utter misery blasted through the receiver.

"What?! What happened?"

"I don't know! I mean she was stabbed! Somebody killed my baby!"

"When, Massimo? When did this happen?"

"I don't know! I don't know! I just came home, and found her!"

"Jesus! Did you call the police?"

"No! I called you!"

"Jesus! Massimo, you gotta call 911! Now!"

"I'm afraid! I'm afraid they'll think I did it!"

"Why, Massimo? Why?"

"Because it's my knife!"

CHAPTER TWENTY SEVEN

Treading Carefully

San Francisco, February 2000

It was 8 1/4" long, a Cold Steel OSS™ that had cut through the tangled web of ligaments, muscles, veins, and arteries at the base of the throat of Veronica Baldestari, cut through, and been left there. Massimo had been doubly devastated when he realized it was one of a matched pair of knives that he really loved—with the satiny double-edged blade, the solid quillon (guard), and the checkered, heavy-duty rubber handles.

Paul wanted to be there before the police arrived, so he told Massimo to do some calming breaths, not to touch anything, and wait for him outside of his house. Massimo's breathing was still quite raggedly when Paul told him that he was on his way. He called the service and asked them to take all of his calls, dashed out the door, and made his way to his client's apartment at Greenwich and Battery.

When he arrived, Massimo was sitting, head down, sobbing, with distress in his blood-red eyes. His apartment was a two bedroom one with a small deck off the backside. Paul looked through the open front door, past the small garden in the back, and saw Coit Tower in the distance. Massimo had blood smeared on both of his hands, and staining the rolled sleeves of his EMT uniform jumper almost to the elbows. The neck of his shirt was sodden, and he had blood stains on his face. As soon as he saw Paul, he started to get up to hug him, but Paul told him gently but firmly to sit back down, and not move. Whether Massimo interpreted this as rejection or not, he immediately started sobbing again, and speaking in an incomprehensible mish-mash of English and Italian, punctuated by sonorous moans. Paul pulled his cell phone out of his leather jacket, and called Northern Station—half-praying that Phil McLaren was not there.

He was a homicide detective at Northern Station on Vallejo and Columbus, just minutes away. Phil McLaren was a Vietnam vet he had met when Paul had given evidence at a murder trial two years ago. He had testified as an *amicus curii* (friend of the court) due to his expertise on trauma and traumatic memory, and because he was a Vietnam vet who had practiced in combat psychiatry in-country. In this case, he had been preferred to other, more seasoned (and expensive) "experts" who were usually only book-learned; or who had been psychiatrists in the military (officers) who had not had any raw, first-hand exposure. (The one psychiatrist he did respect was Jonathan Shay who wrote *Achilles in Vietnam: Combat Trauma and the Undoing of Character* about his experiences there).

Paul thanked his lucky stars and took a deep, deep belly breath before he spoke.

"Phil? Hi. It's Paul Marzeky."

"Hey Paul! How they hanging?"

"Fair to midlands. Listen, I've got a small problem here."

"What? Did you just kill someone?" he asked, and then laughed.

"No, but a former client of mine just came home and found his wife murdered."

"WHAT?"

"He was totally hysterical, speech was incomprehensible, when he called me."

"Called you? What the fuck? You didn't call 911? He didn't call 911?"

"No. He called me, and I rushed right over. Let me give you the address."

"Black-and-whites are rolling! Do NOT fucking move!"

"I only came because I was afraid he might harm himself. I just didn't think!"

"I'm on my way, asshole!"

Paul had told Massimo to prepare for rough handling. They had their hands up when, within sixty seconds, two uniformed officers arrived at Massimo's with guns drawn. He tried to introduce himself as a "friend of Lieutenant McLaren's," but it held no water.

The officers ordered them to their knees, then proned them on the ground, hands on the top of their heads. Still holding his weapon on the pair, the other one of the officers patted them down, and cuffed them. Very shortly another patrol car pulled up, and there were even more sirens in the near distance. Their pockets were turned inside out and examined by several different policemen; and asked repeatedly why they were there.

Paul knew enough to keep it simple until Phil got there. Plus he did not want to have to repeat the story of his presence more times than he had to, knowing that these two were the bottom of the ladder, and that detectives would need to hear it (numerous times too)—and that their stories would have a far more influential effect on the direction of events thereafter.

"And you say that this guy," said the more senior officer, gesturing at Massimo, "called you first? Why was that?"

"He's an ex-client. He called me, and I called Lieutenant McLaren. I was concerned that he," gesturing to the now mute, and withdrawn-looking figure of his ex-client, "might be a danger to himself!"

"Why's that?"

"Officer, I've explained that I have a confidentiality conflict here. Is Detective McLaren here yet?"

Two detectives, who had made a pass through the house, came out and started to address Paul as a very pissed off Phil McLaren pushed through, and immediately got in Paul's face. He unleashed a torrent of cursing, then launched into a list of other potential damages that he might personally inflict upon Paul.

"You stupid ass motherfucker! I could charge you with obstructing a police investigation! You should have called 911 first! You shouldn't even be here at all, you asshole! I mean, what the fuck? I should just kick your ass, but we got too many witnesses!"

Paul knew then that Phil was going to settle down, even though he was still severely riled up. Phil then turned away to speak to the senior officer.

"So whatta' we got?"

The older patrolman told him that they had cleared the house, and that the "vic" was in the back bedroom.

"It's kinda weird, detective. She laying there on the bed with this big ol' knife in her throat, but her hands are crossed over her chest, and her legs are straight out in front of her, like a frikking angel or something!"

"I'll check it out!" and left to do so.

Paul called out after him.

"What about me? Please! Let's talk!"

The detective looked back over his shoulder and said "You had plenty of time to talk before I got here! No! You fucking wait!"

Then he turned to a grizzled looking older patrol officer and said, "Put 'em in separate units! You can uncuff him," he said gesturing to Paul. "And keep the fucking media back fifty feet!"

Phil and his sergeant, Bill Watts, put booties on their feet and double rubber gloves on their hands. Everyone called Bill "Brillo" because of his moderately grown-out Afro. He was half African American, and half-Jewish, so he came by his hair naturally. He got the occasional ration of shit about his hair from the brass (supervisors), but had asked for and gotten a ruling from his union that he was allowed to grow it out for "religious reasons."

He pulled aside another pair of officers.

"You two call for more back up, the ME, and a bus (ambulance). Forensics too! ASAP! Go secure the scene! I want tape all around the whole building! Both the front and back entrances! When back up gets here, I want you two," he said glancing at the name tags for the first time, "Flaherty and Crispin, to start going door-to-door. Get three or four other uniforms too! And reinforce the blue line there—keep those press vultures back! Go!"

McLaren came back out of the house a few minutes later, and deposited his contaminated protective clothing in a red biohazard bag. He opened the door of the squad car and took Paul as far away from the immediate crime scene as possible. Phil grabbed Paul's right shoulder firmly, and pushed him against a wall.

"Just what the fuck do you think you're pulling? My fucking Captain is just a fucking inch away from charging you with Obstruction of Justice! That's a goddamn felony! What the fuck were you thinking?"

Paul got almost nose-to-nose with the enraged detective, and straightened his shoulders.

"Fuck your fucking Captain! I acted in the best interests of my client, er, ex-client! I called you immediately after I got here! Massimo had just found his wife murdered! Don't you think he deserves a little…shelter?"

"Shelter schmelter! What if he killed her? The man is my prime suspect right now!"

"Oh bullshit! He was on duty for the last 48 hours! He's probably got dozens of witnesses!"

"Yeah, well, we'll see. In the meantime, keep a low profile around Captain Ormolo. He is seriously pissed!"

"How'd he even find out?"

"I don't know. Maybe one of the dispatchers told him. Or more likely told another dispatcher who told a sergeant, blah, blah, blah, blah, blah!"

"Now you sound like Lenny Bruce! 'Yes, Your Honor, I said blah, blah, blah!'"

"I better get a quick solve on this one. I gotta get that motherfucker off my back!"

"Look, Phil, I acted in good faith. And, completely off the books, I do not believe he has it in him to kill someone, especially not Veronica!"

"Here we go! Mr. Psychological!"

"Well fuck you very much!"

"OK. OK. Tell me something that'll help me."

"I sincerely thought he might harm himself! That's why I came right away!"

"Yeah? And?" he said, making the "come on" gesture with his right hand, wanting more information.

"Phil, there's certain information that I can't give you without a court order. Patient confidentiality. You understand."

"I'll have a court order this afternoon!"

"Massimo is innocent! I guarantee it!"

"We'll fucking see!"

Paul had seriously been tempted to skirt the edges of confidentiality, but what Phil wanted would come to him in the form of Paul's case notes and the Psychological Eval he would provide as was required by the letter of the law. Of course, there was a whole lot of material that he did not include in his documentation for the insurance company that was very relevant to the case; at the same time he did not feel comfortable releasing his client's history of sexual abuse *carte blanche*. He needed to talk to Massimo privately about this issue, as well as about the resolution in therapy that had led to the dramatic lessening of the paranoid ideation. Massimo had remembered more material about his mother, and her resemblance to his now-dead wife. Unless Phil worded the subpoena exactly right, he was not going to release all of his case notes, many of which had been written to and for himself alone to guide him in the formulation of a treatment plan, and in writing up the Evaluation required by the insurance company. Before he spoke to Massimo, he did not want to release more information than was required. If the authorities were not content to check out his alibi, and accept the findings he had made for the official report, then he might have to dig deeper and decide to release his own notes too.

CHAPTER TWENTY EIGHT
Tidal Surge

Later February 2000

Massimo had spent two nights in a holding cell at the Hall of Justice which depleted his already fragile emotional state. The police had used threats of sending him down to San Bruno (the official San Francisco County Jail was down the 280 Freeway in San Mateo County). Paul had officially re-engaged as his therapist. With some assistance from Phil McLaren and Massimo's attorney (a North beach old-timer hired by his mother), Paul had been allowed to see him once each day for thirty minutes. Phil McLaren had made a somewhat oblique approach, hinting that he would "appreciate" Paul's "cooperation" with the police investigation that was quickly gathering speed, though seemingly only focused on Massimo, the almost-too-perfect suspect.

"He's my client! He has the expectation of confidentiality!"

"Come on, Paul! You know he's guilty!"

"Fuck you! You don't know that!"

"All of the evidence is against him! He had her blood all over him, and it was his knife!"

Not meaning to mislead the detective, yet neither willing to share confidential information without proper process, Paul let the logical response hang in the air as they parted.

"What's his motive, Phil?"

Massimo was wearing an orange jail jumpsuit. The work jump suit he had been wearing had been taken as evidence. He had been placed on paid administrative leave pending the outcome of the investigation. His self-loathing had bloomed as he had now elevated Veronica almost to the status of a saint in his own mind and cosmology.

Paul had been granted the courtesy of using an Attorney Interview Room, which meant that we were able to speak to each other face-to-face without Plexiglas and a telephone receiver. He was acutely aware of the fact that my client had not been showering daily, nor washing his hair.

He looked so forlorn, so miserable, sitting there with downcast eyes and a completely disoriented mien, that Paul almost felt drawn to shed a tear, and attempt a gentler approach, but decided that the situation was far too serious than to allow false sentiment to stand in the way.

He breathed deeply, and then broached the real topic at hand.

"Massimo. Massimo! Look at me! Look at me! We need to talk!"

The young man looked up slowly, bleary eyed, sighing.

"What? What?"

"Massimo, you're in serious trouble."

"I didn't do anything!"

"It doesn't matter! It looks really bad for you!"

"Why?"

"Massimo! Veronica is dead! And you were found with her blood on your hands at the scene! What part of that do you not understand?"

The only response he got was yet another gout of tears.

"Massimo, we need to talk. Before she died, you were really angry with Veronica...thinking she was cheating on you!"

"Fuck you, man! I remember! But I was wrong! You helped me see that!"

"Did I really?"

"Yes! We were going to have a baby! I really didn't trust her, but I loved her! Does that make any sense at all?" as a burst of combined tears and frustration splurted out and he buried his face in his hands.

"We're talking about one of your splits."

"Yeah, yeah! Maybe. I loved her, always loved her, but...I never trusted her!"

"Probably that she reminded you of your mother!"

"Fuck you! I keep wanting to forget that!"

The police had been even more thorough (read brutal), despite (or perhaps because of) Paul's being involved. Good detective work had uncovered a witness who had overheard Massimo threaten her. Tommy Allesandro, a boyhood friend who used to play baseball with him at Di Maggio Park in North Beach, stated that he had heard Massimo threaten to kill Veronica because she was "fucking around on him." Yet another had heard him drunkenly cursing her out one night on Columbus Avenue in front of the Golden Spike restaurant. Three different people *in toto* came forward to make statements. It was also discovered that, while in uniform and on duty, he had tailed Veronica for over an hour as she shopped in and around North Beach. It was a stunt he had been written up, and never revealed to Paul.

"That was pretty outrageous, Massimo!"

He looked at me, eyes wide and pleading.

"Don't you see? I thought she was cheating on me—meeting her boyfriend, her girlfriend! I don't know! But it made sense at the time!"

"And now?"

He rubbed his hands across his face, a sheen of oil in their wake.

"Now? Now it seems completely…crazy, I guess. I mean, I don't think…she couldn't…"

Paul sat and simply observed, as his young client started sobbing again.

"I fucking hate it that they think I killed her!"

Massimo sat twisting his fingers. Paul's inner states vacillated between outrage, disbelief, and concern for his client, but he kept his demeanor blank, with only his eyes displaying any emotion.

"That Lieutenant keeps asking me to repeat 'my story!' Keeps asking if I 'remember anything else!' It's harassment! I want to know who killed her too!"

Paul could not help but feel deep sadness well up within him. Before he could stop it, a tear drop rolled down his cheek. He quickly wiped it away, and said, "I know it's a little early, Massimo, but do you mind if we close? Are you complete for today?"

"Yeah, I'm good Paul. When will I see you again?"

"Have your attorney call me. Probably Friday."

They shook hands. Paul was exhausted by the encounter and decided to go home and take a nap. He hoped he could get up refreshed, make some coffee, and get in a second round of writing today. His thoughts had been a bit choppy earlier, and his visit with Massimo had not helped at at all.

He awakened from a dream involving decidedly not-fresh fish, his two sisters, an auntie (long dead now, his mother's only sister), and some swarthy-looking men with moustaches in what appeared to be 1930's New York, probably lower East Side. It had nothing to do with what he was writing about, but it was always a good sign to have a vivid dream he could remember— especially one that left a lingering literary flavor.

He wrote for two hours, getting up only once to get a second evening coffee, and a snifter of Drambuie. After going to the bathroom, he felt very focused, although he did sense that there was a lot of chaos "in the wind" swirling all around him. It wasn't unusual in and of itself, but today most of it was centered on Massimo. As much as Paul wanted to believe him and his pretty far-fetched story concerning his finding her, he questioned whether or not he might have missed something in the differential diagnosis, something he that might have prevented this tragedy. He knew he was harboring deep suspicions about the man, but he really did not want to ask him directly again if he had, in fact, killed his wife—especially since he was supposed to be a part of the man's support team.

It put him in mind of his continuing feelings of discontent. He sincerely wished he could live with the contemporary conditions of the world, rather than constantly questioning whether he were right or wrong; always asking if there were something more he could do other than just living with the illusion; that he could just be satisfied with what most people seemed willing to accept as "the way of the world and wanting to perhaps promote his own slant on the Big Delusion; make it more real, fill all of the cracks and crevices of his being, and be whole at last. It seemed that "cracking the illusion" was far more work than living with it, being supported by and in the illusion, even if the illusion inspired a certain amount of hope, in which case it might be best called "delusion."

If only it were so easy.

His contacts with Massimo kept triggering an awareness of his lifelong process of attempting to learn to live completely honestly, instead of walking around depressed and hiding his own feelings. No one would have listened anyway. Even though his childhood home was a madhouse, it was Paul who had come away clinically self-diagnosed as "Major Depression, Chronic, Recurrent."

One of the best days of his life was the day he went into the Army—and even better was the day he was liberated from the clutches of the military! The net effect of the many trials and tragedies of his life had been to allow him to find out who he really was, tempered in the flames as he threw off the suffocating blankets of despair and denial that had almost choked him.

He had arisen like a phoenix, born from the ashes of his self-created flames—born into brightness and awareness and the glory of emerging into a new life, leaving behind forever the burnt memories of his former self and the shabby trappings of a completely dishonoring life filed with lies to survive. He had gone underground at the age of eight, and with every passing year, had hidden more and more, fed the fires of the Hell that lived in his heart and belly, attempting to appear "normal," to keep himself from slaughtering the many people who had harmed him.

In retrospect, it had all been necessary and perfect, though experiencing it had been excruciating, chaotic, and punishing. But there had always been something driving him to define himself by his own standards; to acquire a form and manner he liked; to develop real guiding principles by which to live, to see and make his own way through the confusing maelstrom. There had always been guidance, often just nudges from Fate, other times strong, demanding, not-to-be-ignored intimations that showed up in the form of dreams, intuitions, and even physical interventions that pushed him in certain directions. Some had called him obsessed, others simply "crazy."

But through it all he had kept faith with and in himself, even when he seemingly most abandoned this nascent self during the heaviest drug use years that had helped him define who he did not want to be; and showed him lessons he could not have learned any other way.

Drifted, and fought, and struggled, and ran for so many, many years, sometimes without hope, sometimes in great fear and shame, sometimes filled with so much light he thought he might be Jesus' son. But always onward, always moving—sometimes listlessly, sometimes at light speed as if he had geezed up a bunch of amphetamine—but always onward, propelled by the Voice of the Universe, especially that of the Divine Mother, often hidden behind the scenes and props of seeming "reality," always seeking that final curtain that would signal an end to all of his pain, all of his suffering. He always thought of it in terms of a woman, a divinely supreme and superb woman who would come into his life and help him redirect his ship of state, help him continue the pilgrimage of redemption, of reclamation, of ever-continuing, never-ending growth and birth and death arising from the holy flames to continue, always continue the sacred journey, to becoming who and what he truly was.

He sincerely wished he had commemorated the blessed day when he first saw, really saw, his rage and fury concentrated, distilled, purified—and released, revealing to him the innate tenderness he had hidden like a Damascus steel vault, the shattering of which revealed all pretense—and he had surrendered all (seemingly) of his hidden treasures to the glaring light; self-judgments and terror, and everything he had hidden from himself, lied about to himself, denied in his heart of hearts—surrendered it all to the cleansing flames of the love in his heart for the Creator, Manifest and Unmanifest; surrendered it all, heart washed clean of the terrible burdens he had carried for millennia, released to the healing winds of eternal change and expiation; released to arise newborn and whole, to be the man he had always wanted to be, free-born, full-born like Athena from the head of Zeus, fully armored and ready for battle. And it was this magnificent warrior he that he met coming out of the womb of himself, squatting in the desert sands, embracing all of the qualities and character he had worked for so long to perfect, displaying them all with equanimity: peace, gentility, power, strength, joy, wonder, immense mentality, prescience, empathy, wonder, healing ability, wordsmithing—all outshone by a tremendous vitality and *joie de vivre* that he had only known in bursts previously, now flowing in his veins and arteries, pulsing in his heart and penis, vibrating everywhere, and radiating from him without effort.

The magnificent words of Ken Wilber from *Sex, Ecology, and Spirituality* echoed in him:

> And comes to rest that Godless search, tormented and tormenting…gone the madness of a life committed to uncare, and gone the tears and terror of the brutal days and endless nights where time alone would rule. And I—I rise to taste the dawn, and find that love alone will shine today. And the Shining says: to love it all, and love it madly, and always endlessly, and ever fiercely, to love without choice and thus enter the All, embracing the only and radiant Divine: now as Emptiness, now as Form,

together and forever, the Godless search undone, and love alone will shine today.

It was true. It was real. He was grateful.

CHAPTER TWENTY NINE
Deeper into the Darkness

Early March 2000

Despite the particular depth and flavor of his personal work, many of his clients seemed to be seeking reinforcement of their illusions and delusions, as if in some way persistence alone could create the possibility of their manifesting simply by believing strongly enough, holding out hope despite all the odds. It so much reminded him of what had been genuinely called "New Age Thought" at one point, which title had now degenerated into being called "woo-woo" and other derisive terms due to massive misuse and commercialization by lesser minds who did not embrace true wholeness and forward-thinking in their hearts—and could only manage the most banal, superficial reproductions of the essence, and the beauty, the dignity and inspiration, the title once possessed. It all came about, in part, because too many people had wanted to adopt the trappings of hip; wanted to look or sound like they were true pioneers in this dark and lonely age; wanted to feel like they both simultaneously belonged to a special and evolved group, and were uniquely set apart from the vast masses—all by professing to have access to ethereal knowledge and information, the specialized lexicon of genuine seers and believers.

As part of his own particular pursuit of "sanity," Paul had had to dismiss his own fantasies about being a world class author with all its magnificent perquisites—especially when he confronted himself with the statistics of the odds against his becoming a professionally published author. The latest stats were that 300,000 unsolicited (not professionally represented) manuscripts are submitted every year, and of these only one percent ever got read (3000); and of that one percent, only one percent (30) ever got published!

These demoralizing numbers had led him to forsake traditional publishing, after many, many rejections. He did not want to feed the commercial publishing system, yet had a strong desire to be read and appreciated. So he decided to offer free copies of his book on shame (when it was completed) to clinicians and other interested parties—in order to share the wealth of who we was and attempt to satisfy the hunger in his heart to be heard. It was the ultimate declaration of his belief in what he called the "give-away Universe." By giving freely of all that he had, he completely believed that he would be fed by a loving and beneficent Universe, generated by his own small voice in the vast symphony.

He was frequently reminded of something James Baldwin had once said: "In this country it is a crime to be poor. You either make it or you don't. There's no in between. So a novelist who becomes a success becomes a show-business commodity. It is as difficult to survive success as it is to survive obscurity. Both are equally brutal."

Eternal hope kept springing up for him, an almost indoctrinated belief in the miraculous manifesting the wished-for, hoped-for, answers to his personal dilemmas. This process that was so common to much of humankind, reminded him of a citation from Demosthenes: "Nothing is easier than self-deceit. For what a man wishes, that he also believes to be true."

Paul was only too aware that many individuals tended to avoid doing their own personal work, following the predominant contemporary worldview that so viciously and punitively discourages self-examination, self-motivation, and breaking out of the "authorized" and pre-conceived mold. It was the kind of "space brothers are going to save us" thinking that pinned already tenuous hopes and dreams on an even more specious view that the future was going to be far better and more personally meaningful. (Related also to the "pie in the sky" doctrines of all religions and political ideologies). It was part of the mechanism that always got people "hooked" on confidence schemes, and those who plied their trade swimming through schools of smaller, more fearful and more hopeful fish in order to make a meal of them. Such people "professionally" kept the hope of aspirants alive as long as the money was flowing in; and when it wasn't, they practiced inducements, praise, seeming good will, and even "love" to further milk the vulnerable human cash cows.

Seeking recognition had become the greatest addiction of all, the desire to seen and heard, read and listened to, recognized by the vast and faceless public to ameliorate personal emptiness— and very little could be done to dissuade people from following grandiose, delusional pursuits. Paul felt strongly that relinquishing his own small stake in this no-win process was his contribution to making the world a better place.

He always flavored his initial orientation to new clients with a measure of self-disclosure. By opening himself up to them, it started creating the therapeutic bond that would ultimately allow the client to trust him and themselves, and to step through the magic doorway that led to the healing of heart and soul. In sharing freely and releasing shame, clients in effect gave themselves permission to let go of (often) decades' worth of emotional weight that translated directly into their symptomatology. Therapy is a relationship. Both parties have to agree to it; and both parties have to choose it. Without consent, there is no relationship.

Paul subscribed to the idea of "bottoming out" with mental health as much as with any addiction. Eventually everyone came face-to-face with a crisis of one sort or another—some were led there by broken dreams, others as their entire lives collapsed. It inevitably led to despair, depression, and the sense that their "world had ended." When a couple was no longer compatible, and the relationship ended, one party or the other felt abandoned, or rejected. Yet it was this kind of "cracking" that opened up the doors of perception, or at least allowed a little sunlight in, so that the client could sometimes see how rigid and narrow they might have become in pursuit of a dream/illusion that a more objective observer might long ago have seen; and one that would not, or could not, ever materialize, secondary to real, or as-yet-perceived, character faults or other defects, related to emotional or spiritual development. Such experiences inevitably involved the stick tendrils of codependence, the interactive addiction to another's needs that one adopted in hopes one might get one's own met. As Bradshaw had noted: "Codependence is the disease of the disease."

Sometimes Paul felt so goddamn exhausted, dealing daily with all of the venal, greedy people in the world and their dark agendas for domination and control. He believed in his heart that he could be, even should be, a part of a movement to counterbalance the incredibly destructive, rapacious industrial and post-industrial movements of the commercial world, and its rapacious plague of technologization. They, the ubiquitous "they," were even colonizing databases, huge, massive databases to track people and their most intimate preferences, so as induce them to buy even more, often useless products. And add to the shadow government's ability to pry into the most hidden places in citizens' lives in never-ending pursuit of the phantom "national security."

He really identified with Ned Ludd, the 19th-Century English textile worker who feared the end of his trade and started a protest movement against newly developed labor-economizing machines—stocking frames, spinning frames, and power looms introduced during the Industrial Revolution threatened to replace them with less-skilled, low-wage laborers. The movement took on his name, and between the years 1811 and 1816, the Luddite movement was a region-wide rebellion in Northwestern England that destroyed then-modern technology and required a massive deployment of military force to suppress. (Talk about maintaining the established order against the people who are most expected to provide the nutrients for the broken system!)

Paul really resonated with their rage at being replaced by machines, having their skills denigrated and set aside in the name of profit. He had heard of software being designed to make psychological diagnoses based on "yes/no" answers to a survey. What total bosh! It triggered his deep-seated feelings of alienation, even though it was only the proximal cause, not the actual one. God, how he longed to live in a community, a society, on a planet that embraced love and non-competitive sharing as a basis of business, government, and all spheres of human activity. Positively ached for it!

He had recently had an invitation from a senior MKP man, Tom Trevellian to a co-ed workshop in Berkeley he attended. There were five men and three women. Most of the men were MKP brothers, and the women had all had participated in women's empowerment trainings—so none of them were virgins in consciousness-raising. What transpired though, was miraculous. During the final hour before lunch, they were asked to choose someone they didn't know, (or knew least well), and reveal something they had never told anyone before. This really opened the room up energetically. By the time they had had a catered lunch, almost everyone was sitting chatting as if they were old friends. During the afternoon session, they were offered the opportunity to "work" by "taking space" in the middle of the room, or to engage selected members to play roles in a psychodrama. There was a strong sense of connectedness and everyone was eager to share.

One of the women stood and said, "I'd like to work through an old issue. I've spent a lot of time in therapy with this, but I feel like this might be a good arena for psychodrama."

The facilitator asked how she might want to do that. She replied that "Just telling the story in front of everyone" would be a good place to start," and asked that, should it feel proper for her to go further, could she? The facilitator counseled her that there would be time for each person there to have approximately forty five minutes; and that, within that context, she could proceed, and they would go as far as they could.

Jane began describing the early innocence of her childhood, and then being fondled by her brother when she was eleven. He was three years older. At first she told it pretty straight-faced, then tears started leaking out of her eyes.

"He never apologized! Even when I confronted him! The fucker! He denied it ever happened! He's married and got two kids now! I worry about the safety of his daughter!"

Then Tom spoke, and asked if she wanted to have some kind of role play with her "brother," utilizing one of the men willing to play the role. He asked for volunteers. All but one of the men raised a hand, and she chose a rather meek-looking man, then shook her head, and said "He looks too safe!" She then chose a burly-looking fellow, and he agreed to participate.

When asked where he should be in her field and how he should look, she at first put him five feet away on the other side of the circle, facing away. Then she started screaming at him, flailing her arms about. Then she started shouting, over and over: "How fucking dare you? How fucking dare you, you bastard?"

Tom asked if the "brother" had any lines, or did he just stand there?

"Nothing. It's not safe enough yet. I'm just too pissed off!"

She railed for several more minutes, then took a deep breath into her belly and expelled it loudly.

"OK. I think I'm ready for him to have some lines!"

"And what does he say?"

"I want him to tell me why he did it!"

"And why was that?"

She looked at the man playing her brother, and asked him, "Do you have any idea what he might say? Can you tell me what he was thinking?"

The man blushed, and said, "I never did anything like that. But you say he was fourteen?"

"Yes!"

"I don't know, but I'm guessing his hormones were raging! You might have been an easy target!"

Jane stiffened, then started to cry. One of the women went to comfort her, but the facilitator spoke sharply, "No! Let her have her own process!"

In a moment, Jane looked up fiercely.

"You know that sounds absolutely right! That fucking bastard!"

"Would you like for him to confess to you?"

"Yes! Yes! Absolutely!" She stood quietly, and then said, "And I want him to come closer!" When he was about three feet away, she held out her hand, palm out.

"There! That's close enough!"

Tom said, "OK now. Run your lines! Tell her why you did what you did!"

As the man began to speak, Jane's face tightened, then she screamed at him.

"You bastard! You fucking bastard!" And when she made as if to hit him, Tom intervened.

"No overt violence! But you can hit a pillow if you want.

When Jane agreed, they set up a stack of long, thick pillows in the middle of the floor, and gave Jane a plastic baseball bat, with the instruction that she should only swing over her head and down, and not at anyone. She was told she could continue screaming, and asked if she wanted her "brother" to keep running his lines.

"Oh hell yes!"

She started beating the pillows furiously, mostly screaming over and over.

"Bastard! Bastard!"

Fairly quickly, she started getting hoarse, and her voice lowered. Then, just as suddenly as it started, she dropped the bat and started sobbing. At this point, all of the women were crying, and most of the men, including John John, the man playing her brother.

After a small interval, Tom asked if she needed anything else. Before she could answer, John John asked in a tearful voice, "Is it OK if I apologize? I mean really apologize, for all of the men in the world!?"

Jane looked up at him, got to her feet, and approached him. He opened his arms to her, and she fell into his arms sobbing. He softly stroked her back, repeatedly saying "I'm sorry! I'm really sorry!" as the tears flowed down his face too.

After a few minutes, Tom asked, "Is it OK if we all hug you?"

Jane sobbed and nodded, and the rest of the participants linked arms around each other's shoulders, and Tom prompted, "Just breathe what you are feeling into the center of the circle. Don't talk!"

Paul felt an incredible warmth spreading through him as he fell deeper and deeper into a sense of cellular connection with those in the "group hug." Most of the people were either smiling broadly, or crying, or both. Paul reached out his hand and put it on Jane's head. He started laughing, caught up in the deep sense of fulfillment that rolled through him as he said, "You are the whipped cream in our éclair!"

Several people laughed, and they all hugged each other more tightly, seeming to breathe with one breath, one mind, one heart. They were shaken by a sense of love and tenderness as if by the Loma Prieta quake that struck the Bay Area in October of 1989.

Paul was flooded with the awareness that most people do not get to experience unconditional love as infants and children, and therefore often find themselves involved in the paths of addiction, even "mental illness," seeking the kind of love of which they were deprived. He did not discount the many thousands of scams and schemes that smacked of home, or forgiveness, or belonging; all of the cults, and other rip-offs related to the seeking of personal love or "salvation." It was the carrot all religions held out as a reward for enduring all of the iniquities, violence and turmoil, the turbulence, and disorders of the world—to avoid deeper, unresolved personal issues, and obviate what true healing might otherwise come.

And what if this were all there was—loving, being loved, all with no fear or shame. Being honest and open; being embraced and recognized, being real and genuine; and openly sharing one's heart with others, not fearing abandonment? Isn't this what everybody wants? Yet we often run away from offers of love out of fear of being harmed, when the object of the exercise is to reach out and find empathy with others. He sighed deeply and drew in more of the wonderful light he was experiencing.

What if this were all there was? What if, at the center core of all things, Love were really all there was?

CHAPTER THIRTY

Is this the Real Life or just a Fantasy?

Mid-March 2000, San Francisco

Though they had dithered and dallied; though Phil McLaren and his hard-working men had put in a mountainous pile of overtime requests, they had been unable to find enough evidence to substantiate their relatively formidable circumstantial case. They were simply unable to definitively charge Massimo with the crime—and had released him on his own recognizance along with all of the usual warnings not to leave the City and County of San Francisco, and to turn in his passport.

Paul made an exception to his rule, and was seeing Massimo twice a week for an hour at a time, since his insurance company would only countenance two hours a week. The man had continued to deny his culpability, and Paul seemed hard-pressed to break through the walls of his disavowal, despite Paul's intuitive sense that he was lying—though the motivation was unclear, whether from a really twisted pathology or simply deeply-felt guilt.

"What's going on, Massimo?"

The younger man had been sitting silently for several minutes, looking deeply preoccupied. They had been again probing the intricacies of his relationship with his dead wife when his garbled responses and lack of eye contact had trailed off into indistinguishable mumbles before finally leading to an uncomfortable silence—though Paul knew from long experience that such lapses could sometimes be mined for therapeutic gems.

Veronica's death was still a very active case. Phil McLaren and his bulldog partner, Bill Watts, had not stopped pursuing the investigation; and Massimo was still their prime suspect. The fragile therapeutic progress they had made had been shattered when the detective pair had shown up at Massimo's workplace, demanding to re-interview the other paramedics. Other hospital personnel who had provided his alibi were also on their list. Though they had a firmly established time of death as being during the time Massimo was on duty, they were hoping to find someone who had seen him disappear for some period of time (half an hour would have been enough they surmised), or who might have covered for him, who had stated he was there when he was not. At first he had been stunned, then shocked, and finally angry and outraged, accusing them of harassing him while the real murderer was walking around free.

"And that's what I told them! Then the *bastardos* told me to leave my work station, and wait outside while they talked to my co-workers!"

"Jesus! You're not under arrest again, are you?"

"No! No! But I was so fucking pissed off!"

"I'm glad you didn't go off on them!"

"I got to go to work. I'm on until day after tomorrow at 0600."

"Let's make a time for you after you get up."

"Yes! Please!"

"You still sleep in the AM when you get home?"

"Yes."

"What do you think? 1300? 1400?"

"Better make it 1400. That'll be safer."

OK. See you then. Call me again if you need to talk."

"*Ciao. Bene.*"

Phil was still angry with Paul about Massimo calling him first, but Paul felt he had a duty to his client he could not ignore—though in retrospect, he probably should have called it in first. But he couldn't have abandoned his client *in extremis* like that. If he hadn't been there, the cops might even have stitched him up. But that was probably just him being suspicious of authority. He always had been. In fact, he usually vacillated between suspicion and hatred that those ostensibly in authority had assumed the power that society granted to its "guardians," and with it the belief that they had the right to pry into his life, and ask intrusive questions. It really irritated him, especially as more and more civil rights were being ignored and abrogated. But then, it had never been "the land of the free and the home of the brave," had it?

Paul had been working on reversing the effects and artifacts of the weird energy he had created throughout his life, of the energies he magnetized into his life. He had always felt he had paid intense dues, though it was always just feedback from the Universe. For some reason beyond his paygrade, the massive dysfunction that represented the current state of cosmic affairs—the communal inner energies of all of the individuals that equal the shared manifestation of ALL in this moment, in this dimension. It was the headline announcement on the front page (under the fold) of the *San Francisco Chronicle* that Jeb Bush was under investigation for his part in stealing $5.2B in the "savings and loan scandal." On the very next day's front page, this was eclipsed by the 72-point bold font when "Daddy"

George launched "The Ground War"—and Jeb's name mysteriously disappeared from public scrutiny forever.

That night, Paul started a list of those he considered criminals against humanity, true war criminals in the sense that they were responsible for the destruction and defoliation of the planet, and the ruination of millions of lives. His list started with George H.W. Bush and Dan Quayle. Certainly as President and Vice-President they had to be held accountable. Then he added the entire of Congress, any and all politicians, lobbyists, and other assorted political intriguers, financiers, backroom-schemers, and assorted toadies—and, by extension, their families and associates. By the time the dawn broke, he had approximately half of the people in the United States, and twenty seven foreign countries, on his list. Even for him, it seemed grandiose and excessive!

But it brought him to a moment of truth. The system itself was totally corrupt. Eliminating the placeholders would do nothing to change it. He wracked his brain for an immediate and impactful way to have an effect on both the system and his own felt-sense of powerlessness. Within moments of contemplating it, like a lightening flash across a midnight sky, he came to the illuminated understanding that by choosing to step off the wheel of exploitation in every possible way, he could empower himself and quit feeding the extant system of corruption and misuse.

It started with the decision to stop eating meat and exploiting animals, though this was relatively superficial compared to the scintillating understanding of the vast and extraordinary power of shame shaping world events, and what R.D. Laing called "ontological insecurity," the questioning of one's right to even be alive (one's origins). It eventually led to his writing his second non-fiction book, called *Crucible of Shame: Trauma and Transformation*. He saw that the world society's web was held together, at least on one level by the power of shame to confuse, manipulate, demand, order, terrorize, harm, shadow, coerce, cajole, manage, use, damage, ruin, fill with fear, and generally cause havoc in the lives of others by creating continuous generations of children who are discouraged from looking within themselves lovingly for value because they have been so inundated with shame and its sequela (all addictions, especially greed addiction). "Mental illness" was also deeply shame-based. It was what Thomas Szasz called the medicalization of "problems-in-living," a quasi-credibility that the medical establishment used to assume the right to profit from the continuing projections of an insane, corrupt, debilitated, and merciless global society.

Paul continued to explore these topics in therapy, seeking clarity and release from the pervasiveness of his past as if it had a separate existence, acting upon him without his volition. In a recent session, he consented to some body work to help elicit places in his body where he was holding pain, to connect his old pain with his injuries, and let them go. On that particular day, Tim had elicited a mixture of grunts and groans, both pleasure and pain—and starting to congratulate himself on not screeching aloud when Tim lifted his left arm and put his fingers on a nerve plexus in his shoulder.

Paul screamed as his body torqued off the table, bowing up and coming down in one motion.

"Oh! Oh my God! What was that?"

"Just old stored pain releasing!"

"Oh Jesus fucking wept!"

"You been carrying it for a long time!"

"But what is it?"

"Doesn't matter! You're releasing it," he said, and replaced his fingertips.

Paul screamed, then moaned. Then his tears erupted, a vicious, viscous stain spreading down his cheeks, a cascade of drool running from his mouth as incoherent broken syllables tumbled out.

Paul sought some kind of mental and verbal traction, and began to speak to his long-suffering body through a mouth full of slobber.

"Oh God, I am so fucking sorry! I always thought you were the problem! I was so, so wrong! Please forgive me!"

He realized that he had much more work to do in forgiving his precious body for all of the harm it had experienced working for him (though there was no real separation). He'd had a lot of body work, and experienced other therapy modes like Primal Therapy, but this was an especially deep experience. (Paul thought that Rolfing was overrated, a process for masochists!) He realized yet again that locking up his old pain was another of the "lose to win" strategies that he had adopted in order to maintain some kind of sovereign territory within himself, to be free, to be who he really was. It was admittedly a deeply flawed, but one that had worked. He had survived. He had escaped. Living well every day now was his revenge. As Niccolo Machiavelli once said, revenge is a dish best eaten cold—and he ate his meal in pleasure every day. Even though they had healed the rift years before his father died, there were still layers and layers of shame and pain buried in the antediluvian regions of his soul and brain that were still occasionally triggered in him.

He made his way home slowly, and had a quick meal before falling exhausted into bed. When he awakened four and a quarter hours later, he felt refreshed, though still a little groggy and mildly shocked that he had slept as long as he had. When he stretched and yawned, happily pandiculating before he put his feet on the floor, he felt as if he'd had had a pair of microcephalic dwarfs using him for a trampoline in his sleep. He ached all over, and thought again about the incredible power of healing, releasing what had been held in stasis for so long in his bones and body, using his primal energy supplies to stay alive. Considered in this way, it made perfect sense that his muscles and ligaments would be protesting like a bunch of students during the Days of Rage in October 1969 when The Weathermen and the Students for a Democratic Society decided to "bring the war home" to the streets of Chicago.

After a cup of his coffee (this week he was experimenting with a French Roast/Sumatra blend), Paul reflected on the downside of fame (public appearances; lots of travel; being really visible [exposed] to the public; open to judgment and ridicule; dealing with serious business types, and serious business—all things he really despised. Then, of course, there were all of the projections, about which Frank Herbert had spoken so eloquently:

Greatness is a transitory experience. It is never consistent. It depends in part upon the myth-making imagination of humankind. The person who experiences greatness must have a feeling for the myth that he is in. He must reflect what is projected upon him. And he must have a strong sense of the sardonic. This is what uncouples him from belief in his own pretensions. The sardonic is all that allows him to move within himself. Without this quality, even occasional greatness will kill a man.

He had always craved fame in order to be seen and heard, his life and work becoming public property in order that he might become a literary and literate adult, recognized as special, to redeem the frustrated genius who had felt overlooked, denigrated, spurned, rejected, repudiated, and ignored despite his brilliant mind, and now his distilled wisdom, a compilation of thought and philosophy that certainly went radically counter to the "mainstream" (whatever the fuck that was!), a realm wherein he was likely to be labeled revolutionary, a "kook," a "weirdo," or, at best, (and delightfully so in his estimation), a visionary or futurist. Visibility was what he had always wanted. He vividly remembered his parents having conversations about him with him standing right there—leading him to the conclusion that he was simply just a piece of furniture that talked!

He realized the fallacy of seeking fame when viewed through a psychological lens. It was only his own love, recognition, faith, clarity, and acknowledgment he had sought; his own love and forgiveness that he needed—yet it rankled him when he saw many who he judged to be far less talented, far less intelligent, being given honors and prestige, elevated and acclaimed by the current culture. Of course, that was part of the problem. To become acclaimed in spite of the ubiquitous "they" who ruled and controlled, who elevated insipid literature with prizes and power celebrating the consensus reality they sold to others while themselves living in a far more rarified strata. It was practically impossible. Sometimes he feared he secretly wished he were one of them! Jesus! What a fucked up revelation! Next thing you know he might want to be as rich as Donald Trump!

CHAPTER THIRTY ONE

Center Everywhere, Circumference Nowhere

San Francisco, April 2000

On a chilly, foggy morning like today, Paul fell easily into reverie. He felt more than heard his joints creaking as he levered himself out of his leather executive office chair, and went to the kitchen. He filled the kettle and set it to boil while he lined the ceramic one-cup holder with a filter paper and five teaspoons of coffee. He laughed, thinking of the many night shifts he had pulled at San Francisco General on psych unit 7-A. It seemed odd to be making a single cup when he and his two fellow "mole people" on the shift were all heavy coffee drinkers. Each night one of them brought in a fresh ground pound of high quality coffee to brew the hundred cups they collectively drank every night! Crazy! Now for him it was usually just a pot in the morning while he wrote until two in the afternoon; then another pot after he woke up and wrote until he had to leave for work at ten in the evening.

As he waited for the water to boil, he started speculating about a new client he was treating—making superficial comparisons to his ex-girlfriend Marlene who delighted in presenting a constantly shifting panoply of costumes and cosmetics, always playing different characters, different nail polishes and lipsticks, even whole make up arrays, and using different props to support the roles she chose. It had always been fun and exciting, like dating a variety of women at the same time! The new client, Lorraine, though she seemed to play different roles, wore different sets of clothing, had different tones of voice, and exhibited different personality characteristics. He had only had the three sessions with her, but he felt that she was not choosing her roles purposefully.

She had been referred to him on a consult to establish for a differential diagnosis, not for long term treatment. She had been shopped around to a variety of therapists, none of whom seemed able to establish a diagnosis that met the array of her presenting symptomatology. Her insurance company wanted a "proper diagnosis" so her psychiatrist could bill for fifteen minute "medication management" sessions. Paul suggested that they fork out the bucks for a proper Psychiatric Evaluation, but they seemed unwilling to spend $800 to do so—their interest being primarily financial, not therapeutic.

She had been in and out of therapy for many years, and had had eight different diagnoses. She'd had trials of almost every drug available in the psychopharmaceutical nostrum: anti-anxieties; anti-psychotics; anti-depressants; beta-blockers; Lithium and carbamazepine; even psychostimulants (Ritalin and Adderall) in the mistaken notion and the empty hope that they would work—all to no avail. After reviewing the case documents, and her plethora of diagnoses, he had his first session with her. He came away feeling strongly that he needed to investigate further. After the second session, he requested and received permission for a fourth session, though he was pretty clear about his conclusions. She had previously been diagnosed with various forms of schizophrenia, PTSD, and the full spectrum of anxiety disorders. He believed that none of them were correct.

He was leaning strongly toward Dissociative Identity Disorder (DID). The literature indicated that most people who were so diagnosed had an average of eight previous diagnoses; and had been given trials on numerous medications, none of which worked. (This latter was also true of an Axis II diagnosis of Borderline Personality, the most refractive of character disorders). Previously known as Multiple Personality Disorder (MPD), the diagnosis had been made famous by the treatment of a woman who had become known as "Eve" in the movie *All about Eve*, depicting the treatment of a woman who initially displayed three distinct personalities whilst in treatment with the eminent psychiatrist Corbett Thigpin in the early 1950s. (It was rumored that she went on to eventually manifest 27 different personalities).

He sat down with the newly released DSM-IV (Diagnostic and Statistics Manual, Fourth Edition) to review the symptoms. it indicated that the most necessary symptom was the appearance of at least two distinct and relatively enduring identities (or dissociated personality states), that alternately control a person's behavior; accompanied by memory impairment for important information not explained by ordinary forgetfulness. Further, these symptoms could not be accounted for by substance abuse, seizures, other medical conditions, or by imaginative play in children.

The name had been changed from MPD to DID. First, the original name had been misleading, prompting many to associate it with schizophrenia (coined by Bleuler in 1910, it translated from the Latin as "a splitting of the mind,"). Instead, DID is the lack of a single, unified identity with an emphasis on different identities as centers of information processing. The other reason was the reference to the term "personality" usually referred to "characteristic patterns of thoughts, feelings, moods and behaviors of the whole individual." A patient with DID, conversely, switches between identities and behavior patterns that are, in fact, the mainframe personality which lack an independent, objective existence.

Amnesia was another symptom, because patients may experience "amnesia for the amnesia," and fail to report it. (In a chilling aside, psychiatrist Colin A. Ross noted that, based on documents obtained through the Freedom of Information Act, psychiatrists linked to Project MKULTRA in the 1950s and 1960s claimed to be able to deliberately induce MPD using a variety of aversive techniques in so called volunteers).

The diagnosis is most common in North America, and three to nine times more so in females than in males. Other prominent symptoms could include: loss of time, (classically called "dissociative fugue"), although that was not always present though identities could be unaware of each other, and compartmentalize knowledge and memories, resulting in chaotic personal lives.

The vast majority of patients eventually diagnosed with DID retrospectively report childhood sexual and/or physical abuse, usually before the age of three—though the accuracy of these reports was considered controversial because individuals with DID were often reluctant, even unable, to openly discuss traumatic memories.

The primary personality often carried the person's given (or birth) name, and was often seen as passive, obedient, dependent, guilty, and depressed while other personalities may manifest as more active, aggressive, or hostile, often lacking memories of the primary personality's childhood. A specific relationship between childhood abuse, disorganized attachment, and lack of social support were thought to be a necessary components of DID.

She had arrived twenty minutes early for her first appointment, neatly dressed, immaculately clean and polished. She had been pleasant and seemed forthcoming about the biographical facts of her life; and genuinely perplexed as to why she had been referred to him. She seemed even more mystified, and unable to relate to, the large shopping bag full of medications, previously prescribed for her, that she had brought with her. Though he had not actually observed a classical switch, and she had been cleared neurologically, she did exhibit some quirky, idiosyncratic hand and facial movements, akin to tics. Her mood fluctuated some (labile), though not in a markedly bipolar way.

Her history included a number of hospitalizations dating to the age of thirteen, for depression and suicide attempts—tempered to some extent by her intermittent attachment to a fundamentalist church she attended weekly; a general lack of motivation, except with her children (two girls, ages 12 and 9). He probed this, and she blushed when she admitted making public proclamations about her shortcomings, trying to discern her inconsistent pattern of obedience and conformity versus areas where she seemed to manifest fear and anxiety.

She was ten minutes late for the second session, and came in dressed in a shabby mismatched sweat outfit, and a beat up pair of tennis shoes. She wore no makeup, and looked otherwise disheveled. Her language was coarse, with frequent cursing. Her mood was angry, edgy, and bordering on aggressive. She challenged Paul several times wanting to know why she had been asked to come—and made oblique references to a "her" who she herself did not like very much, who was always "playing by the rules."

"Not enough money!" was the only problem she would own. Although she looked to be twenty to thirty pounds overweight, she stated that she sometimes skipped her meals for days at a time.

"I don't know. I'm just not hungry!'

She rolled her eyes when he asked how she'd been feeling.

"Look, Doc, I've got some things to do today. So let's cut it short, OK?"

He summoned up the best arguments he could muster to convince her to stay, but she stood, picked up her large, oversized purse, and farted loudly.

"You can talk her into staying! Or that goddamn meddling Church Lady! But I'm not fucking staying!"

In a huff, she left, slamming the door to his office, leaving a foul wave in her wake.

Stunned, he sat at his desk and made quick, precise case notes, and again pondered his provisional diagnosis. Although he had seen radical shifts in bi-polar clients before, they had never been as deep and mysterious. And there was something unsettling about the mention of a "her," that left him more convinced than ever that he was moving in the right direction diagnostically.

Their third session was like entering another dimension. The woman who entered the room looked vaguely similar to the woman who had previously visited, but there was such an extreme variance in her aura. She looked taller. Her hair was red, not dark brown. She was wearing a very stylish green silk blouse and a black gabardine skirt below her knees; she had a cloche hat on her head that reminded him of the 1930s, but did not seem at all odd on her. She came in, carrying what appeared to be a real Prada handbag clutched in her left hand. She looked around as if she had never been there before, and surveyed the room until her eyes lit on Paul.

"We've met before, haven't we?"

"Yes. Hello, Lorraine. Please have a seat."

"I'm not Lorraine. I'm June, her older sister."

Paul tracked quickly through the encyclopedia in his head, and said, "Of course. Please have a seat."

"She couldn't make it today, so she asked me to come."

"Wonderful."

"She trusts you, you know. That doesn't really happen very often."

"I see."

"She said you seem trustworthy, so when she asked me to come, I did."

"Thank you. That's very kind."

She started to pull a long, lavender-filtered cigarette out of a gold case, but Paul stopped her.

"No smoking allowed in here, I'm afraid."

A dark look crossed her face, and then something like a snarl came out of her throat.

In a deep, snarling, cruel voice, the woman said, "You're all alike, you fucking men! Use a woman and then don't let her have what she wants!"

Paul made the intuitive leap and asked, "Excuse me. Who are you?"

"I'm Maggie! Not that it matters to you!"

The woman looked around, and made a moue that transformed her face into a caricature of her former well-made self.

"What exactly in the fuck am I doing here?"

"June was due here to continue our evaluation."

"Fuck her! She's so goddamn prissy and sophisticated! I mean, she does OK—for Lorraine. I'm the one who does the heavy lifting, you know?"

"Actually, no, I don't. This is the first time we've met."

"I've been here every time Lorraine has come. I've been watching you, waiting for you to slip up. Men always do!"

Paul decided to allow his intuition to carry him, and just tell the truth.

"I don't like cigarette smoke in my house!"

"If it hadn't been that, it would have been something else!"

"So what is your job?"

"Isn't it pretty obvious? I'm the Protector! None of them would know how to get along without me! I'm always watching!"

"I bet you're really good!"

There was a long silence. Then a velvety voice issued forth that was almost seductive.

"Hi, Doctor Paul. It's me, Lorraine. Shall we begin our session for today? I don't know why it took me so long to get here today."

Paul decided that he had better get her home safely while she was still in her primary personality, and suggested that they cancel today's session—and, by the way, could he call her a cab?

As soon as he had bundled her into the backseat of a Deluxe cab, he wrote up his case notes for the shortened session in great detail. Paul then took the next two and a half hours to summarize his conclusions, add them appropriately to the sections of the ongoing framework of his evaluation, read through it, print, and sign it.

Then he broke his longstanding tradition of only drinking alcohol either with or after a meal, and poured himself a snifter of Drambuie. He sat for a long time contemplating what had just transpired as he sipped the liqueur along with a freshly brewed cup of coffee. He knew he was duty-bound to call the therapist who had made the referral, even though he felt that the man was not of sufficient depth and experience to properly manage the woman's treatment sensitively. He also considered calling the insurance company because it was likely that anyone who would be appropriate would likely be out of network, and very expensive. He decided he would research clinicians before calling them to refer her, much as he himself would have loved to delve into the labyrinthine hallways of her mind.

CHAPTER THIRTY TWO
Rolling On

San Francisco, May 2000

It seemed that the patterns of his life flowed regularly from less intense to more intense. The periods when he was less tumultuous allowed him the opportunity to explore more deeply the ancient mysteries he believed lived within himself, as if he were someone loving and kind having a relationship with himself—and the words of Rainier Maria Rilke reverberated in him: "I hold this to be the highest task of a bond between two people: that each should stand guard over the solitude of the other...Love and friendship are there for the purpose of continually providing the opportunity for solitude."

He intuitively felt that everything he wanted to know, perhaps even everything that he could know, was contained within himself; and his true and perhaps only task was to discover the hidden mystery of Self; to prove to himself that he contained the cellular awareness of the living vibrant library of the Universe; that by virtue of his being alive, simply by breathing, that he was star-seed material. Sometimes he believed it was the only thing that would satisfy him, could ever satisfy the aching in his heart of hearts.

It was a strange mixture of exuberance and despair that drove him—even though the desire of attaining mystical Wholeness was coupled with an equal (sometimes even far greater) fear and despair that he would never make it, would never get there, never have the strength, the self-love, the determination and power, even the joy required to persevere, to win through to this greatest, most to-be-cherished state. He always called it a state even though he intuitively believed that the term was less than truly descriptive, inadequate to embrace the depth, richness, and beauty it might entail.

Perhaps that was the problem—one had to be in the desired "place" to adequately describe, not even it itself, but it was perhaps a "condition" (too ephemeral), or a "way" (too limiting), even "path" was too discriminatory—it seemed that one had to embrace "IT" as a totality, perhaps even let "IT" enter into and become one's very Self (maybe it already was), the higher order beingness, an infinite number of steps up the virtual food chain from where "normal" (whatever that was) consciousness reigned. He couldn't help but wonder if perhaps the terminology or the syntax in which humans attempted to describe "IT" were the very factors that limited one's being able to embrace "IT." One had to live "IT," whatever the hell "IT" was because "IT" was all there was, and one could no more define "IT" than a bird could describe a worm. "IT" just was.

It was relatively clear that Providence provided everything in a way that required no real personal power or authority per se. It was always a matter of letting go and receiving rather than asserting and taking. One could describe one's arm or leg as an appendage, a part of one's body, but one could not adequately describe the relative wholeness of one's body without reference to something greater or larger, the next level of wholeness. Wilber had it right when he discussed "nests of beingness," like an infinite set of concentric circles, each senior "holon" being contained in and by, and having all of the powers and qualities of the next previous junior "holon," with, of course, each "holon" being whole and complete within its own boundaries. Center everywhere, circumference nowhere. The earliest mention in an extant manuscript is only the beginning of the thirteenth century, whereas the original concept is ascribed to the fourth-century grammarian and philosopher Marius Victorinus (*Liber XXIV* philosophorum, a Latin booklet by an anonymous author that consisted of 24 commented definitions of what God is).

Getting immersed in the "God process" often left his head spinning, his heart aching—feeling that he had somehow "missed the boat" in this life. The enormous weight of knowledge and esoteric wisdom he felt hovering just out of sight, just beyond his grasp, but so near as to touch it. Sometimes he felt so constrained by the bulk of humanity's being suspended around his neck like an albatross, but Paul tried to be generous and compassionate, as Plato had long ago offered: "Be kind. Everyone is fighting a hard battle."

He just really and truly wished sometimes that it could be, would be, just a little simpler, a little easier. If he could take his own good advice, rendered to clients all the time, to take a deep breath into his belly—breathe deeply every time anxious or angry thoughts arose; breathe into them, wherever they were in the body, fill them completely with love, and release the energy down through their feet into the molten heart-core of Mother Earth. It was the single most powerful, and simple, breathing technique he had ever used. It worked anytime, anywhere, but you have to have enough presence of mind to use it.

He was grateful he'd given himself a day completely off. He would take a walk in Golden Gate Park; go to the Hall of Flowers, or Stow Lake with the Portals of the Past. Or if he got really ambitious, walk all the way out to Ocean Beach, maybe go to the Beach Chalet. It was part of The City's Heritage Trust. It stood on the Great Highway facing the cold and foggy Pacific near the Dutch Windmill at the furthest western end of Golden Gate Park. Designed by Willis Polk, it opened in 1925 with a lounge and changing rooms on the first floor; and a restaurant on the second. The murals, mosaics, and woodcarvings were completed in 1936 as part of a Works Project Administration (WPA), with many of the frescos by Lucien Labault depicting life in San Francisco during the Great Depression—including scenes at The Embarcadero, Fisherman's Wharf, Baker Beach, Golden Gate Park, Land's End, the Marina, Downtown, and Chinatown.

Labaudt also designed and directed the tile work, created by Primo Caredio, and magnolia-wood carvings done by sculptor Michael von Meyer, including the intricate balustrade along the stairs leading to the second floor, with octopus newel posts, mermaids, deep-sea divers, old ships, and a sea monster. In 1981, an extensive restoration of the structure and artwork began, with the chalet being listed on the National Register of Historic Places that same year. It finally reopened in 1996, with the ground floor housing the Golden Gate Park Visitors' Center. Upstairs was the Beach Chalet Restaurant with sweeping views of the Pacific that had become so popular that even locals needed a reservation for lunch. But he had gotten lucky that day, and returned to his office after an outstanding shrimp platter with fries and vinegar coleslaw, musing about the state of the world and his own mind.

Paul leaned back in his executive office chair, doing a final review and edit of his most recent case notes. He had let them go for a few days, and had finally caught up that morning. He was just settling into a light trance that threatened to become a nap, when, of course, the phone rang. He ignored it, and let the service pick up. He had just re-settled himself when the service's special ring cut through the air. It seemed that there was just no escaping it today!

"Dr. Marzeky, a man is on the line. He says he's Massimo Baldestari!"

Paul sighed and told them to ring him through.

Massimo was frantic. Despite hearing far more frequently than he would have liked from the police detectives, he had still been working diligently with his squad, and had not been visited in person for several weeks. Then today, just a few hours ago, the detectives had casually dropped by his apartment, wanting to ask "a few questions." They were just doing a "routine follow up"—which did not, of course, sit well with Massimo, whose paranoid antennae went up immediately, and had stayed in place ever since.

"The assholes didn't have anything new! They were here harassing me! Those *bastardos* still think I killed my Veronica!" Though he had been born in San Francisco, he inevitably inserted Italian equivalents into his speech when he got upset.

"Calm down, Massimo! Just tell me what they wanted."

"They asked me if I had any further knowledge of the death of 'the decedent,' as if my baby was just a dead person!" Paul decided to let him rant, knowing that more good would come of it in the long run.

"Then they wanted to go through my alibi again! This is goddamn harassment!"

"Did they say why?"

"They tried to tell me it was 'routine follow up,' but I don't believe them for a fucking second! Fucking liars!"

"What did you tell them?"

"I told them they had my statement; that we had talked about it many times; and I was not going to go through the whole thing again, especially without my attorney!"

"And?"

"They told me I was 'not being very cooperative,' and then he, that sergeant—what the fuck is his name? Williams? Watts! That it! He had the *testicoli* to ask me 'Don't you care if we don't ever find her killer?'"

Oh shit!

"And?"

"I started to go after him, but that lieutenant, your friend, McLaren, pushed me back into my chair, and told the sergeant to 'get the fuck out!'"

Thank God for Phil McLaren! Paul thought to himself.

"And?"

"I…couldn't help it! I started crying! I told him 'I miss her every fucking day!' I cry all the time, still!"

"What else?"

"I don't know anything! I really don't!" Paul heard the catch in Massimo's voice.

"What? What was that? That hesitation?"

"Oh, it's nothing! Probably just me being 'paranoid' again!"

314

"Tell me anyway!"

"There's this guy, Ted, I work with. He's on another bus (ambulance), but we been working together for four years or so…never more than to say 'Hello' to. You know?"

"Yeah."

"Well, ever since Veronica…died, he's been sort of friendlier. We even had a couple of beers twice, down at Gino and Carlo's. Shot some pool. You know. Casual."

"And?"

Massimo shifted gears, and Paul had a sense that he was about to hear something significant. He had no reason to suspect, just pure intuition.

"Paul, I don't want you to think that I'm getting worse. Or lost in my grief again."

"Go on, Massimo. It's OK!"

"Well, the last time we went to Gino's, we had more than a couple of beers. Got pretty blasted. Ted started asking me all kinds of questions about Veronica, personal stuff, you know? And then—I know I wasn't that drunk—he called her 'Ronnie!'"

"'Ronnie?!'"

"Yeah. She never called herself that! Liked her name! So did I!"

"That sounds weird. He could have just been him creating a nickname for her."

"Yeah, I know. But I thought I should tell you."

"Did you tell Phil, Lieutenant McLaren, about this?"

"No, I wanted to talk to you first. Then they showed up and that *stronzo* Watts started in on me, I completely forgot!"

"I understand. Give me a minute to think about this."

Paul put the line on speaker, and set the receiver on his desk. He straightened his posture, and took a series of deep breaths from the bottom of his belly. The first breath relieved him of most all of his stress, creating a clear, sparkling field of stars all around him, and a tremendous, enveloping silence—although he remained aware of his surroundings, including all of the noises, especially Massimo's presence on the other end of the telephone line.

After some time, he spoke.

"Do you mind if I pass this information along to Lieutenant McLaren? He might be more receptive with it coming from me."

"You think it might be important?"

"I don't know Massimo, but let's find out. They might want to talk to this Ted guy. What's his last name?"

"Struthers. Ted Struthers."

"Do you know anything else about him?"

"Not really. Lives in the Mish. Alone, I think. At least he never talks about a girlfriend."

"OK. I'll get back to you. How are you feeling? Right now?"

"I thought I was doing better. But this stirred up my shit again!"

"Maybe we ought to schedule some time, do some more grief work. Sounds like you're still pretty stricken."

"Yeah I am! I miss the hell out of her," he said, and then started sobbing again.

Paul considered making an emergency appointment for him later that afternoon. Paul let him go for a minute, then asked "Are you feeling OK for now?"

Massimo sniffed a couple of times, and then replied in a much heartier voice. "No. I'm good for today. How's Tuesday? I'm working but I don't start until 2000."

"Excellent! I could give you either 1100 or 1500. Your choice."

"Let's do 1500. That way I can do some errands before I see you."

"Good. Glad you called."

"Ciao. Bene."

"*Bon journo*, Massimo!"

Paul sat back and contemplated his next move. He wanted to talk to Phil McLaren, but not to Bill Watts. Not right now. So he'd have to finesse this a little.

He called him on his direct line at the Hall of Justice. Now officially divorced after a long legal separation, McLaren had an apartment out near Golden Gate Park on the Sunset side, so he figured an invitation to a very local watering hole might not go amiss.

"Phil. Paul Marzeky here."

"I thought I might be hearing from you."

"And, magically, here I am!"

"What do you want?"

"Like to get a beer? I was thinking of The Shamrock."

Open since 1893, it was San Francisco's second-oldest bar, trailing only The Saloon in North Beach, which opened in 1861.

An antique wooden clock still hangs on the wall above an inscription that reads, "No tick since April 18, 1906." It had also withstood the 1989 Loma Prieta earthquake, even though the lights went out, the TVs fell, and patrons ran outside. At that point, they lit candles, the bartender went behind the stick, and business kept going. It was the favorite of writer John Lescroat who has featured it in almost all of his novels.

"Now why might you be thinking of The Shamrock?"

"I know it's close to home for you, so if you have more than one, you can walk home. I'm driving so one is my limit!"

"Not taking any risks, are you?"

"Not with the eagle-eyed SFPD cracking down on drunk drivers!"

"I'm getting ready to leave anyway."

"Where's your partner?"

"Took off early. His son had a Little League game this afternoon."

"So I'll see you at The Shamrock. Thirty minutes?"

"Sounds good."

It had always been a neighborhood bar. Following the demise of Henry Africa's, one of the first "fern bars" in San Francisco, The

Shamrock had undergone a transformation to create a more "social atmosphere" with Tiffany lamps, potted plants, big screen TVs, a pool table, and a darts room—though many regulars still went there simply to drink.

Paul arrived first, and secured a table in the back near the darts' room. There was a weekly tournament scheduled, but it was an hour away, depending on the general laxity of individual players' timekeeping and level of intoxication.

Paul decided against his usual choice of a dark brew, and decided on another of his favorites, the original Anchor Steam beer. It had been brewed in San Francisco since 1871, under a variety of owners, in different locations all over The City. Though they now produced many varieties, the original beer is still made with a blend of pale and caramel malts; fermented with lager yeast at warmer ale temperatures in shallow open-air fermenters; and gently carbonated in their cellars through an all-natural process called kräusening.

While the origin of the name remains otherwise shrouded in mystery, Anchor Steam® likely relates to the original practice of fermenting the beer on San Francisco's rooftops in the cool climate in lieu of ice. The foggy night air naturally cooled the fermenting beer, creating steam off the warm open pans. It was a very San Francisco taste. Paul enjoyed it year 'round, though he loved Anchor Steam Porter, and the Christmas Ale too (usually only available for two weeks either side of the holiday).

He and Phil talked sports (the 49ers, the Giants), the weather (delightful), his practice (coming along smartly), Phil's job (overworked, underpaid, underappreciated as usual), and danced around the one topic they had in common, but both resisted mentioning. Paul was still nursing his first when McLaren ordered his second beer, and then Paul broached the topic.

"So I heard you were around to see my client Massimo."

"'Client?' I thought he was a former client."

"Was former. Is currently—since you guys stopped by and got him all agitated this afternoon with fucking Watts', he made air quotes, "sensitive interrogation techniques.""

"Hey! The guy's a good cop!"

"Maybe so, but he's got all the finesse of a berserk eighteen wheeler!"

"We just stopped by because of the anniversary thing!"

"It isn't even close!"

"And Watts practically accused him again of being the perp!"

"Your client is too sensitive!"

"Fuck you, man! His wife was murdered, and he found the body!"

"Well fuck you too! He's still our prime suspect!"

"Oh Jesus! Talk about an unenlightened attitude!"

"That's your department! Mine's being a cop!"

"Watts is an asshole!"

"That's what your client called him, in Italian!"

"He's still really hurting! Watts' antics today cost me an hour calming him down! Maybe I should bill you guys for it!"

"Good fucking luck! I'm still waiting for my overtime check from last month!"

Paul sat up then, and took a deep breath before looking McLaren in the eyes.

"I might have something for you."

"Client's holding out on us, huh?"

"No! Watts got him so pissed off he forgot!"

"'Forgot,' huh? Bullshit!"

"OK. So maybe he didn't feel like talking in front of Watts. Thing is, he told me something interesting that you may want to check out."

"OK."

He told him what had transpired between he and Massimo.

McLaren sat for a moment, absorbing the information, then sighed before he spoke.

"Well, I've pursued more obscure information! I'll be in touch!"

Paul had provided this with his client's permission, so it did not break confidentiality. They had begun treatment again, probing the edges of the shadow states that had gotten triggered, or more accurately, re-stimulated, by the recent turn of events. He also started excavating more of his unexpurgated grief surrounding his ex-wife's history. Pursuing this, he had at times had to become quite stern with Massimo, because the young man kept retreating into victimhood.

"Massimo! Massimo! Listen! You cannot keep blaming yourself! It's not going to work on me! No matter how much you blame yourself, she's not coming back!"

When Massimo looked up through tear-stained eyes with a mixture of hatred and extreme sorrow, Paul smiled, and continued in a gentler voice.

"But there's good news too!"

His client still looked at him completely unable to fathom the crazy fucking guy smiling at him, this nut-bag who was supposed to be his therapist! He couldn't find any words to respond as Paul kept smiling at him.

"I want you to really look at me when I say this! The good news is that you, my man, are still here, still alive!"

His client looked blearily at him as he attempted to grasp the possibility that anything could ever be good again. She was fucking gone!

"I'm not full of shit! You've survived one of the most horrible shocks any person can experience."

Massimo started to speak, but started crying again.

"You're very, very strong! I know! I walked through it with you! when you were suicidal!"

The younger man raised his hands in supplication toward Paul, but still couldn't find adequate words.

"Remember, 'To whom much is given much is required.'"

Massimo started crying even harder, almost doubled over for a moment, his head going down deeply into his chest, and then he fell off the couch onto the floor, and sobbed for some very long minutes. Paul sat quietly and did his deep breathing, occasionally turning his palms out toward the young man, arms extended, radiating support and connection. When Massimo finally sat up, he looked dazed, disoriented; and radically shifted.

He coughed briefly into his hand, and then said, "Paul…I'm just so…fucking sad. I miss her so much…every fucking day. You…saved my life. I'll never be able to thank you enough."

Paul took a deep breath before he spoke.

"You're welcome. And," said Paul, tearing up himself, continued "I am grateful to you, too. I have learned a lot working with you!"

Stefan J. Malecek, Ph. D.

CHAPTER THIRTY FOUR

Stepping into the Same River Twice

San Francisco, October 2000

Paul had never been reluctant to give a client an extra ten or fifteen minutes; or cancel a social event to squeeze an extra client session, even if it wasn't an emergency, but hey! He loved his work.

Emergencies did occasionally happen. They were far more rare in private practice than when he worked for a Community Mental Health Agency (CMHA), and was on regular call every Wednesday night from 5 PM until 8 AM Thursday morning. It didn't matter if he had slept all night, or been in the ER all night long sorting out suicide attempts, drug overdoses, or hysterical people who had come to the ER as a court of last resort—he was expected to show up and start seeing clients.

During that period, he invariably kept his Thursday mornings free so as to manage the paperwork that always seemed to build up, case notes that needed to be written, or responses to letters, even the odd summons—anything to avoid having to see clients, especially if it had been a long, rough night. Once he had been called out to the ER on three separate occasions in that single night—though one had been such a simple resolution that he was back at home in bed inside of twenty-three minutes! Since he had to bill half (or twenty hours) of his weekly time in client contact hours, he filled in the slots in his schedule to accommodate it. It was a point of pride to him that he very rarely found his name on the end-of-the-month report listing those who had late or missing paperwork.

In private practice, though, getting called out in the middle of the night was pretty rare. It depended, in part, on the manner in which one selected those who populated one's caseload. He had always been up front about refusing potential clients who were verbally abusive or aggressive; or who seemed sleazy and manipulative (a hearty "No thanks" to straight up Borderlines!); and especially with those who believed they could (or should) dictate the terms of treatment (especially when court-mandated).

Paul very rarely took anyone who was prescribed psychiatric drugs. They were usually the most unstable, and more likely to quit their meds; and/or end up in the ER in the middle of the night, even if they were medication compliant. The drugs were designed to block or distort true emotional responses, and therefore made it far more difficult to establish therapeutic rapport, and elongated the healing process (especially since releasing stored traumatic memories and other toxins was key to Paul's approach), Paul always considered cognitive approaches to be bosh as front line methods!

He never took anyone with an active drug or alcohol problem; and no one who claimed to be "clean and sober," until they had at least a year in recovery. He had found that anything less in clean-and-sober time was fraught with difficulties. (He had read a study in which the brains of former alcohol addicts were sectioned at autopsy, and they had found traces of alcohol derivatives in the brain pan seven and a half months after the person had quit drinking). But, in spite of all of his best precautions (or even misguided empathy), he did still have that rare emergency. One in particular stood out in his memory.

He'd had a client who had been taking anti-depressants for a number of years, and desperately wanted to stop taking them—against the best advice of his doctor, another former therapist, and Paul himself. The man had convinced himself that the "only thing wrong" with him was the shame he associated with taking "psych drugs," and the fear/anger/rage/deficiency he associated with this situation. Paul took him on initially because he was a pretty interesting fellow, a professor of geology at UC

Berkeley. (Besides, he had good insurance, and was willing to travel; and did not want to risk any of his colleagues finding out that he was getting professional help). He was obsessed about quitting, and had resisted every previous attempt to get him to talk deeply and extensively about his childhood.

Paul surmised that since society itself was so sick and corrupt, it was a pretty safe bet that there had to be some kind of childhood dysfunction. Paul was on the verge of terminating him for non-compliance (he refused to do his "homework" between sessions), when he finally agreed to a month without constantly insisting on quitting meds. Paul offered to refer him to an MD-type friend for titration, so he would not have to go cold turkey. Even after he had explained (from the Physicians' Desk Reference [PDR]) the range of possible side effects from such a radical choice, the client seemed unconvinced, though he verbally agreed.

A few nights later, he got a call at 0221 from the ER at Herrick Memorial Hospital in Berkeley. They had his client there, and that he was complaining of some bizarre somatic symptoms, most notably "lightning bolts in his brain." He had been declared medically clear, with no drugs or alcohol on board; his labs looked good, though his affect was very labile, and they were considering admitting him against his will to the psych unit.

When Paul asked about antidepressants, the doctor said "No, he didn't mention them!" Paul explained about the man's obsession (bordering on delusion) about meds, and asked to speak to his client.

"Paul? You gotta get me out of here! They want to put me on the psych unit!"

"'Lightning bolts in your brain!' Sounds a little…off, don't you think?"

"But it's true!"

"When did you stop your meds?"

A long silence ensued, and then he heard "Three days ago."

"Didn't we talk about this very thing? How potentially dangerous it was to just quit? And you agreed to wait a month so we could do this properly?"

"Uhh, yeah, I guess so!"

"Not good enough! Did you or did you not agree? None of this 'I guess so' bullshit!"

"Well, I agreed, but I didn't really mean it!"

"Do you want to be admitted to the psych unit?"

"Oh God no! I'd probably be fired!"

"Are you willing to cooperate—and mean it this time? Take the meds every day until we agree that you're ready for detox?"

"Ummm…"

"OK. George. Make your choice. I will either tell the doctor to put you on the psych unit for 72 hours on a legal hold, or you will totally and honestly agree with every single item I have just outlined? Clear?"

"Well, can't I just…?

"No! No more bullshit! No 'I crossed my fingers' crap like you're a little kid! Choose! Now! One way or the other!"

"But…"

"Choose!"

"OK. OK. I agree."

"And no more bullshitting around! We are going to explore your childhood issues!"

"But why?"

"Because I am your therapist! You asked for help! If you don't want to follow the plan, I will refer you to somebody else!"

"No! Don't do that! I...I'll tell you all about it!"

"And you agree to do your homework between sessions?"

"Yes, I guess so."

"No guessing. It's either full commitment to my program, or I recommend three days on the psych unit! Don't you realize how crazy you sound?"

"OK! OK! I agree!"

"And you will come to see me tomorrow! Without fail! No cancelling! What time do you get out of class?"

"I have a lecture until 1100, and then a lab until 1400."

"Can you be at my office by 1600?"

"OK. OK."

"Do you really mean it?"

"Yes! Yes! Get me out of here!"

"I'm going to ask the doc there to give you a double dose of your meds, and a prescription I want you to fill before you leave the hospital—at 0800! I'm going to ask him to keep you there until then. You're in no condition to drive. You might want to consider having your assistant take the early class."

"But, but…!"

"No 'buts!' You agree or you don't. Simple."

Another long silence, then, "But you are going to get me off these drugs?"

"I'm not invested in you taking them. I am invested in you having a more stable life, one without 'lightning bolts in your brain!'"

"You promise?"

"I'll do better than that. I will give you my intention to do so. Without fail!"

"OK, then."

"'OK' what?"

"I agree with your terms. I will take the meds until you tell me I can start getting off of them safely. I will spend the night here, and get my graduate fellow to take the early class. And I will see you tomorrow at 1600."

"Good. Now put the doctor on!"

Paul explained the situation to him, and he agreed, reluctantly at first, and then with more vigor as Paul continued to explain the circumstances, and the cold turkey.

"And can you get him to sign a release for me so I can get copied on this visit?"

"Absolutely! You take care now!"

"You too! And hope I don't have to talk to you any time soon!"

CHAPTER THIRTY FIVE

If He must Stand Alone, He is Undaunted

San Francisco, December 2000

He took the bottle of Drambuie from a kitchen cabinet, and poured a healthy measure into a small balloon snifter before settling himself in the chair in front of the coffee table, when he turned on the television for distraction. He was in one of those weird places he got into once in a while where he just did not want to be inside himself. He immediately muted the sound, and allowed himself to be distracted by the flickering images. He took a first sip, and allowed his anxieties to escape down through the bottoms of his feet. The second sip brought to mind the legend of his by-far favorite liqueur.

Prince Charles Edward Stuart (popularly known as Bonnie Prince Charlie) was on the run, pursued by the King's men across the Highlands and through the Islands of Western Scotland, bravely aided by many Highland Clans. The defeat at the Battle of Culloden (April 1746) had ended his hopes of restoring the Stuarts to the throne of Great Britain. John MacKinnon, Clan

Chief, helped the Prince escape from The Isle of Skye. In thanks for his bravery the Prince gave him the secret recipe to his personal liqueur, a gift that the Clan thereafter treasured. In 1873, the recipe was passed on to John Ross of The Broadford Hotel on Skye, who started making it to serve there. It became known locally on Skye as *dram buidhe*, "the yellow drink." Customers who tasted it commented in Gaelic *an dram buidheach*, "the drink that satisfies," which became shortened to Drambuie.

God! If the fucking world could be as easy and simple as it was in 1745! Or a thousand, or ten thousand years ago! He was so goddamn sick of "progress"—just a new name for corporatized bullshit rip-off profit grabbing savagery disguised as commerce!

As often as he felt well and truly connected with his Wildman brothers, he often felt depressed, alone and alienated from the rest of the world. It seemed sometimes as if part of his brain were actually stuck the in the silent violence of his childhood, constantly re-creating it, hoping to magically drink the essence of what he had missed. One of his constant internal pursuits always seemed to be what he called "tracking down the archetype." On some level, the "reality" that he could see was just not enough. There was always something deeper at work, some underlying fundament that fed the more superficial level.

Most often he tracked it back to "Big Mom and Dad," most usually the government or other institutions acting in loco parentis, especially when making decisions for him (or the populace) as if it were the parent and he (or they) were all small, undiscriminating, uninformed, supposed-to-be-unaware (and remain that way) malformed children who needed to be protected "for their own good" (almost always corporate bullshit-speak for protecting the profits). It was a very hot button for him, one that he revisited over and over, seeking to create a different, more beneficial outcome—and always landing in the same exact spot of it being true that this vast, tentaclular monster, in essence, controlled the world. There had to be more! He worked assiduously to crack that barrier, despite all of the barricades and obfuscations "the world" seemed to throw up. Somehow he knew he attracted to, and allowed, all of the distractions, including addictions (how convenient for the corporate mindset!), they were still ultimately choices—that supplanted his quest for higher states than the ordinary "normal," and all of its concomitant mindlessness.

Sometimes he felt as if he were drowning in the shit of modern civilization, on the verge of taking his very last breath. He was so confused about what he doing with his life; about how he could be so unhappy when he had a thriving practice, and beautiful women who loved him; when he had more and better sex than he had ever dreamed possible during all of those lonely, bitter, angst-filled teenaged years; about the direction he wanted his life to take, and really, ultimately, in many ways, did it fucking even matter at all?

More deeply: was anything he could say or do ever going to have any positive impact, ever going to shift the world in the slightest one way or another into a better, richer light? In these moments of the clearest light, when his naked soul was most fully exposed to him, he feared greatly that his greatest suspicions were being realized. In spite of all the beauty and wonder to which he had had access, there were dark appendages running through his life like a bad film that one could not stop watching despite the terrible acting, the predictable plot, the boring dialogue, and the awful denouement.

It was part of why he rarely drank. He had really lost his taste for alcohol in any but the smallest quantities. He honestly did not like being intoxicated on substances any longer, though he did still have very occasional fantasies about smoking some of the holy weed he had so long known and loved. The other reason was that too much alcohol was initially uplifting, it ultimately depressed him, and could induce his flashbacks, even though some were simply generic.

The edges of his vision blurred. Then, like the fog creeping in under the Golden Gate Bridge toward The City until it surrounded all of the neighborhoods—Sunset, Richmond, West Portal, Haight, Ashbury Heights, toward Mount Davidson and the Miraloma District, and finally Twin Peaks, were all buried in a sodden blanket. Then indistinct sounds—chirps, tweets, blonks, honks, tiny shrieks, muted shouting, bells, chimes, arrhythmic thumping, percussive staccato noises like jackhammers, syncopated drums, even atonal flutes and saxophones wailing, and children's cries rising to screams of agony—all suddenly gave way to the sound of explosions: automatic weapons, hand grenades, mortars, rocket-propelled grenades (RPG), artillery rounds impacting, then a fucking arc light (B-52) strike lighting up the world, the entire earth heaving up under him, being flung around like an insignificant bag of shit.

Into the shocked, unable-to-hear, grateful-to-be-alive hush, tympanic membranes vibrated beyond any possibility of hearing, flushed with the all-encompassing altered state into which he had been so rudely shoved, all senses scrambled, synesthesia rampant, colored notes dancing through his head even though he couldn't even hear the voices of his buddies shouting at him from a foot away; tasting the air filled with cordite and all manner of unidentifiable particulates, odors colored or filled with sound. He felt special, extremely special, because for those few moments, he had been transported to a land, perhaps not God-like, but at least godlike, as if elevated to another realm wherein all of the nascent and occluded powers of human existence were present and available for immersion and consumption. He was actually there, living them, feeling them, breathing them. They were real, absolutely real. Then, in a blink, as if a huge lens or a filter had been removed, like a cataract from his eye, it was all gone. Hearing returned first, insect sounds, then birds' crescendos trilling, finally the voices of the other survivors screeching and tiny as through a damaged megaphone.

He popped out as neatly and quickly as he had left. Seamlessly. No commotion, no compunction, no disruption of the world-as-we-know-it. His slightly dented glass of Drambuie was still sitting there, inane used car and cosmetics commercials flashing across the muted screen—the blessed mercy that had shielded him from immense pain and massive confusion, a brain contusion, all fell away in one enormous sheet of clarity, the utter truth of matters standing clear before him.

Thick sheets of heavy rain fell intermittently all afternoon. He stopped to admire the beauty of it as he had twice made his way to the bathroom.

He had barely opened his eyes from his erstwhile nap. He needed some food, but coffee more so. He showered and shaved, then had a strong black cup before deciding to go to one of his favorite restaurants, The Tandoori. Its massive clay oven reached a temperature of 900°, and seared food to perfection, keeping all the wonderful juices and flavors in. They also made good strong Turkish coffee, but you had to ask. It was not on the menu.

He already knew he was going to have the Tandoori Lamb, Biryani rice with raisins and almonds, and onion Nan, with two sides of raita. Even though his brain was in turmoil, he began to see last night's flashback as a positive thing in retrospect. He felt much better today, and it had certainly contributed to his getting what was really one of the best night's sleep he'd had in recent history. Sipping his second Turkish coffee, he contemplated his situation. He was left him feeling like a splitting wedge stuck in the middle of a fibrous oak log, firmly emplaced, unable to move in any direction. He called the one client who had left a message with the service, and made an appointment with him for the following day, then he called the psychologist from Ohio. They talked for about ten minutes (after he acknowledged that he had the man's sister's written permission to do so, and he would fax it later in the day). She seemed like she might be a good fit for his style of work—motivated, ready to work, previous history of therapy and self-empowerment work. Paul told the man to give her the office number and they could talk. His food arrived shortly before he ended this call, so he put off whatever other calls he had to make, though he knew Massimo would be next.

He strongly felt a need to contact the man. He breathed a sigh of relief when he got the man's answering machine (now devoid of Veronica's voice). But his relief was short-lived. Massimo picked up. He was excited and hyperphrasic. His words were coming so fast, and were so volubly pronounced, that Paul thought the man might be having a manic episode.

"Whoa! Whoa! Slow down!"

"They just came and arrested that motherfucker!"

"Who arrested who? What 'motherfucker?'"

"Struthers! That *bastardo!* I told the cops about him, and they just showed up here and arrested him!"

"Wait a minute! Wait a minute! You're moving too fast for me!"

"OK! OK! Listen! Remember I told you he called Veronica 'Ronnie' that time when we were drinking? At Geno and Carlo's?"

"Yeah! OK! Yeah!" Paul's brain was spinning, but he was getting on track.

"They showed up here, apparently just wanted to talk to him. But he refused, and started fighting with the cops. Then your friend, Lieutenant McLaren, arrested him!"

"Damn! You sound completely amped up!"

"Been up all night. Had two runs. One was a fatal crash down on Geneva Avenue. Took forever. Fire guys had to use the Jaws of Life to get the vic out!"

"Jesus! Are you gonna be able to get some sleep now?"

"I doubt it. Probably just drink some more coffee," he said, his energy still hyperthymic and restless.

"Just a suggestion, man. But you might want to try to sleep. When do you get off?"

"Not until tonight. Eight o'clock."

"That'll be tough!"

"You know that old saying, 'I'll sleep when I die!'"

"I hear you man, but we're all getting older!"

"Fuck you, Jack! I'm still a young man! Ask any of the ladies!"

"Yeah! OK! Right!"

Paul took this as a good sign. Perhaps his extended grief process was starting to wane.

"Keep me in the loop on this, OK?"

"You're the one's friends with the cops!"

"Bullshit! Just friendlier than you at are the moment!"

––––––––

Paul tried to settle his mind, racing, skipping from topic to topic—almost as if he had been infected by his client's mental state. He sat back in his favorite chair, and drifted off into a disturbed and all-too-brief slumber. In his dream, he breathed a sigh of relief. He had just breathed another deep sigh when the phone rang again, and brought him back to a different reality.

"Paul? Paul? It's Massimo!"

His voice was strained, almost strident. He sounded like someone from another planet. Massimo was clearly stressed. His enunciation was uneven, and the contents of his speech were punctuated with small utterances of extreme disbelief and sorrow—not unlike the strangled release of oxygen from a drowning man.

"What the fuck? Massimo?!"

The response was a huge burst of tears, and again the strangled voice.

"They're saying he did it! He killed her!"

"What? Who?"

"Struthers! They're saying he killed her!"

"Are you fucking shitting me? Oh my God!"

"Can you believe it?"

"No! When did this happen?"

"Just a few minutes ago! I don't think I'm supposed to know. An EMT I know was at the Hall of Justice. She overheard two cops talking. They said that he confessed! Oh my fucking God!"

"Wait! Wait! We don't know this is true! Let me check! Stay by your phone! OK?"

Fuck! What a thing to happen! He had had only a few minutes relief from his own dilemma, and now this! Shit! He called Phil McLaren's desk, then his office. Voice mail. Then, he figured, fuck it! Can't lose, and called his mobile—and actually got an answer on the fifth ring!

"Yo, Phil! Paul Marzeky here!"

"What the fuck do you want?"

"Good to hear you too!"

"Seriously! What the fuck do you want?"

"A little bird just told me you arrested Ted Struthers!"

"How the fuck did you find out?"

"You know what they always say: 'San Francisco is just a small town!'"

"Well fuck you and your bird!"

"Seriously, man! My client told me!"

"Oh shit! How much does he know?"

"What do you mean?"

"If I say anything to you, you cannot, repeat, cannot, tell your client!"

"I...OK!"

"Struthers says he was Veronica's lover!"

"What?"

"He got jealous! She wouldn't break up with what's-his-name, Massimo!"

"Not a fucking chance!"

"What he says!"

"He confessed?"

There was a long silence, followed by a deeply indrawn breath.

"He denied everything over and over! We had him in the box for three hours. He got jumpy, crying, and shit! Then he blurted out 'I loved her! I didn't kill her!'"

"Aw, Jesus!"

"Keepin' him in a cell overnight should do wonders for his disposition! Does your client know she was cheatin' on him?"

"Shit! I'm just not buying it! I worked with the both of them in couples' therapy for four months! You should have a psychologist examine him!"

"The DA will probably ask for a psych exam!"

"If you use a shrink, all he'll do is determine if he's capable of assisting in his own defense! He won't say anything about his fabricating evidence, or being a pathological liar!"

"How do you know he is?'

"I don't, but I know my client isn't!"

"I don't even know how he heard we arrested Struthers!"

"He said a female paramedic was at the Hall of Justice, and heard two cops talking about it. She called him!"

"Jesus! Is nothing sacred anymore?"

CHAPTER THIRTY SIX
Prelude

San Francisco, The Next Day

He felt a serious urgency to give Massimo full disclosure about Ted Struther's arrest, but to do so properly, he'd need to set up an appointment. So he called him, asked how he was holding up; where he was; and could they meet for just a few minutes?

"Sure. I'm on until 2000 tonight. Unless a call comes in, I've got plenty of time."

"Problem is, I don't. I have something really important I have to do at 1900, so if we could meet right away, it would be great!"

"No problem! You want to come meet me at the bus?"

"I'd actually rather talk privately."

He told him he couldn't be too far away from his working vehicle, or his partner, in case a call came in. They were both hungry, so they decided to meet at The Taqueria at Mission and 25th where they could get a quick *lingua* (tongue) burrito.

"I'd rather talk first. I really just have maybe twenty minutes. No charge," Paul chuckled, trying to inject some humor into the situation.

"I'll get my food and meet you. I'll call my partner and I out for dinner break at Mission Delores Park."

"Works for me. Thanks!"

The ambulance was just pulling to the curb in a "No Parking Zone" as Paul scored a rare and lucky parking spot just down the street on 20th.

Massimo was smiling when they met, and they went to sit under a tree where they had relative privacy. He started munching hungrily on his burrito, chatting about the 49ers' chances this year, and being generally amiable. Paul was so preoccupied with the information he had to impart that he had absolutely no appetite, zero. He figured Massimo would very soon be losing his appetite too, and Paul ended up feeding his burrito to one of the many dogs wandering round the park chasing Frisbees.

Massimo couldn't help but notice Paul's preoccupied, brooding silence.

"What's going on, Paul? You look like Rodin's *The Thinker*, only depressed!"

"I got some heavy shit to tell you, and I'm not quite sure how!"

The younger man took another bite of his burrito, and then put it on the aluminum foil, but close enough to discourage marauding canines.

"Just tell me straight up! What, my insurance denied payment? Look, I'll cover it out of pocket if that's it!"

"I wish it were so easy!"

"Then what? What?"

Paul turned to look him fully in the eyes, and said, "I don't know any other way to tell you this, but you need to know before you hear it through the grapevine."

"Now you got me worried! Am I getting fired? What?"

"It seems that Struthers…"

"That *feccia*!" he said referring to the man as scum.

"It's not that simple! Listen, he said that he and Veronica were lovers!"

"*Impossiibile!*"

"No, he confessed that he was her lover!"

"*Egli fa sesso con la madre!*"

"I'm not sure what you said!"

"He would have sex with his own mother!"

"I'm just telling you what Phil McLaren told me!"

"*Madre di Dio!*"

Looking around to be assured they still had privacy, Paul said, "Look I'm sorry to have to do it this way, but it couldn't wait until we had a full session!"

"It's OK, Paul. I appreciate it!"

"Are you sure you're OK?"

"Yeah. I'll be fine."

"You're sure? Because I really have to go!"

"I understand. And *grazie, grazie molto!*"

He looked broken, forlorn. Paul sincerely wished he could stay with him, give him human comfort of some sort. As he walked away, he looked over his shoulder—and was surprised to see Massimo sitting with his legs stretched out in front of him—a huge smile on his face, voraciously chomping away at his burrito. It seemed kind of strange, but then, he decided, we all react to grief in different ways.

CHAPTER THIRTY SEVEN

More Questions...

San Francisco, January 2001

He'd been served a subpoena for Massimo's records, and had properly refused, noting client confidentiality and mental health provider/client privilege. Then wiseass Bill Watts (undoubtedly going behind Phil McLaren's back) called, and threatened him with a search warrant, if he did not "voluntarily hand them over right away." All of this was in preparation for Ted Struthers' upcoming court appearance, even though he continued to adamantly deny killing Veronica Baldestari; continued to claim that he loved her deeply, and would never have hurt her.

Paul felt a need to disclose his fears about confidentially to someone appropriate. He was still bothered by the intuitive "hit" he had had when he walked away from Massimo sitting under a tree in Mission Delores Park, after he had delivered the terrible truth about Veronica—acting as if her were famished, wolfing down massive bites of his burrito, and smiling a most radiant smile, white teeth flashing in the sun like a row of tombstones.

He couldn't help ruminating on it. It haunted him, and he decided to call a colleague for a confidential consultation.

He and Claire Winthrop had a longstanding collegial arrangement. They had tried a "trial date" once, setting aside their professional relationship, and decided they were better off as friends and colleagues.

"I don't want to believe Massimo is a murderer! I mean, I have no real evidence, just this terrible feeling." He sat for a moment, and took a deep breath. "OK. Look, I saw my client…we met out of the office so I could tell him about Ted Struthers, the guy they're holding for Veronica's murder. He was eating a burrito. When I told him, he looked freaked out and sad."

"And?"

He then told her about the bizarre, almost surreal experience he had had as he walked away.

"That doesn't mean anything in and of itself. But I can see how you might be suspicious…and concerned!"

"But what should I do?"

"First let's review the regulations and take it from there. OK?"

"Sure."

"We inform clients of the limits of our relationship; that we cannot maintain their confidentiality if there's suspected child abuse, elder abuse, or abuse of a person with a disability (if we know who the person is); also if they are planning on killing themselves or killing someone else. We promise to keep their other secrets, their fantasies, crimes, pain, dreams, failures, and moral dilemmas confidential. We do not speak of them. Never. Ever. They are free to explore with us everything that comes up within the limits of that relationship free from worry. That is our job as psychologists."

"Right."

She opened one of several large volumes lying open on her desk, some with sticky-tabs marking certain sections, and began to read.

"We want clients to make informed decisions. We want to make sure they know the benefits and dangers of any individual choice. I also believe that it is our job, our duty, our moral requirement even, to allow our patients to have the dignity of risk—knowing the benefits and dangers, having the freedom to succeed or fail. You are a psychologist, not an officer of the court. It's not your job to turn people in for their behaviors, or to prosecute them for their crimes. It's our job to help them understand themselves, to learn tools to make effective choices, and to support them to make effective choices. It's difficult to see people make 'bad' choices (she made air quotes). We have to tolerate those feelings, even if we don't agree with them, because our job is to be helpful—not to prosecute, or dictate the choices our patients make."

"I'm with you."

"Reporting someone for a crime that has already happened to a person who is currently alive, and not in jeopardy of death or abuse, would prevent a client from being able to talk freely about what they are doing. They could be forced to incriminate themselves in the process of seeking help. They would likely not come to therapy."

"Absolutely!"

"In California, therapists must disclose statements only when, either the client presents a risk of serious harm to others; or disclosure is necessary to prevent that harm. The therapist's required course may involve notifying the potential victim, the police, or both. If the client is sufficiently mentally ill, the therapist may be required to initiate an involuntary hold."

"Even if the statements are made outside of the therapeutic environment?"

"He's still a client!"

"My best understanding is that a therapist would be required to maintain confidentiality if a patient has already murdered someone, and is not currently homicidal."

"Wow! I didn't know that!"

"A criminal defendant may not claim therapist-client privilege when she or he has voluntarily made their mental state an issue in the criminal case. In other words, the defendant either: Argues that she or he is not guilty by reason of insanity (i.e., the "insanity defense"); or argues that she or he is not mentally competent to stand trial.

"Confidential communications between a therapist and a client are not protected by the therapist-client privilege if the client sought the services of the therapist in order to commit a crime or tort; or to escape detection or arrest after committing a crime or tort, any wrongful act done to someone else for which the victim could claim damages in a civil court proceeding."

She switched to a leather bound volume.

"Like other evidentiary privileges in California law, the psychotherapist-client privilege can be waived by the patient in writing. This means that the client can make the privilege disappear, by either: Disclosing a significant part of the privileged communication, or consenting to the disclosure of the privileged communication by anyone else. However, the client will not necessarily waive the therapist-client privilege for the content of communication with a therapist merely by disclosing the fact that said client is seeing a therapist, or divulges the purpose of his or her visits to the therapist. The court could order disclosure of such records if they were 'necessary to the proper administration of justice.'"

"Wow! How do you know so much?"

"I research a lot! I actually really love it!"

She lifted the huge book from which she was reading, one of a series of dark blue covered volumes. California Criminal Code. She also had copies of California Regulations for psychologists, and the Federal guidelines. She took up yet another, yellow-covered tome and read.

"The particular criminal charges for which psychotherapists are often thought to be at risk when they fail to report their patients' confessions of criminal activity, belong to a class of offenses referred to as 'inchoate' crimes, and include the crimes known as 'misprision of a felony' and 'accessory after the fact.' Also the closely related offense of 'obstruction of justice.' These 'inchoate offenses' originated in English common law, when the Norman Conquerors placed obligations on their captive populace to help deter crimes against the hated rulers, effectively forcing others to testify against accused people. They were originally adopted by American courts, and incorporated into American common law. They have somehow managed to find their way into contemporary American criminal statutes—a statutory offense under federal law since 1790."

"What? That's incredible! How can that be?"

"At least two federal cases have held that, although 'mere silence' is insufficient (i.e., there is no obligation to notify civil authorities), the giving of an untruthful statement to authorities is a sufficient act of concealment to sustain a conviction for 'misprision of a felony.' Thus, it appears that when therapists respond to investigators' questions, they have an obligation to do so truthfully. There does not appear to be an obligation, however, to say anything at all; and a therapist could respond to an investigating officer without incurring criminal liability by stating that he or she is unable to provide any information because of the confidential nature of the therapist-patient relationship."

She went to another section of the same volume and continued.

"In some instances, once the 'duty to warn' has arisen and the therapist has divulged the statements, those statements may be used at trial. However, several courts have held that the duty to warn is distinct from the admissibility of the client's statements in court—in other words, a therapist must still warn of a dangerous client, but may not testify about the statements necessitating the warning. Reporting a client's confession of a crime is still a breach of confidentiality, but there are some exceptions: Cases where the defendant chooses to make his/her mental condition an issue—by pleading not guilty by reason of the California insanity defense, or claiming that she or he is not competent to stand trial; cases where the defendant sought or used the psychotherapist's services to enable the commission of a crime; or to escape being caught or arrested after committing a crime; or a situation where the psychotherapist reasonably believed that the client's mental condition makes him or her dangerous to him- or herself, to someone else, or to someone else's property."

"That's a little confusing!"

"It really relates to the intention of the client in divulging whatever is expressed. In addition, the psychotherapist is required to 'claim the privilege'—that is, refuse to disclose the confidential information, even when she or he is not directly instructed to do so by the patient. This means that privilege only covers information that is transmitted as part of the therapeutic relationship—including information obtained from the therapist's examination of the patient, the diagnosis, and any advice given by the therapist. Further, privilege only covers communications made in confidence—meaning that they were not disclosed to third persons outside of that relationship."

"All of which leaves me…"

"Basically, you cannot officially report your suspicions."

"Damn! You are so right! And I am so grateful! You're a peach!"

CHAPTER THIRTY EIGHT

...Than Answers

San Francisco, February 2001

Paul was depressed. His mind kept presenting him with pictures that felt forced—persistent and insistent—to examine the debacle in which he was involved. A creeping anxiety invaded his thoughts like a colony of alien microbes. Massimo and that fucking weird smile kept haunting him! He just couldn't get it out of his mind. He made a decision to see if he could subtly pry the lid off of the man's not-so-tightly capped brain in a session—though what good could it do in any case was really a moot point. But he had to know. He badly wanted Massimo to be innocent, but his intuition kept bugging him, telling him over and over, at the oddest times, that he was guilty—not like an external hallucinated voice, but an adamant voice nonetheless.

He rationalized his curiosity, and couched it as good client care. Massimo often looked as if he were wearing the same clothing for more than one day, pants dingy and un-pressed; shirts wrinkled and occasionally stained (at least his mother seemed to be feeding him); perhaps he was not even bathing daily—and he had appeared unshaven for sessions several times. The decline in Massimo's appearance had been gradual, certainly not like a Market Street panhandler, but increasingly obvious—and never in evidence prior to the death of Veronica.

It may have been simply part of his grief process. Paul knew from long experience that grieving took different forms for different people. He had seen clients who had been amateurishly diagnosed by family members or friends as having a "protracted grieving process;" who had encouraged the client to just "get over it"; to go to community events; even start dating again, when the person was just really not yet ready. As far as he knew, there were no "official" parameters that separated healthy, "normal" grief from the more pathological varieties. It all depended on the person or relationship that one was grieving, as well as the intensity of the grief, and the impact the grief was having on an individual's life in terms of ability to function, do daily care, and so on, was the significant factor.

It was broadly conceded that five years might be a roughly defined as the "outer perimeter," as it were, for intense grieving (social withdrawal, diminution of self-care, frequent references to the loved one, sleep disturbance, depression), though he knew a woman who had been married for over fifty years who had been intensely grieving for her husband for eight years. Her children had petitioned the court to get medical power of attorney so they could have her hospitalized for ECT (electroconvulsive therapy), a barbarous treatment to which Paul was violently opposed, having assisted in such treatments hundreds of times when he was a Licensed Psychiatric Technician. Paul had been contacted by one of the woman's oldest friends who was concerned about this possibility, and Paul agreed to meet the woman. He quickly came to see that her grief was protracted, but did not feel that the proposed treatment was warranted. He agreed to testify on her behalf, and the court ruled against her children, who were seriously upset with him. The client though, was quite pleased, and started sessions with him the day after court to complete her process, which she did delightfully within six months. She came to realize her former relationship had never been perfect; that her dead husband had many foibles; and that she was allowed to have a life of her own finally. The capstone comment that told him that she was complete—after many sessions of tears and the recapitulation of their relationship—came when she gave him one of her sparkling smiles, and said, "You know, I never could stand his snoring! I don't miss that at all!"

Beyond his "itchy" curiosity, he was concerned for the younger man, though what he could do for him therapeutically remained an open question. If he were to take his usual approach, and work at helping him clear the traumatic memories that were haunting him, Paul might inevitably prove himself right and uncover the murder. Shit! Then what? It might save an innocent man from being convicted; and he might even be able to demonstrate mitigating, even exonerating, circumstances for his client—emphasize his obsessiveness, his suspiciousness bordering on paranoia (though his fears had turned out to be founded apparently) —though the latter, if successful would only terminate with him being committed to psychiatric care, should he be deemed to have killed her as a result of his mental illness—not a sure thing by any means. It was such a fucking conundrum!

It was enough of a puzzle that it drove him to seek therapy for himself, in the form of a follow up with Claire, who he knew so well and trusted. Besides she very well knew the case material he wanted to discuss further. She had fortuitously just had a cancelation for the following afternoon.

"Claire, thanks for squeezing me in!"

"You had perfect timing! My client had just called about ten minutes before you did!"

"I'm grateful!"

"So what can I do for you today? Your problem client again?"

"Yes and no!"

"O-kaaaay!"

"No, I mean, partially. It's also about my stuff that is coming up in relation to the serious problems with this fellow."

"So. Tell me more."

"I'm having a hard time carrying around the burden of what I believe I know! It pisses me off and it's confusing! I'm not sleeping well again. I'm depressed—mostly because I feel so helpless to do anything! It's...sort of bringing up all my childhood shame again! I've worked so hard to get free of all of that, and now it's up in my face again!"

"What other symptoms are you experiencing?"

"I get triggered by little stuff!"

"Like what?"

"Any time I feel like I'm being disrespected, or invalidated, I go immediately to rage! Or when I feel intruded upon!"

"'Intruded upon?'"

"I get nutty with telemarketers! When they call, sometimes I end up screaming at them! Fucking Jehovah's Witnesses! Oh shit! I cannot stand them!"

"What do they do that's so bad?"

"They're so goddamn intrusive! I didn't invite them, yet they call me! Or show up at my fucking door uninvited! It always feels like my fucking mother!"

"Go deeper!"

"I...feel invaded! Raped! Like they're putting shit inside me!"

"How?"

"Doing things to me! Things I didn't invite! Things I don't want!"

"By calling you?"

"I didn't invite them! They're doing it against my will! Without my permission!"

"And that reminds you of your mother's behaviors?"

"Yes! Her using me...sexually! I did not fucking ask for it, and I certainly did not want it!"

"And that triggers you?"

"It's like a flashback! Every single time!"

"This has happened before? In your life?"

"Oh God! For the longest time!"

"And you react instantly? Without thought?"

"Yes!"

"Sounds deeply regressive to me!"

"Me too! But I can't get beyond it!"

Paul just sat there, and started sobbing, perseverating, asking over, and over, and over, "Why? Why? Why? Why did you do it? Why? Why? Why?"

Anger and shame poured out of him in great gouts, the more he remembered, feeling the utter helplessness of his analog three year old being sexually attacked by his mother—unable to do a goddamn thing, totally entranced, completely under the spell of her power and sexual allure, wanting to resist it, yet totally wanting it, needing it, craving it, as if his very blood depended upon it, this facsimile of love that he experienced, needed to continue breathing—yet it felt so wrong, so wrong, his young brain could not comprehend as she caressed his rigid little penis, repeatedly kissed his face in a sexual flush, and parted her legs as

373

she gently pushed his little, completely trusting face down, down, down, deeper and deeper into the mystic triangle of her crotch.

"That's it, darling! That's right! Just kiss Mommy there!"

And he did, tentatively at first, then with increasing ardor and intensity of focus, urged on by her voice and her hands on his head, pushing and twirling his little head, as she taught his lips and tongue to move in ways most favorable for her, unaware and uncaring of the damage she was doing, of the ways she was disrupting his neural pathways forever; imprinting him, sentencing him to a lifetime of distorted, dysfunctional relationships with women, seeking their favor, seeking to give all women everything they wanted all the time, every time, to the complete and utter disregard of his own needs, his own well-being, his own identity, sundering his sovereignty, his dignity, his essence, his very selfness with every caress, every lick, every flicker, every movement of his little tongue, his previously unaware self innocently drawn ever more fully into the slavish web she was weaving, now only her instrument, there to satisfy her raging needs, arousing in him a false and salacious sense of connection, losing the awareness of what love is, a "seeing" by his sponge-like soul, indelibly implanting a template to which he would be inextricably bound as if with chains and iron straps, to follow, to obey, in his every waking or sleeping moment for many decades that followed, seeking the dream of connection, the sense of melded hearts and minds that he "knew" to be love, for which he would sacrifice his individuality, his autonomy, hungering for that sensation of fulfillment for which there is no other, when one's soul has been stolen and mesmerized into believing untruths and disinformation; when one has utterly surrendered custody of his own personal safekeeping into the hands and mind of one who had no real consideration for his sovereign needs and desires.

He felt an inner loosening as a tremendous energy poured out of him, gouts and chunks, and agglutinated gobbets of the foul, vile bile of decades of fermentation and degradation spilled, rushing like a torrent through a cataract, releasing him for the first time in his life from the caustic, acidic rage he had always felt at the shame and misuse, and the continuing self-disavowal it had created, the utter betrayal of his innocence, by the one person who should have held him sacrosanct, who should have held his well-being, health, and growth as her highest and most sacred values. Should have, could have—and hadn't.

He took the glass of water that Claire offered, and emptied it in one motion, and the refill she brought next.

"I…guess I had no real idea that I was still carrying so much!"

"Sometimes it's hard to know."

"I…I'm grateful that you helped me get there."

"You were ready. I just facilitated."

"Guess we got off track a little about my client, huh?"

"There must be some relationship to that situation."

"I don't see it right now."

"Give yourself some time. It'll come."

"It just all revolves around me telling my truth, or not. Or more, feeling 'permitted' to do so. I think my conflict here is personal versus professional and legal."

"I guess that, given the way things are set up, you may have to choose professional and legal over personal."

"Yeah, I know."

"The other path might include you losing your license and maybe being prosecuted yourself. Minimum some form of censure. You really are bound to protect your client's confidentiality."

"I feel a little like an early Christian martyr!"

"But you don't really know he's guilty!"

"You're right. But my intuition about it is very strong!"

CHAPTER THIRTY NINE

A Strange Summons

San Francisco, Late February 2001

After that dramatic session with Claire, he experienced such relief, a lightness in his chest, a loosening of tension in his body, and even moments of sweet and unadulterated joy. He had even started eating less, and exercising. It felt like an incandescent rebirth was sprouting beautiful flowers in his heart.

His interest/obsession in cracking Massimo's potentially specious alibi had decreased considerably also. Perhaps the old saw about pain and depression being necessary to create art might actually have some substance. Perhaps it was the pain that drove one to a deeper introspection, which, in turn, led one to releasing the pain that looked like a solution, but was actually just a shift in one's consciousness and perspective. He had told Massimo that he was available as needed, but the man had failed to call again. Paul actually felt a much greater sense of peace, a more profound deepening in the overall continuum of inner quiet. All in all, he was feeling better and stronger than he had ever felt in the longest time.

He started taking walking tours around The City. Today was an early spring day compared to the previous day, giving him a break from the Arctic chill and accompanying icy rain. He was working his way through *Stairway Walks in San Francisco* by Mary Burk (with Adah Bakalinsky). He had walked from his new apartment on Green near Stockton (Thank God for good references and lots of cash!) to Coit Tower, then down the Filbert Street Steps all the way to Levi's Plaza on the Embarcadero, and back! Exhausting, but what a joy! Then he had then stopped at Café Malvina to have a double espresso and a chocolate biscotti. As he walked in the doorway of his new place, the phone was ringing.

"Paul Marzeky here."

"Dr. Marzeky? It's your service."

"Hi. Is this Maria?"

"Yes, it is! You recognized my voice!"

"Years of training! What's up?"

"The police have been trying to reach you!"

"Oh shit! Now what?"

"A Lieutenant McLaren has been trying to reach you!"

"I just got home. Give me his number please."

Paul called Phil McLaren, and caught an earful of shit.

"Where the fuck you been?"

"I didn't have my cell phone with me. It's goddamn Saturday! Who in the fuck has a crisis on Saturday?"

"Your boy Massimo!"

"Oh shit! Now what?"

"He's got a knife and he's talking suicide! There's a negotiator here, but he's asking for you! You just better get over here."

"'Here?' Where's 'here?'"

"His place, on Greenwich."

"Be right there!"

Paul's brain dashed from thought to thought seamlessly as he made his way to Massimo's. The police negotiator was clearly not making any headway. Suicidal ideation plus knife in hand equals intense. Massimo would have be put on a 5150 hold.

Wonder if he's having some more flashback stuff. What a way to blow a great Saturday—at least he had had some premier time to himself first! Screw carrying his cell phone all the time! So many people were completely nuts about lugging the damn things around these days! Too ugly and bulky!

As Paul neared Massimo's, he was struck by the amazing number of people who seemed to have magically materialized. Most of the by-standers were neighborhood residents, many Italian, but, like the true melting pot of North Beach: Greeks, Russians, Dominicans, Persians, Saudis, Ethiopians, Germans, Egyptians, Poles, French, Nicaraguans, and Swiss—and of course, the Caucasians, even though most were not actually from the Caucasus!

Following an anonymous 911 call, two uniformed officers had arrived, appropriately assessed the situation to be way above their pay grade, and called dispatch—and all of the vast facilities of the SFPD went into deployment. Uniformed officers from Central Station had set up a perimeter to maintain crowd control, facilitate traffic flow, and constitute the outermost ring of organization. The surrounding neighborhood streets were blocked off, and traffic diverted. Neighbors in the immediate vicinity were evacuated, including one eighty-five year old woman who was both blind and hard of hearing who took her cane to one of the officers before her sixty-eight year old daughter calmed her, and they left their apartment without further incident. Then a Hostage Negotiator and his backup had been summoned, and a Special Weapons and Tactics (SWAT) team put on stand-by alert.

When Paul reached the outermost ring, he was brusquely asked his name. When he gave Phil McLaren's name, he was asked for his ID, and told to wait. Moments later, his erstwhile friend came toward him, parting the tightly packed circles of activity as if he were a modern day Moses and they the Red Sea. He quickly identified the pattern of rings of increasingly greater security to be negotiated the closer he got to the center.

The Hostage Negotiator and his back-up had made no headway. They had tried all of their standard tactics—establishing contact; attempting to develop rapport; attempting to join with the person's position; using first names, not titles or ranks. Being reassuring. Not pressuring. Being empathic. Reframing in order to create alternate tacks for action; asking what the hostage-taker wanted. They had relieved each other every thirty or so minutes to stay fresh with the man acting as support providing water, coffee, and other fluids flowing to the man talking, as well as providing a shadow watch on the transference and countertransference issues—making sure that the primary negotiator was not getting too involved with the victim, or attempting rescue him or her; or attempting to get his or her own needs met (i.e., be a hero or heroine), albeit unconsciously. He also provided coaching, and provided fresh ideas for any behavioral modifications that might be useful in order to keep the active negotiator from responding to taunts, silences, verbal affronts, or bizarre behaviors. When the active man had asked if there were anyone to whom Massimo would like to talk, Paul's name came up.

As Paul arrived, he was handed a telephone receiver, and heard the phone ringing. Massimo answered.

"What?"

"Massimo? It's me, Paul Marzeky."

"Hey, man. I guess I fucked up this time, huh?"

"What'd you mean?"

"All the police and shit! I bet they got SWAT out there ready to shoot me!"

"Swear to God! SWAT is not going to shoot you!"

"I don't believe you!"

"Have I ever lied to you, Massimio? Ever?"

There was a long pause, followed by a weak "No!"

"OK, then. Take me at my word—no one is here to shoot you! We're all concerned about you!"

"It's all your fucking fault!"

"Whoa, whoa! What is?"

"Everything!"

"Wait a minute! Wait a minute! What 'everything' are you talking about?"

"All of this shit I'm in!"

"What 'shit' are you talking about?"

"This fucking mess I'm in! If you just hadn't pushed me to remember about Veronica and my mother, none of this would have happened!"

"What do you mean?"

"We were doing really fine! We were going to have a baby!"

"Calm down, Massimo! We can work this out!"

"I'm so fucking sad, Paul! So fucking sad!"

"I understand, man! I really do!"

"I don't know what to do, man!"

"We can work it out!"

"How? What?"

"Let's just get through today! We can set up a schedule for you to come and start seeing me again."

"No! I don't fucking want to remember anything else! That's what started this shit!"

"Massimo! Massimo! Slow down! Are you saying that remembering your childhood got Veronica killed?"

"They're related! Can't you see that?"

"Tell me about it! How are they related?"

"I knew that fucking bitch was cheating on me!"

"Veronica?"

"Yes! Of course! What other cheating, lying bitch did I know?"

"You just mentioned your mother a minute ago!"

At this the Hostage Negotiator and his partner both glared at him, and made to take away the telephone. Paul acted as if he didn't see them, and continued with his process.

"Fuck my mother! She was a fucking bitch too!"

"I know she lied to you too, Massimo!"

Loud sobs came through the speaker now, followed by sniffing, and finally the sound of a nose being blown.

"Well, she's fucking dead now! And so is that bitch Veronica! She was cheating on me!"

"Your mother's dead? When did that happen?"

"So you don't know everything, do you?"

"What are you talking about, Massimo?"

Paul made a gesture, and wrote "Mother?" and her address, then shrugged his shoulders.

"Ted Struthers confessed to cheating with her. But he says he didn't kill her!"

"The fucking bitch! She said she wanted to have a baby with me!"

Paul decided to take an intuitive shot and asked.

"Do you think Ted killed her, Massimo?"

Again the glare from the Hostage Negotiators, but Paul turned away, shielding the phone with his shoulder.

"I don't know! Ask him!"

Now switching tacks, Paul asked, "What can I do for you, Massimo?"

"Nothing, man! It's over!"

"But why? You were making real progress!"

The sobbing started again.

"She's gone! And I loved her so!"

"But there's still so much more for you to do!"

"I don't deserve to live! And it's all your fault!"

Paul reacted to this jab in a way that was less than therapeutic.

"Hey, man, I'm not responsible for how you feel!"

"Not how I feel, *bastardo*. For getting me to remember!"

"Massimo, you were carrying a lot of old, bad memories! You told me you felt a lot better when you remembered!"

"But now I can't forget!"

"You mean you keep remembering?"

"Yes! Yes! I cannot stop!"

"Let me help! Please!"

Yet another burst of sobbing came, followed by a moaning dirge that ululated hauntingly through the phone and the speaker on which the police were listening.

"Please Massimo! Talk to me!"

"I'm...it's...too late!"

"No, Massimo! It's never too late!"

"You don't understand! She reminded me so much of my mother!"

"I understand! I really do!"

"No! No! You can't!"

"But I do! I do!"

"No! You can't! You can't!"

"I can help you, Massimo!"

"Nobody can! She...I...*Paulo*, I..."

"What, Massimo?"

"She reminded me so much of my mother! She cheated on me!"

"I know! I know! I'm sorry!"

"Paul…You don't know!"

"What, Massimo? What?"

"I killed her, Paul! I fucking did it!"

Paul was stunned into silence, a silence that carried to the Hostage Negotiators, who exchanged a glance. As the backup man called the Incident Commander to convey this latest information, he was handed a note. He read it, then a second time before he showed it to his partner, who, in turn signaled to Paul.

They had found Massimo's mother lying on the kitchen floor of her home stabbed multiple times in the throat, exactly as veronica had been found.

Massimo stepped through the door of his apartment house, carrying a bloody, double-edged and dangerous, beauty-of-a-blade, the twin to the knife that had been found in his dead wife's throat—a Cold Steel OSS™ that he was gripping tightly in his bloody right hand as tears poured down his emaciated face.

Ancient sorrow wafted thickly off of him, as if with the whirling, swirling gases of an emotional hurricane were permeating the air all around him.

Paul rose, as if in a trance, and started walking toward his emotionally lost client, wanting to save him, yet another wounded warrior who needed him. An officer intercepted him, then another, before he had taken two steps. Massimo stared at the bizarre *pieta*, displaying the most eerie, twisted rictus of a smile Paul ever seen.

"Paul," he croaked. "She reminded me so much of my mother!"

And with a single swift motion, in a glistening glissando that punctuated the very air itself, he jabbed the super-sharp blade into the soft "vee" of his throat, the superior thoracic aperture, in an incision mimicking a bizarre tracheotomy from which immediately spurted a gush of arterial blood that shot out four feet out from his face, and splashed in a crimson waterfall on the sidewalk. Massimo crumpled into a sodden heap with the strange, almost preternatural smile still on his face, still looking at Paul, as his eyes glazed, and the life force left him forever.

CHAPTER FORTY
Aftermath

San Francisco, June 2001

The often misattributed Mark Twain quote about the coldest winter he ever spent was a summer in San Francisco, might certainly have found at least a modicum of validation that particular summer, but it was a matter of some indifference to Paul.

Following the dramatic incident of Massimo's suicide, he had shut down his practice—at least put it on hold for two months while he recovered some semblance of sanity and order within himself. He took daily walks all over The City—Golden Gate Park, Alta Vista Park, all of the pristine natural hide outs—and Marin County, most often Mount Tam and Muir Woods, where he could lose himself for hours at a time in the presence of the massive trees and luxurious displays of plants and flowers—the Universe providing an enormous balm for his wounded soul.

A variety of women had volunteered to accompany him on his perambulations. Some offered the ultimate grace of their precious bodies, but Paul was still overcome by what he had witnessed—stunned, overwhelmed, hyper-sensitized. But the greatest, most heart-warming, and supportive response he had had was from a group that had formed around Phil McLaren, who had rallied to him and provided a sort of extended family of police officers, paramedics, nurses, psychologists and other mental health professionals, assorted crisis workers, trauma therapists—and lots of MKP men and Woman Within sisters. They all met regularly and irregularly in groups of various sizes in different peoples' houses. There were parties, dinners, meetings, gatherings, softball games, bowling nights, and a plethora of activities that helped Paul slowly release the massive guilt he felt, all of the "what ifs" and "if onlys" that had been haunting and taunting him since the horrid demise of his client.

One night, after they had eaten a sumptuous pot luck meal at a small gathering in the Sunset District, their work bordered on doing a Gestalt process, a kind of psychodrama. There had been tears and fears, even some minor screaming, after which they had gathered in a large circle in the back yard, arms wrapped around each another. Some were sad; some were happy; some were crying; some were laughing, as they held each other, affirming their basic humanity and desire to help one another and wished for the planet to have a better, brighter future.

Paul felt all of his bitterness, rage, and despair well up in his chest—and resignation and acceptance filling him as his breath deepened, and he entered into a most exquisite quiet. He remained aware of the noise from the street, cars and buses streaming by; the sound of conversation drifting up from the restaurant next door; the irritated screeching of cats battling for sex or territory; even the yapping of little dogs that he normally despised, and usually instantly irritated him. All of it seemed like no more than distant background noise. Tonight none of it really mattered. Everything seemed so superficial as to not even exist; so meaningless that none of it could penetrate the sea of silence in which he swam—deeper, ever deeper, into the impenetrable fathoms of the ocean of consciousness itself. What if this love, this beauty, were truly all there was?

www.ingramcontent.com/pod-product-compliance
Lightning Source LLC
Chambersburg PA
CBHW072302020726
47501CB00002B/353